Farewell to Hollywood

a Red Carpet Romance
Book Three

Farewell to Hollywood

a Red Carpet Romance
Book Three

MICHELLE KEENER

AMBASSADOR INTERNATIONAL
GREENVILLE, SOUTH CAROLINA & BELFAST, NORTHERN IRELAND

www.ambassador-international.com

Farewell to Hollywood
A Red Carpet Romance - Book Three

ISBN: 978-1-64960-116-2
eISBN: 978-1-64960-166-7

Cover design by Hannah Linder Design
Typesetting by Dentelle Design
Ebook Conversion by Anna Riebe Raats
Edited by Katie Cruice Smith

AMBASSADOR INTERNATIONAL
Emerald House
411 University Ridge, Suite B14
Greenville, SC 29601, USA
www.ambassador-international.com

AMBASSADOR BOOKS
The Mount
2 Woodstock Link
Belfast, BT6 8DD, Northern Ireland, UK
www.ambassadormedia.co.uk

The colophon is a trademark of Ambassador, a Christian publishing company.

For my mom

Chapter One

YOU'RE FIRED.

Kate stared at the computer screen with a mix of relief and dread churning in her stomach. That was the end of her legal career. Dear Ms. Sullivan, you messed up, so clear out your office and have a nice life. The email was much more professional and legal-sounding, but that was the gist. Her services were no longer required at the esteemed law offices of O'Brien, Shae, and Collins—one of Boston's most prestigious firms—for "inexcusable absences, dereliction of litigious duties, and willful negligence of client and firm needs." In all of her twenty-six years, she had never been fired before. Not from a babysitting job or the food court at the mall or even working in the bookstore at Harvard. She may have been wild, but she had always been dependable.

She wasn't dependable anymore. Not since that one glance, that spilt second of recognition. There was nothing more important than that now. No job, no career—not even the wrath of old Mr. Collins himself was enough to change the course she had decided on two months ago.

She rubbed her hands over her eyes and tried to ignore the anxiety that filled her stomach. The email was the end of everything she had spent the past six years working for, everything she thought she wanted. She leaned back in her chair, balancing on the back two legs, testing how far she could go before it fell. She had pushed her luck with the firm too far, but there was nothing she could do about it now. She'd made her choice.

The email wasn't a surprise. She had known it was coming. She had used up all of her vacation time and sick days weeks ago. When that was gone, she said she had a family emergency and asked to telecommute for a short time. They had given her a month of unpaid leave instead. That had ended two weeks ago. Her voicemail was full of increasingly irate messages from her supervisor and her supervisor's supervisor and, finally, a message from one of the senior partners. She had tried to come up with an explanation they would understand, but no one cared, no one knew the depth of her pain and the length she was willing to go to end it. She'd offered to take a leave of absence; she'd even volunteered to take on all of the firm's pro bono cases, but it hadn't been enough. Mr. Collins had left a message demanding that she return to work immediately or face termination. It had been an easy choice but one that flipped her entire world upside down. With one email, Kate Sullivan's status had changed from promising up-and-coming corporate attorney to soon-to-be-homeless, unemployed lawyer.

And for what?

A glimpse. A passing glance that lasted less than three seconds.

But that one glance had been enough. She knew. She knew in that one look she had found the right man. After years of searching, countless dead ends, and one single memory burned into her brain, she had found him.

The man who killed her sister. He was in Los Angeles. After all this time, she had finally found him in a dark and depressing night club called Norma Jean's.

There was no way she was could walk away—not after years of waiting for this chance, not when she had been just steps away from the man who had murdered her sister, destroyed her family, and ruined her life. The partners at O'Brien, Shae, and Collins could take their law briefs, contract negotiations, and depositions and toss them in Boston Harbor. She wasn't leaving Los Angeles when she was so close to ending the nightmare she had been living with for six years.

She had spent the past two months since that night in Norma Jean's chasing down every lead she could find. She talked to the club owners; she pestered the waitresses; and when she started talking to the customers, the bouncer tossed her out and threatened to call the cops. Thanksgiving and Christmas had come and gone, and she had barely noticed. She helped bake pumpkin pies and decorate Ben and Lily's Christmas tree, but her mind was always somewhere else. As the New Year rolled into Hollywood, Kate was stuck in the past, her memories all focused on the face she saw in the car window on the night her sister died. She couldn't leave now. She owed it to her sister. And if the cost was her job and her reputation, so be it. She would pay any price to put an end to this nightmare.

She probably should have been more upset about the demise of her career, but as she stared at the ivory wall of Ben and Lily's guestroom, she couldn't think about anything but finally getting justice for Megan. Everyone else had moved on, forgotten the sweet, nineteen-year-old girl who had died on that lonely canyon road. Everyone but her. It was up to her to finish it. It was her responsibility to make someone pay for stealing Megan from the world. Her dad had his career with the Los Angeles Police Department to focus on; her mom . . . well . . . her mom had chosen her own way to forget about Megan. Kate was the only one left who was willing to keep fighting, and she wouldn't let Megan down again.

She drummed her fingers on the smooth surface of the cherry desk as her mind whipped up a to-do list. She'd have to find a dignified way to respond to her firing. Her legal career at O'Brien, Shae, and Collins was done; and given the relatively small corporate law community in Boston, word of her firing had no doubt already spread through the city. Once her search for Megan's killer was over, she wouldn't be able to find another law job anywhere in Boston. Her life as a California exile on the East Coast was done. She was going to have to fly back to pack up her small apartment and clean out her office at the firm. And she'd have to tell her dad.

Of all the loose ends that were facing her, that one hurt the most. After everything she and her dad had been through since Megan's death, they were finally reconnecting, finding a way to talk without yelling. It hadn't been easy, but they were trying. With one email, that was all going to change. He'd been so proud of her when she'd been accepted to Harvard Law School. He'd driven her across the country and helped her move into a tiny apartment within walking distance of the school. He'd hugged her and told her he loved her; then he'd driven away with tears in his eyes. Guilt gnawed at her when she thought about him driving home alone, returning to an empty house, and spending the following years on his own, walking the halls of a house that had once been the center of their family and now was little more than a museum of broken relationships. She hadn't felt guilty at the time. All she'd wanted to do was get as far away from Los Angeles and the memory of Megan's death as she could, but even snowy winters in Boston and sleepless nights in the law library couldn't erase the past.

Her dad wanted her to let it go, to move on and focus on building a life of her own, but how could she? She had been in the driver's seat that night; she'd watched her sister's life fade away, and she'd seen the face of the man driving the other car.

Two months ago, she'd seen it again, silhouetted against the door of a dingy club the night they rescued Hannah. It was as if a figment of her deepest horrors had escaped onto the streets of Hollywood. She'd seen him walking out of the club—the line of his jaw, the shadows under his eyes—and she'd known. The image was as clear to her as it had been the night of the accident. That face had followed her across the country, taunted her, dared her to find him. That was him. The man who had killed Megan and gotten away with it for six years. She had searched legal records, tried to piece together the events of that night, but every door had been closed to her, every avenue of recourse shut off. Until that one glance. Now that she had found him, she would make him pay for everything he had taken, for every life he had destroyed. If that meant losing her career and disappointing her father, she would do it. Nothing was going to stop her getting justice. The legal system had failed Megan. She would not.

A doorbell chime echoed down the hallway and drifted into her room, drawing her out of her memories, away from the faces that haunted her. She closed her eyes and took a deep breath as she tried to focus on the present. Lily was hosting brunch, and Kate was under strict orders from her best friend to attend.

She tucked away her anger and worry about being unemployed and put on the mask she'd been wearing since she fled California for the East Coast. Confident, brash, put-together Kate. A woman who had it all together. Unshakable in a board room, unbeatable in a courtroom, and utterly broken on the inside. She stood and closed the laptop. Bad news didn't need to be shared. She would handle this like she handled all the other tragedies in her life—on her own. Reflexively, she fluffed her hair, giving the long, red waves volume, considering for the millionth time if she should just chop it all off, and then headed to the kitchen to eat pancakes and pretend like everything was fine.

She stepped into the sunny kitchen, awash with light from the panoramic windows in the living room that overlooked the Hollywood Hills. Deep, male laughter greeted her as her bare feet left the polished hardwood of the hallway, and she stepped onto the chilly, marble tile. Ben and his best friend Chris Johnston were standing by the coffee machine, while Lily flipped pancakes on an iron griddle on the large chef's stove.

Kate stood in the open space for a moment, caught in a middle ground between the anger within her and the loving family in front of her. She watched the scene in the kitchen like she was watching a movie, a spectator instead of a participant. It still took her breath away to see Lily standing. She'd been with her in the hospital after the fire, had seen her sitting in the wheelchair, confused and hurting, questioning everything she believed and pushing away the people who loved her. Kate had sat beside that wheelchair, making small talk and trying to help Lily find her faith again, which was the ultimate irony since Kate had long ago decided that God couldn't be trusted. Seeing her best friend effortlessly stand in front of the stove, shuffling her feet as she flipped a pancake and slid it onto a plate, was amazing. It was almost enough to make her believe that God did answer prayers.

Across the kitchen, the coffee maker sputtered and steamed. As Chris took his mug and stepped away, his gaze met hers.

"Hey, Kate," he said, lifting his coffee mug in salute. The bright blue of his eyes shone over the rim of the cup. The movie director had become a fixture in her life since she had come back to LA. He was Ben's best friend, and he tended to show up whenever and wherever they were meeting. They were the unattached friends stuck tagging along with the lovey-dovey couples.

If she was honest, Chris was an excellent option to avoid being a third wheel. With his sun-bleached hair, richly tanned skin, and board shorts, he was a perfect fit for Southern California. He looked like beach towels and sunscreen, summer days on the sand, and the chilly kiss of the Pacific waves she had spent years trying to forget. He was tall and tempting with his thoughtful expression and reserved demeanor. If she was a raging tempest, he was a calm sea, and the pull of that peace was almost too much for her. It was for that very reason she kept him at arm's length. She didn't have time for a distraction. Blue eyes and sun tans would only get in the way of her search for Megan's killer.

Ben and Lily turned toward her, and she was struck again by the sense of family, the feeling of belonging. Her own family had splintered and broken under tragedy, but Lily's family had grown stronger. Megan's death fractured her family beyond repair, and it was only with Lily, Noah, and their dad that she had ever found that sense of home again. She envied whatever invisible force it was that kept the Shaws together. They gave her a piece of what the accident had taken, but that comfort only highlighted how much her family had lost and how deep the chasm had become. It was why she had to leave Los Angeles completely. Not even the Shaw family could replace what she had lost, but all these years later, Lily was still there for her.

After she had spotted the man in the club, it had only taken her a split second to decide to stay in LA. She had been stuck without a place to live, alone in the city she had once she called home. She didn't want to go back to Boston, but she couldn't face the prospect of staying with her dad. Being in her childhood home was too painful, and there were too many conversations she wasn't ready to have. Ben and Lily had invited her into their home, making her feel welcome and loved and never pressing for details. She had tried to stay out of their way—they were still newlyweds, after all—but they never made her feel like an intruder. Fortunately, Ben's movie star house was plenty big for all of them, and it had been easy to give them their space.

"I thought you had forgotten about us, Sleepyhead," Lily said and switched off the burner. The flickering blue flame disappeared with a pop. Lily passed the plate of pancakes to Kate, and the smell of butter and vanilla made her stomach growl. Maybe hiding in her room all morning hadn't been the best choice after all.

She carried the pancakes to the dining room and set the plate on the table beside a ceramic bowl filled with fruit. "I was just catching up on some work emails."

The dining room was on the front side of the house, and through the open curtain, Kate watched the fountain in the middle of the circular drive bubble and sparkle in the sunlight. Lily had been talking about remodeling the house, tearing down some of the walls and giving it an open-concept feel. Whenever she brought it up, Ben smiled and agreed, though Kate was pretty sure he would agree to just about anything Lily wanted. Seeing the two of them together was enough to soften even Kate's bruised and battered heart.

Ben brought over a bottle of syrup and a plate of butter. "They must be getting anxious to have you back." His hair flopped into his eyes as he bent over the table. He was letting his hair grow for his next movie role, and it was already hanging past his ears. Kate wondered how long it was going to get before he lost his patience and cut it. Although, how long it would get before Lily lost patience with the shaggy waves was probably a better question.

She sat on the fabric-covered chair and focused on arranging her napkin in her lap, keeping her eyes on the pretty blue and green checkered pattern. "Not as anxious as you'd think."

Chris sat beside her, his arm brushing against hers as he pulled his chair in, and she scooted her chair further away. It wasn't that she didn't like him; she did. He was funny, and kind, and—if she was willing to admit it—handsome. Very handsome. He had broad shoulders that seemed to suck up all the space between them and sandy blond hair that was too long for a courtroom lawyer but not long enough to be a rock star. It hung just above his shoulders, and Kate resisted an impulse to reach out and twist her fingers through the ends, just to see if it would feel like sand running through her hands. He was comfortable and easy-going, and she admired the way he blended into any situation, as if he as was always watching, waiting for the right moment to call "action" and start the scene.

He was also obsessed with his faith and frequently found a way to work God into the conversation. More than once, Kate had caught herself getting annoyed with him simply because he didn't understand what it meant to beg God for help and hear nothing but silence. God might be nice to have around when things were going well, but He wasn't much help when people really needed Him. Kate tucked her arm against her side to avoid touching him. He might be funny and handsome, and maybe she did notice him more than she should; but she didn't have time for a relationship, and she certainly didn't have time for God. Not when she had something much more important to do.

As Ben, Lily, and Chris bowed their heads in prayer, Kate stared at the empty plate in front of her. Ben's words droned in the background, like a radio station in the car, background noise for the frantic mess of her thoughts. During her first year in law school, she had used all of her newly acquired skills to track down any information she could find about the accident. Records had been sealed; paperwork was missing; mistakes had been made. Her dad had tried to shield her, encouraged her to let it go; he'd even forbidden the investigators in his department to talk to her. Her search went cold not long after that. The paper trail ended. The man simply vanished. She had searched obituaries and surrounding counties, thinking he must have died or moved, but now she knew he was still here. Still nearby. Still driving the same streets where her sister had died. She would find him this time. She just needed a place to start.

She was focused on her plan, so her amen was a little late, but no one noticed. As they dug in to Lily's pancakes, friendly banter filled the room. The Shaws had been her bonus family ever since she and Lily had met in college. When her own family fell apart, it was the Shaws who had kept her together. She looked at Ben and watched as he tucked a stray strand of hair behind Lily's ear. It was so gentle, such a tiny bit of sweetness, that her heart melted like the butter on her pancakes. Her pieced-together family was growing. Ben was a great husband to Lily. The two of them had happily ever after practically written on their foreheads.

And Chris. She snuck a glance at the man beside her. He was gesturing to Ben with his fork as they discussed a movie that had opened over the past weekend. Well, Chris was part of the package, she supposed. He wasn't bad company; he was just . . . distracting. Warmth radiated from his shoulders, a nagging reminder of his presence beside her. He was always there. Always by her side whether she wanted him there or not. She didn't think Lily was trying her terrible matchmaking skills on her, but how could she focus on what she needed to do if this six feet of muscle and humor was always around?

As she drizzled more syrup over her breakfast, she tried to figure out where he fit in the puzzle. He was successful, respected in the industry—at least as far as she could tell—and he seemed like a genuinely nice guy. He was also exceedingly single.

Too bad she wasn't looking for a nice, exceedingly single guy.

"So, Chris," Ben said as he poured himself more orange juice from a pretty, crystal decanter that had been a wedding gift. "What's up next for you?"

Chris scrunched his face like he was thinking about something unpleasant and shrugged. "I'm not sure. There's nothing really interesting coming my way."

"Seriously?" Surprise colored Ben's words. "I heard you were getting scripts sent over almost every day."

Kate turned to the director and smothered a laugh as she watched him fidget in his chair like a child who'd been caught sneaking a cookie. It was hard to imagine the guy she split a piece of pie with at Thanksgiving, the guy she had seen spend four hours untangling Christmas lights, was the same guy who directed movies that made millions of dollars.

"I am getting scripts," he said, choosing his words carefully. Too carefully. If they'd been in a courtroom, Kate would have immediately started making notes for her cross-examination. He was hedging. Not quite lying, but not spilling the truth either. "They're just not what I'm looking for. They're all . . . " He set his fork on his plate, then lifted his hands in exasperation. "Shoot 'em up, save the world, action stuff. They're all the same."

Lily put her hand on Ben's arm, her soft pink nails resting against his forearm. "You know, honey. The stuff you do."

Ben laughed and planted a loud kiss on his wife's head. "Thanks for that." He looked across the table at Chris. "Then what are you thinking? No more big-budget action films?" Ben put his hand over his heart as if he'd been deeply wounded, though Kate knew perfectly well he'd just finished filming a sappy, romantic movie a few months ago. "Are you looking for something artsy? Drama? Romantic comedy?"

Chris folded his hands and set them on the table, suddenly serious. "I've got something in mind, but it's risky. And I'm pretty sure no one will want to fund it, much less distribute it. It's most likely a career-killer."

Silence descended on the room. Kate looked from Chris to Ben, trying to gauge the seriousness of the statement, knowing she was out of her element. Movies and publicity, Hollywood politics—she didn't care about any of it, but now that her best friend was married to a movie star, she was getting a crash course in the behind-the-scenes secrets of Hollywood. It made her most contentious corporate negotiations look easy by comparison.

Chris leaned forward, like he was about to share a secret. "I'm thinking of making a documentary. On human trafficking here in LA."

Ben whistled and crossed his arms over his chest. "That's definitely a new direction."

"It's been on my heart for a while," Chris said, passion filling his voice. "I started thinking about it after Hannah told us what she'd been through. Once I saw it for myself, once I knew it existed, I couldn't ignore it. I kept seeing news stories and articles about how bad it is, how many people are being trafficked, and how many lives are being destroyed." He paused, his voice dropping even lower. "I feel like God is calling me to speak up for them."

Kate tried not to roll her eyes. God. Always God. Did he really think God cared about his career? That God was sending telepathic messages about what movie he should make? God didn't care about things like that.

Ben rubbed his hand on his chin as he stared at Chris across the table. Kate waited, curious to hear what Ben would say. He knew the ins and outs of Hollywood. He was a box office draw and highly in demand. His words would carry weight with Chris—not just because of their friendship but also because of his influence in the industry.

"Then you should make it," Ben said simply, as if it was settled.

Chris exhaled, and his shoulders relaxed. Ben's support obviously meant a lot to him. It gave Kate one more reason to respect the movie star she had once threatened to sue and/or murder. "Noah told me the same thing when I mentioned it to him."

Lily laughed. "Well, that must be a sign because Noah would usually be the one campaigning for the car chases and explosions." A pang hit Kate's heart as Lily talked about her big brother. Noah was happily in love with Hannah and moving on with his life. Hannah was perfect for him, and with their wedding only a few months away, Kate found she didn't mind being happy for them. She thought she'd be jealous if she stayed in LA and saw the two of the together all the time, but she wasn't. Truthfully, Noah had been her back-up plan, a safety net, and that had never been fair to him. She couldn't fault him for finding someone who made him her first choice.

"Oh, he made a good case for them," Chris conceded. "But in the end, he told me to follow my passion, and I think this is it."

"Sounds like you've made up your mind," Ben said.

Chris nodded, but his lips were pursed in thought. "Unfortunately, I don't think anyone will fund this film. It's not exactly box office gold." He picked up his coffee mug, sipping it as his pronouncement hung in the room.

"I'll do it," Ben said, and Chris sputtered into the mug. "Lily and I have been talking and praying about starting a production company. It would give me more control over the films I want to make and let me be more hands-on in the production side. Why not start with this one? I already know you're a great director."

Chris stared open-mouthed at Ben. As the seconds passed, Kate wondered if he was breathing or if she should smack him on the back to jump start his heart just in case it stopped beating. "Ben, this might be a huge loss. A disaster. You could lose everything you invest."

"I believe in you, Chris. I . . . " Ben looked at Lily. She smiled and nodded excitedly. "We would be happy to finance the film."

The director shook his head. "I don't know what to say. Thank you,"

"Tell me you have a place to start," Ben said as he reached across the table to shake Chris' hand. Just like that, the deal was done.

"I do," he said. "It turns out that club where we found Hannah was a front for a human trafficking ring. They were moving girls in and out every week, bringing them up from the border and then passing them further north. I'm going to start by investigating the men who were in the club that night, seeing if I can find a connection to the larger criminal circle."

Kate dropped her fork. It clattered against the plate, and she caught it before it could bounce to the floor. "How are you going to find them?" she asked, her heart thundering in her chest.

"Your dad said he could give me some leads—names of suspected criminals, men who might be tied to this. It isn't much, but it's a beginning. I'll start researching there."

Her head spun. Clues and connections and possibilities raced through her mind. If she could get a list of names, a list of the men who were there that night, she could figure out which one was the man she sought, the man who had murdered her sister.

"Then we're in business," Ben said. "Let's start on the legalities and get the funding sorted out, and we'll trust that God has a plan." With a decisive nod, Ben went back to his breakfast as if he hadn't just completed a business deal over pancakes and orange juice.

"I can help with that." Kate spoke up quickly, anxiety and excitement making her voice squeak. "I have plenty of experience in corporate law. I can be on hand to make sure . . . " She searched for a way to make herself indispensable, to be a part of the project, and to guarantee that she could get her hands on that list of men from the club. "To make sure all the legal mumbo-jumbo is taken care of." Chris turned to her, his eyes curious and puzzled by her sudden outburst. "You know, so you can focus on the creative side. I'd be happy to help."

Kate held her breath. She needed this. She needed that list. She tried to calm her racing heart. She couldn't reveal what was really going on.

Lily clapped her hands. "Kate, that would be amazing! But don't you have to get back to Boston?"

She forced a smile on her face. "Turns out, I've got some time on my hands."

Chris smiled, and guilt wound its way through her veins. She held his gaze, hoping she wasn't blushing, twisting her hands together on her lap as she tried to keep her face impassive. He couldn't know why she was doing this. He wouldn't understand. No one did.

"Thank you," he said. The whisper of his voice touched her cheek, and nerves danced across her skin. Had he always been this handsome? He was focused on her, his gaze holding hers with excitement and honesty, and she wondered if he could hear the deception in her mind, the game she was playing, the lie she was telling. She nodded and turned away, swallowing the confession that leapt to her lips.

He was a means to an end and nothing more.

Though the words in her heart were heavy, filled with a disappointment she didn't expect, that was all he could ever be.

Chapter Two

CHRIS LEANED AGAINST THE LOPSIDED desk, the sharp edge pressing against the back of his legs, and stared at the blank, beige walls. The room was small and windowless, not quite claustrophobic, but pretty close. The smell of fresh paint was so strong, it made the air itself feel wet and thick. The newly applied, nondescript mocha color matched the rest of the interior at the Hollywood Mission. It was a color meant to blend in, to be unnoticed and unobtrusive, to provide a plain background so that the artwork and decorations could have the spotlight. Only, there wasn't any artwork on the walls of this tiny, tucked away room—just blank, beige walls.

He scratched the stubble on his chin. If he thought about that metaphor too long, he'd get depressed. Blend into the background, set the scene so someone else can shine—wasn't that exactly what he'd been doing for years? Hanging out behind the camera, following someone else's script, turning the lights on the actors, and then fading into the shadows once the production wrapped. He was the behind-the-scenes guy—important, but invisible.

He blew out a long breath, the sound echoing in the small space. It wasn't that he wanted the spotlight. It wasn't fame or money or awards that lured him. He'd experienced most of those on some level. It was something else, some longing that pursued him like an itch he couldn't reach—persistent, annoying, and elusive. He wanted . . .

What?

He stepped away from the teetering desk and paced the tiny room, while the question followed him. What did he want? It was five steps from one side to the other, and when he reached the other wall, he still didn't have an answer.

He wanted to be useful, to do something worthwhile, to make a difference. He was tired of special effects and explosions and movies that people forgot as soon as they tossed their popcorn in the trash and drove home. He was a good director. Maybe not like the legends he studied in film school, but he was good. He stuffed his hands in his pockets. What was the point of being good at something if it didn't matter? If it didn't make a difference?

Last night on the phone, his mom had told him he was being too hard on himself. When he'd shared all of this with his parents, they'd argued that his films entertained people. They brought a bit of happiness and sometimes laughter into the world. He was using his talents to the best of his ability, and that was what mattered.

But was that all that mattered?

He paced across the room again. If he was using his gifts to the best of his ability, why did he have this itch? The feeling that there was something more. He wanted to take the gifts he had been given, the things he'd learned, and use them to help people, to change lives. He could do something more than blow up a car or stage a prison break. This documentary was the way. It had to be.

Laughter echoed down the hall, and Chris smiled. Hannah and Noah were working in the church office. The closer their wedding date got, the gigglier and mushier they became. Not that he blamed them. After everything they'd been through, they were allowed to be blissfully and ridiculously happy. Given how lonely this room was, he should be grateful for the company . . . even if that company was a love-struck couple down the hall.

Chris shook his head and sat on the edge of the desk. The uneven legs buckled under his weight and collapsed. He scrambled to keep from falling as one end of the desk hit the floor with a loud crash.

He frowned as he looked at the broken desk, tilted and askew like the *Titanic* going down. His production company was not off to a great start.

Noah poked his head in through the open door. "You okay?" He looked past Chris to the desk that leaned precariously to one side. "Sorry about the desk. It's older than the church. I'm pretty sure it was here when my parents bought the building." He stepped into the room and stopped. His nose wrinkled as he sniffed. "And sorry about the smell, too."

Chris laughed as he bent to inspect the damage to the desk. Both legs on the right side had broken clean off. "It's a room, and it's free. I'm not going to complain. You didn't have to paint it just for me."

Noah shrugged. "Dad insisted." He disappeared out the door and reappeared a few minutes later with a rolling chair. "I know it isn't what you big-time Hollywood directors are used to, but the room is yours for as long as you want." He slid the chair across the floor, and Chris stopped it with his foot.

Chris sat on the cushy chair, correcting his balance when it threatened to fall backward, and looked at the first pieces of his production company. Blank walls and broken desks didn't matter. It was his. His film was going to start here. He probably could have called in a few favors at the studio. With Ben as the primary investor, he was sure they would have let him hang a shingle on the lot. He might have had a fancy office with access to the studio's resources, but favors like that came with strings, and Chris was done being a puppet. He didn't want the studio suits looking over his shoulder, muttering about profit and reputation and public relations. All he wanted to do was make his documentary and trust God with the outcome.

This was the project that had been wiggling its way into his heart for over a year, the something more he'd been looking for. Once the idea had taken root, it had followed him around until it haunted his dreams. Now, it was time to get started. He was certain God was at work in this, that He had called him to this moment and this project.

A spark of anxiety twisted in his gut. He was mostly certain God was at work.

The anxiety grew, and his stomach churned.

Pretty certain.

He rocked in the chair as his thoughts bounced from one extreme to the other. What if he was wrong? What if he wasn't called to this? What if he was throwing away his career on a film that no one would ever see?

"I know that look," Noah said as he leaned against the doorjamb and crossed his arms. He was wearing torn jeans and a t-shirt from a 1980s rock band under a flannel shirt Chris knew he'd seen Hannah borrow. A smirk lingered on his face, and Chris knew what was coming. Noah was warming up to lecture him. Noah had been the first person he'd shared this idea with and the first person to encourage him to do it. "You're overthinking this."

Chris ran his hands through his hair, scratching his scalp as if he could chase the whispers of doubt away. "Is it that obvious?"

Noah grinned. "You'd make a lousy poker player, that's for sure."

Using his feet for leverage, he twisted the chair from side to side, tempted to spin it all the way around and only resisting the urge because Noah was still watching him. "Well, then, it's a good thing I don't gamble."

"I don't know about that," Noah said. The smirk was gone, and his expression turned serious. Noah may play the comic relief most of the time, but he had gone through his share of darkness. Just like Ben, Noah had come out of the trials with a deeper faith and a woman he loved. It was more than Chris had. The last time he'd gone through a rough patch with a woman, it hadn't ended well at all. It ended with public humiliation and getting fired from a film. It was a mistake he still regretted and would never repeat. "This documentary sounds like a bit of a gamble."

Noah didn't know how right he was. Chris had turned down two big-budget projects in the past three months. Projects that could have brought in major money. If he'd been able to negotiate a piece of the back end, he could have walked away with more money than he would know how to spend. Certainly, more money than his two-bedroom townhouse, frozen dinners, and paid-off car needed. He had several charities he donated to regularly, and the money would have helped them a great deal. Wiggles of doubt resurfaced as he thought of what the profits from those big-budget films could have done.

But he'd turned them down, walked away from contracts he'd dreamed about when he was in film school. For what? The chance to make a one-man documentary about human trafficking that had no distribution deal and no audience. If it crashed and burned, he wasn't just risking every dime he'd sunk into the film, not to mention the money Ben and Lily invested. He was risking his name in the industry. He had worked hard, clawed his way up to almost the top of the Hollywood food chain, and now he was putting it all on the line. It only took one wrong move, one box office flop to slip back down to obscurity and end up right where he had been as a new film school grad crashing on friends' couches and living off ramen and canned soup while he prayed for a paying job. He'd used up all of his favors after the break-up with Tessa. If this film went sour, he didn't have anything except Ben's friendship to fall back on, and he would never want to put Ben in a bad spot. After all he had been through, Ben deserved some peace and happiness. No, Chris would let his reputation rise or fall with this film.

In spite of all the rational and logical reasons why this was a stupid idea, why he should scrap it all and go make *Protectors of Earth Part II*, he couldn't shake the feeling that this was what he was called to do. He was choosing to trust God's leading. God had never failed him, and if this was the end of his film career, he believed God would lead him to something new. Given the choice between being obedient and being safe, he'd choose obedient every time. It was an easy choice, but terrifying just the same.

Wanting to sound more confident than he felt, he grinned as he looked at Noah. "God is already providing. Look at the fabulous—and free—new office He has given me."

Noah gave the walls, the broken desk, and the smiling director an appraising glance. "You know this was supposed to be a storage room, right?"

A storage room. His production company was headquartered in the unused storage room of a church. Perfect.

"Hey, stop harassing my client."

Chris lost his balance, and the chair tipped back dangerously. Noah laughed as he fought to avoid ending up on his rear end next to the broken desk. There was only one person who could fluster him so badly.

Kate.

She breezed into the office like wildfire and autumn winds. Her red hair fell behind her, trailing sparks that leapt straight to his heart. His throat went dry, and all mastery of the English language left him. In fact, if he'd had to introduce himself at that moment, he doubted he could do it. He'd given interviews on international entertainment shows. He'd rubbed elbows with award-winning actors and writers. He'd once held his own in a debate over symbolism in film with a man who directed one of the biggest blockbusters of all time. He was an intelligent, articulate, and capable man.

Except when Kate was around. When she walked into the room, he tripped over his own feet and said things like "Howdy-do." It was beyond embarrassing.

She'd toppled him the first moment he saw her, and he was still the same blabbering fool now that he was then. They'd spent the past two months hanging out with the Shaws, going out for burgers and celebrating the holidays, and yet he was still as dumbstruck by her as he was the first time he saw her. Shouldn't he be immune to her by now? She was the most beautiful woman he had ever met. She was feisty and stubborn and brave, and she barely noticed he was alive. The only reason she knew his name was because his best friend was married to her best friend. And yet, his heart still drummed; his palms sweated; and his stomach flipped like a surfer wiping out whenever he saw her. She was his impossible dream. Always near but forever out of reach.

"Hey, Taller Brat." Noah wrapped her in a hug, and envy twined its way through Chris' body. Noah got to hold her. Noah got to laugh with her and tease her while he struggled to remember his own name around her. "What are you doing here?"

Kate stepped back and waved a legal-size manila folder in his face. "Legal stuff. Lots of whereases, heretofores, and forthwiths."

Noah's face contorted into a mix of disgust and fear. "Well, I want no part of that discussion. Call me when there's pizza involved." He tossed Chris a quick wave and vanished down the hallway.

Kate stood in the doorway and glanced around the storage-room-turned-office. Her crisp, black suit radiated confidence and professionalism right down to the shiny high heels with sparkly crystal buckles on the toes. She looked like she could have been strolling into the conference room of a billion-dollar corporation ready to take over. Instead, she was here, looking at his broken desk and blank walls and inhaling paint fumes.

Once again, he looked like a fumbling buffoon.

Standing, he took a deep breath. Then she turned her green eyes to him, and he forgot to exhale.

"I brought the incorporation papers, business license, tax forms, and basically everything else the state of California requires for you to start a movie-making empire." She held the thick folder out to him.

"That was fast," he said, swallowing past the desert in his throat. He tried to concentrate, to read the papers in his hand, to ignore the stunning woman in front of him. *Be cool. Relax. It's just Kate.*

But the fact that it was Kate was exactly the reason he couldn't relax.

He flipped through the pages, relieved that his hands were steady, noting the stickies she'd used to indicate where he needed to sign.

They were color-coded, yellow for signatures, blue for initials, green for places he needed to fill in information. *Name of business.* He was going to have to work on that one.

"Efficiency is part of the service." She tapped her foot as he scanned the papers, the crystal bows on her shoes catching the fluorescent light. He wondered if she had someplace to be or if she was just anxious to get away from him. All of the hard work she'd done putting the paperwork together was probably less about helping him and more about doing a favor for Ben and Lily. She'd done her good deed, and now she was ready to get it over with and move on. He wasn't a fan of pity, and he didn't want to be just a good deed.

Peeking up from the papers, he noticed the firm set of her jaw, the calm but tense way she carried herself, as if she was always ready to leap into a fight, a warrior in search of a battle. She would take over any room she walked into—not just a freshly painted, unfurnished storage room populated by one overwhelmed film director. From what he'd seen, Kate was perpetually in motion, jumping from one activity to the next, never slowing down. Her shoulder shifted toward him, and he dropped his gaze back to the legal documents in his hand, worried she would catch him staring at her. Again.

He was as bad as a middle school boy with a crush. Actually, he was worse than a middle school boy because he should know better. Blinking twice, he forced himself to focus on the words on the page. He was reading so slowly, she was probably wondering if he could read at all.

The word *payroll* caught his eye, and he stopped. He didn't have any employees; why would he need a payroll account? He read the form, his heart thundering, and he wondered if he should sit down.

He leaned back against the desk, forgot it was broken, and nearly slid off the sloping side. There was only one name listed as an employee of his as-yet-unnamed production company.

Kate Sullivan.

Chapter Three

KATE PINCHED HER THUMB AND forefinger together. Growing up, she bit her nails whenever she was nervous. She'd never had long, beautifully painted nails like Megan. She'd had stubby, jagged nubs of anxiety. Her mother had tried cayenne pepper, dish soap, and everything else she could think of to get her to stop biting her nails, but nothing worked. The habit followed her to high school, college, and all the way to Harvard Law School. During a mock appellate argument in her first year of law school, her professor noticed the habit and called her out on it in front of the entire class. "Never show weakness," the stern professor scolded her, and the lesson stuck. Now instead of biting her nails, she squeezed her fingers together. It gave her worry a place to go. As long as she kept her hands behind her back or hidden under a table, no one would know how nervous she was. Hiding her emotions had become an artform for her. As long as she could keep up appearances, it didn't matter how much she kept locked inside.

She waited as Chris read the form authorizing a payroll account to be set up. She'd seen the way he'd stopped shuffling the papers when he got to that one. He was quiet as he read the form over and over again. The silence in the small room was as oppressive as the smell of paint. She would have leaned against the wall to look casual and unconcerned, but she didn't want to risk getting paint on her suit. When she'd gotten an interview with O'Brien, Shae, and Collins during her final year of law school, she'd been determined to make a perfect first impression. She'd scoured an outlet mall for hours trying to find a classy suit at a discounted price. The shoes—well, the shoes she'd splurged on, but they were so cute, they were worth every penny. Boston had been expensive, and even though she'd been careful with her funds, there was no way she was going to risk ruining her favorite outfit, not when she didn't have a job . . . yet.

Worry rippled through her as he continued to stare at the form. She probably should have asked him first. She could have presented her offer and gone about it more traditionally, explaining the benefit of having an attorney on staff, sharing her qualifications and experience, using every trick she knew to convince him to hire her, but she didn't have time for traditional. There was too much riding on this. She needed to be close to the production and have access to the information he got from the police. She couldn't risk him saying no. So, she assumed the sale and hoped he would go along with it. Besides, she had reasoned with herself as she drew up the papers, she would be helpful to have around. In a lawsuit-happy industry, every production company needed a lawyer, right?

The longer he read, the more she pinched her fingers together.

He was going to say no.

She would be unemployed, stranded in Los Angeles, and no closer to finding the man in the gray suit than she had been all those months ago. She kept her expression impassive, as if the outcome didn't matter to her, keeping her anxious thoughts from reaching her face. It was a look she had perfected in her years of law school and corporate practice. "Casual indifference" one of her board room opponents once called it. She could have taken offense at the terminology, but since she wiped the polished floor with him and got everything she wanted out of the negotiation, she took it as a compliment instead. Don't give anything away. Keep your opponent guessing. Wait for the right moment to pounce. Take no prisoners. It worked in her legal career, and she would make it work here, too.

A wisp of guilt slithered through her, and she tried to ignore it. She'd never felt bad about any of the tactics she'd used in law school or in her work at the firm. Winning was winning; that was all that mattered. She had never been dishonest—not really—but she refused to be weak. There were rules, of course, but Kate had learned that when facing an opponent in the courtroom or conference room, those rules were extremely flexible.

Except, her conscience whispered, Chris wasn't her opponent. He was a friend, and she didn't have many of those. Like her, he'd been basically adopted by the Shaws, included in the family, and swept up in the love and warmth of their home. He was the one who had encouraged Ben to keep fighting for Lily when she had pushed him away. He'd stood by Noah and had been willing to fight for Hannah. He'd been faithful and supportive of the Shaws, and he'd been nothing but nice to her, yet she was willing to use him and his film to get what she wanted. She squeezed her fingers tighter. She hated who she had become. This wasn't who she wanted to be, but she didn't know how to stop. The end justified the means, no matter how bad she felt about it, because the end was the only thing that mattered to her now. Ever since the accident, her life had been on a collision course, and it was too late to change course.

She'd done the same thing in law school. Fighting for every grade, maneuvering her way into the best internships, willing to sacrifice friendships in her quest to be the best. She'd never stooped so low as to hide books in the law library or intentionally sabotage another student, though she'd known other students who resorted to such tactics. There was always a line she refused to cross—a faint, but inviolable, code of honor that had kept her in check—but now, as she watched Chris's forehead crease into wrinkles as he stared at the paperwork she'd given him, she wondered if she had crossed that line. She pinched her fingers together and reminded herself again why she was doing this. This was bigger than a law school assignment or an internship. Megan deserved justice, and if no one else was willing to get it for her, she would do it herself.

Seconds ticked by filled with silence and uncertainty. She couldn't predict what he would do, and that unnerved her. She thought she had him pegged. Easy-going, relaxed, willing to go with the flow. Maybe she had been wrong about him. Narrowing her eyes, she tried to assess him as if they'd just met, as if he had just walked into a conference room representing a competing firm. Casual dress, long hair. Clearly, he wasn't concerned with impressing anyone. Quiet and a little reserved, but not a pushover. He was starting his own company and had turned down lucrative offers, so he was grounded in his own vision and willing to take risks to get there. It took a confidence and courage to have that kind of boldness, and . . .

She stopped.

Faith. It took faith.

Chris closed the folder and looked at her. His blue eyes were thoughtful and more piercing than she remembered. There was a sharpness in them she hadn't seen before, and for a moment, she thought he had seen through her charade. She stood still, fighting the urge to tell him everything, to lay it all on the table and hope he would help her. What would it be like to have someone to rely on, someone to fight beside her instead of against her?

She stuffed the confession back down, tucking it away in the shadows of her heart. She wasn't willing to risk him saying no. She had put her trust in authorities and the legal system in the past, and they had all disappointed her. The man who drove the car that smashed into them six years ago—the man who had left them bleeding and alone on that dark canyon road—was still out there, living his life without any consequences, as if Megan's life hadn't meant anything. Her death was ruled an accident, and he'd been given a slap on the wrist for leaving the scene. Her sister deserved more, and if this was the only way to get justice, she would do it.

She tilted her head and met Chris' gaze, drawing on every ounce of confidence she portrayed in the board room when she wanted the opposing counsel to give up. There was too much at stake to risk the moral high ground of a Christian movie director, who had access to the information she needed.

He crossed his arms, tucking the folder against his side. "Why would you want to work for me? I thought you were going back to Boston."

Kate shrugged, ridiculously happy that he hadn't said no right away but careful not to show it. If he was talking, that meant there was room for negotiation, and she was very good at negotiation.

"I decided to stay in LA for a while. I've been on the East Coast for five years. It's been too long since I've had a chance to spend time with Lily and my dad, and we have a lot to catch up on." It wasn't exactly a lie, but it wasn't really the truth either. She ignored the squeak of her conscience and plowed ahead. "So, I figured while I'm out here, I should find a way to be helpful. Honestly, I'm not very good at doing nothing. I like to keep busy." She flashed him the smile that had gotten her out of contempt of court charges . . . twice.

When he hesitated, she pushed forward. "Plus, it wouldn't hurt to have chief legal counsel to a major film production company on my resumé."

He laughed, and Kate relaxed. "You drew up the documents. You know there's nothing major about this company right now. We'll be lucky to find one theater willing to screen the film. Forget straight to streaming; we might be looking at a straight-to-the-trash-can disaster."

A twinkle of excitement rushed through her when he said *we*. Whether the director knew it or not, it was a done deal. The only thing left was to finalize the details and sign on the dotted line. "All the more reason to have a competent, experienced, and efficient lawyer on your side."

Chris pushed the rolling chair around the broken desk and offered it to her. When she sat, he excused himself and left the room. Kate's foot bounced in an excited staccato as she waited for him. The first step was done. She would have access to the information the police had. She just had to be here when Chris got it. A quick photocopy of whatever they gave him and she could investigate the men herself. Chris would never know what really brought her here; and if he never found out, then he'd never get hurt, and it wouldn't matter that she had fibbed her way into the job. As long as no one got hurt, the tactics didn't matter.

Chris returned with a metal folding chair. He sat across the lop-sided desk from her and opened the folder again.

"Nice desk," Kate said.

"It's a work in progress," he said as he read the paperwork. She had enough experience in contracts to know that he wasn't just scanning it. He was reading it carefully. She filed that bit of information away. Beneath the board shorts and surfer hair, Chris was an intelligent and competent man. He was being smart with his new company. She respected that.

"You know," he said. "With this salary, you'd be making more money than I am right now."

"And how much are you making?" she asked, as she crossed her legs and smoothed the impeccable black fabric of her pants.

Christ rubbed the back of his neck self-consciously and grinned. "Nothing."

Kate laughed. "So, gas money would actually be more money than you're making." She leaned forward, ready to make her closing argument. "But with me on board, just think of how much money you'll be saving by not getting sued."

Chris reached into a backpack by his foot and pulled out a notepad and a pencil. He held it down with one hand to keep it from sliding off the desk and scribbled on it. While Kate waited, he used his phone for a calculator. Her elation at a sure victory started to fade. She had underestimated the man. He'd always seemed so mellow and relaxed, like the beach bums she'd known in high school, but there was far more going on under his tan skin and good looks. He was proving to be an astute business man.

"How about this," he said as he looked at a number on his calculator app. "Drop your salary requirement by thirty percent, and we've got a deal."

"Thirty percent?" She asked, less concerned about the actual salary than she was about losing a negotiation. She watched his face, searching for signs of deception, but there weren't any. She wasn't entirely sure what to do with that. She knew how to deal with men who tried to get their own way, using leverage to their advantage, manipulating sentiment, but she didn't get any of that from Chris.

"I don't actually need an attorney on staff," he said. "I could put someone on retainer and do my best not to get sued. That would be a lot cheaper than hiring you."

Kate straightened her shoulders. He wanted to play hardball; she was ready to play. "But this salary is much lower than paying billable hours. If you make one mistake, you'll be out half your budget before the case even gets to court."

"Do you think I'm going to make a mistake?" he asked. His voice dropped, the playful tone gone, replaced by something raw, a sincerity that dove straight to her heart. He was alone in the fight, feeling every inch of that solitude; it was a loneliness she recognized.

"No," she said. "I think you're going to do something amazing." She meant it. His drive and his talent were undeniable.

He leaned forward. "Then be a part of it."

She was about to agree, forget the salary, and forget the resume padding; she was being sucked in by his passion.

"For thirty percent less," he added with a grin.

"Twenty percent," she said.

"Done."

His quick agreement stunned her. She'd completely misread the situation. His honesty had thrown her, and she had the distinct feeling he'd gotten exactly what he wanted. She squinted her eyes as she watched him write the new number on the employment contract and then sign it.

As he passed it across the tilted desk to her, she changed her evaluation of the director. He wasn't as naïve and easy-going as she thought. There was something strong and confident lurking underneath the sweet exterior, something that made her heart beat a little faster.

She checked the new salary and signed her name with a flourish. She smiled as she handed it back to him. He may have won this time; but she knew him better now, and she wouldn't fall for his tricks again.

Chapter Four

THE FLUORESCENT LIGHT IN THE storage-room-turned-film-produc-
tion-office buzzed faintly as Chris leaned against the finally dry mocha
painted wall. The paint fumes had dissipated, and the small room was
looking a little less forlorn now that he and Ben had started bringing in
office supplies. That morning, they hung two large whiteboards and a
framed corkboard on the previously bare walls. The colorful dry erase
markers and pushpins provided spots of color against the nondescript,
beige backdrop. Chris was going to use them to storyboard the film.
He had a stack of index cards, along with colored pens, pencils, sketch
pads, notebooks, and everything else the office supply store had avail-
able sitting in bags and boxes that were strewn around the room. As
he looked at the pristine whiteboard surfaces, he couldn't wait to start
marking them up. He loved the process of plotting and planning his
shots. The colored markers helped him step back and see how all the
pieces would fit together; the index cards let him rearrange things;
and the sketch pads helped him think.

Thanks to Ben's willingness to put his construction experience to
use, it hadn't taken them long to get the boards up on the walls. Chris
had mostly held things in place while Ben used the drill, but it was a
system that worked for them. Chris knew his way around every camera,
lighting rig, and sound set up in the industry; but he was something
of a health hazard around power tools. He didn't mind admitting his

weakness in the area of handyman things. Maybe someday, he'd ask Ben to give him a crash course on how to do household repairs, but since he didn't see a wife or a house in the near future, he figured that could wait.

Chris waited for the verdict as Ben stared at the sad, broken desk, still tilted in the middle of the floor. Ben's hands rested on the tool belt around his waist as he surveyed the squashed legs. They splayed out from under the desk like the legs of a spider that had been stepped on.

"Are you sure you want to save this thing?" Ben asked, as he nudged one of the legs with the toe of his work boot.

Chris shrugged. Sentiment has gotten the better of him. "It was a gift from Pastor Evan. I'd hate to lose it. Aside from you, the church is my only partner on this project."

Ben lifted the sagging side of the desk and scooted it to one side so he could squat down and examine the broken legs. They were mostly intact. The desk may be ancient, but it had been built well. "I wouldn't say your only partner," he said, as he turned one of the desk legs over in his hand. His eyebrows rose in speculation as he glanced up at Chris.

Chris shifted on his feet and started rearranging the multicolored pushpins on the cork board. He lined up all the blue ones, then the red ones, studiously ignoring the silent question on his friend's face. That hadn't taken long. Of course, since Kate was staying with Ben and Lily, he should have expected it. Kate no doubt told Lily, and Lily probably hadn't wasted any time telling Ben. Which was fine, he reminded himself. They didn't have anything to hide. It was perfectly acceptable for Kate to work with him on the film. He jabbed a green pin into the cork. If it was perfectly acceptable, he wondered, why was he as nervous as he'd been when he asked Ella Chu to prom?

It didn't help that Ella had said no, and he'd gone to prom alone.

When he ran out of pushpins, he turned back around. Ben was still squatting by the desk, holding the broken leg, patiently waiting for Chris' answer. He wiped his hands on his jeans and searched for a way to change the subject and go back to talking about Ben's new film. Ben had campaigned for Chris to come on board as the director, but he'd refused. It was another action flick that Ben would be great in, but he had already been praying about this documentary. Ben had been disappointed, and truthfully, Chris would miss the crowded set and the large crew. He'd miss having skilled assistant directors and technical experts, and he'd miss the security and safety of having a studio behind him. It was lonely being out on the limb by himself.

He paused, reminded by Ben's raised eyebrows that he wasn't alone. Kate had joined him on this tenuous limb. He cleared his throat. "So, when do you start shooting?" he asked, but Ben just shook his head and refused to take the bait.

Given how much unsolicited advice he'd offered Ben when he was falling for Lily, he doubted Ben would give up the topic of Kate easily. Lily was a romantic at heart, and she loved a good matchmaking scheme. She just hadn't proven to be very good at it yet. He tried to imagine the conversation between Ben and Lily once she found out about Kate joining the production company. If there was the slightest chance for a happily ever after, Lily would be all in. She was probably already planning a double date. Ben would be more cautious.

Ben set the wooden desk leg on the floor and stood. "Help me flip this thing." He grabbed one side of the desk and waited for Chris to take the other. Together, they turned the desk over, so it was resting on its top. Ben opened a small toolbox and began digging through a pile of screws. "You know," he said as he searched through the mismatched collection of different sized screws. "I like Kate. I do. She's Lily's best friend. And aside from the time she threatened to sue me and then kill me for what I put Lily through, she's been a good friend to me, too."

Chris remembered that first meeting. It was after the fire that ravaged the Hollywood Mission. Ben and Lily had barely escaped. When Lily woke up, her legs were paralyzed. Angry and confused, her entire faith shaken, she had refused to talk to Ben or even see him. He spent every day in the hospital waiting room, desperate for news about Lily. Chris sat beside him. Getting coffee, bringing him food he wouldn't eat, convincing him to go home and get some sleep, only to meet him there the next day and do it all again. He stayed by Ben's side, and he was there the day Kate stormed in, her green eyes flashing fire and assessing Ben like a hostile witness . . . or like the man who had nearly gotten her best friend killed. Kate had barely noticed him, but he noticed her. She was the only thing he saw from the moment she walked in until the last wave of her red hair disappeared down the corridor. She'd taken his breath away, and he'd never recovered. Like a lightning bolt straight from Boston, she'd zipped in and lit up the room. Now everything else paled compared to her.

At Ben and Lily's wedding, she'd been the maid of honor and he the best man. The wedding party dance was the only time he'd held her, the only time he'd ever been close enough to touch her, to feel the softness of her skin and inhale the apple scent of her hair. She had fit in his arms like she had been made for him, like they were a matching pair. He couldn't remember what they talked about as the song played, but he remembered the sound of her voice and the warmth of her hand in his. She'd been so close, only a breath away, and even that had been too far. The song ended, and she had breezed away like he had been nothing more than a temporary stop on a journey to somewhere else.

The realization hurt then, and it hurt now. He'd been there one time before. Tessa has used him as a stop on the road to fame and fortune. What he thought had been love had been nothing more than calculation. When he had refused to give her a part in his first major film, she went behind his back and got cozy with the producer. He fell for her charms as surely as Chris had. In the end, Tessa got the role, and Chris got fired. His big break had turned into public humiliation, his name whispered through the studio halls and used as a punch line. Bitterness still engulfed him when he remembered the snickers and giggles that followed him as he cleaned out his trailer. It had taken a year and calling in every favor he had in Hollywood to get another chance to direct a major studio movie. He'd mostly stayed away from dating ever since. Most of the women he knew were tangentially tied to Hollywood or the film industry, and he wasn't interested in getting played again. He'd briefly dated a woman he met in Michigan when he visited his sister and her family, but he quickly found out he wasn't made for long-distance relationships. He had been happy to focus on his work ever since.

Until Kate had flown into his life and shown him everything he was missing. Funny and sassy—and nowhere near the world of Hollywood—she had ignited a fire in his heart that refused to be extinguished. He didn't hate the idea of jumping back into the dating waters, but he did hate the idea of getting his heart squashed again.

Ben dropped a handful of screws in the front pocket of his denim shirt, and the sound ripped Chris from his memories. He blinked to focus on the room, the broken desk, and the gaping hole where Kate could have been.

Ben unhooked a power drill from the tool belt. "Hold this," he said as he handed the drill to Chris. While Chris held the drill, keeping his finger far from the trigger, Ben set one of the legs into place on the bottom of the desk and assessed the damage. Sharp, splintered pieces of wood speared up from the desk. Ben used a file to smooth the rough edges. "Listen, about Kate—"

Chris put up a hand to stop him. "You don't need to give me the big bother talk. She's just working with me on the film. I promise."

Ben laughed. "I'm not trying to protect her from you." He blew the sawdust from the bottom of the desk. "I'm worried about what she'll do to you."

As Ben went back to filing, Chris considered his friend's words. He and Ben hadn't been friends when his relationship with Tessa had imploded, but Ben knew the story. The producer she left him for was still in the business, and even though years had passed and Tessa had eventually dumped him for a multi-millionaire who owned a string of wineries, he had never even sent Chris a script. That bridge wasn't just burned—it was a pile of charred ash. Chris took Ben's concern as a sign of friendship, rather than a comment on his demonstrably poor judgment with women.

How much did he really know about Kate? Nothing. She was a successful lawyer. She'd grown up out here and met Lily in college, but then she left California to go to law school. She was Lily's best friend, and she'd proven herself to be fiercely loyal and as stubborn as an Irish mule. She had hard edges, as if she had been broken and the jagged pieces were still there, but he didn't know why.

More concerning, though, than hard edges and jagged pieces, he knew she didn't share his faith in God. She hadn't said anything outright. She was always polite when they talked about God and the church, but he could sense the shift in her attitude, the stiffness of her body language, and the aloof distance in her tone, as if she was sitting out the conversation, holding her tongue and waiting for a new topic to come around. She rarely attended Sunday service at the mission. In fact, the only times he could remember seeing her there was when Noah preached for the first time and when Ben and Lily got married.

Ben smoothed the now-level desk leg with his hand and blew off the excess dust. The sharp edges were gone, softened and smoothed by a master's hand. God could do the same thing with Kate. The question was, would she let Him?

Chris held the wooden leg in place against the desk, while Ben used the drill to secure it. Ben was quiet and focused as he worked. Ever since his friend had met Lily in that unexpected twist of fate at LAX, Ben had been different. From the first night he met her, his heart began to change. Chris had been praying for his friend for years, and he had been running out of arguments to try to convince Ben to come to church with him. In the end, all it took was a chance meeting with a pastor's daughter at the airport to change everything.

When Ben and Lily told the story of how they met, they described it as their first fight. When Noah told the story, he called it a catastrophe. But that one conversation had changed the entire course of Ben's life. Lily's, too. A simple mistake had turned into an incredible blessing for them both. Not that it had been easy, but they had held onto God and to each other, and they had made it through.

It was like puzzle pieces fitting together. Piece by piece, the big picture was coming into focus. It was in all the little details that God's plan emerged. As Ben moved on to the other broken leg, fitting it back into place, smoothing the rough edges, restoring what had been broken, Chris wondered if Kate and this film were some of those little pieces in his life that would lead to something bigger. Was he moving closer to God's purpose for his life or farther away from it? Was Kate supposed to be a part of it, or was she a distraction he couldn't shake?

"All done," Ben declared, and they flipped the desk right-side up. It was sturdy and level and didn't wiggle at all as Ben pushed on it. He set the drill on the rolling chair and pressed his hands on the faded desktop. "Here's the thing," he said, leaning forward to look at Chris. "Kate is incredible. She's smart, successful, funny, and as feisty as they come, but she's been through a lot." He paused and stepped back from the desk, his gaze serious and his voice quiet. "It's not my story to tell, but Kate isn't as tough as she pretends to be. She's blunt and confident, but deep down, she's fragile. That level of hurt makes people do stupid stuff."

"And you think I might be 'stupid stuff'?" Chris asked, haunting pangs of Tessa's manipulation stinging with each word.

"No," Ben said. "I think the right man at the wrong time is still the wrong man." He crossed to the do-it-yourself bookshelf Chris had bought. The long cardboard box was lying on the floor beside the only remaining empty wall. Using a flathead screwdriver, he cut through the tape.

Chris sat on his heels beside him and helped peel the box open. "You know, Kate working here was her idea." They pulled the pre-cut, pre-drilled pieces, and sorted them on the floor according to size. "I wasn't trying to talk her into it."

Ben laughed as he knelt in the middle of the scattered pieces and unfolded the endless instructions. "If there is one thing I've learned about Kate, it's that no one can talk her into doing something she doesn't want to do."

As Ben glanced from the instructions to the pieces they had laid out, Chris' thoughts went back to Kate. He didn't know all of her story, but he made a living observing people and bringing out the emotion of a scene. Kate was carrying around some heavy baggage. He'd seen it the moment he met her. Well, maybe not the first moment. When she strode into the hospital waiting room and interrogated Ben, he'd been too shell-shocked to notice anything other than the fire in her eyes and the stuttering of his heart. It was like the mornings he spent surfing, sitting on the calm water, waiting for a wave to break. She had broken over him in a cascade of sass and sunlight, and he'd been trying to stay upright ever since.

"Hand me that one," Ben said, pointing at one of the long boards. Chris passed it to him, wondering if he was going to say anything more about the lawyer who had taken up residence in his dreams, hoping he would share something from her past, something that would give him a bit more insight into the woman he spent far too much time thinking about but knowing that Ben wouldn't do it.

The high-pitched whir of the drill hummed in the air as Ben screwed the shelves into the side board. When the drilling stopped, he rested his arm against the half-constructed bookshelf and looked at Chris. "I guess what I'm trying to say is, it's dangerous to love someone who doesn't know what they want." He motioned for Chris to pass him the final shelf. "That was me not too long ago. Lost, confused, and angry. I was making a mess of everything and hurting the people around me. You saw it."

Chris reached for a short, pressboard shelf, remembering how Ben had struggled before he found his way back to God. The bad decisions, the scandals that almost ended his career, and how close he'd come to losing Lily. If anyone could recognize pain, it would be Ben. He should listen to him, hear what Ben was saying, and accept it as wise advice. He should stop thinking about the woman with fire in her hair and ice in her heart. She was his lawyer and his partner on this film. He could be her friend, nothing more. He would be polite and respectful, and that would be it. They would finish the movie; then she would go back to Boston and her corporate life, and he'd . . . well, he'd go wherever God led him next.

He nodded to himself. That was the way it had to be. He had a movie to make, and he needed to focus on that. It wasn't like God was using this film to keep Kate in his life.

Or was He? Was that even possible? Or was it wishful thinking and fantasy?

Ben cleared his throat, and Chris looked at his friend's outstretched hand, waiting for the shelf he was still holding. How long had he been lost in his own thoughts? Embarrassment crept through his body. He had lost all of his common sense. Kate didn't even need to be in the room for him to turn into a lovesick teenager. This was bad.

Sympathy radiated from Ben's face as Chris handed him the shelf. Ben could fix a broken desk, so what were the chances he could fix his confused and misguided heart, too? Ben shook his head. "It's already too late, isn't it?" he asked.

Chris wanted to deny it—to laugh it off—but he couldn't. Kate's face was burned into his brain, seared into his heart, and he didn't know how to stop it.

"Well, this is going to be interesting," Ben said as he reached over the bookshelf and slapped Chris on the shoulder. "Looks like you just went to the top of my prayer list."

Chapter Five

KATE SAT IN THE BLACK, rolling chair, drumming the fingers of her right hand on the padded armrest. The muted thump of her nails against the fake leather material echoed in the small office. Chris was sitting at the desk, his chair set at a right angle so he could stare at the two blank whiteboards on the wall to her left. Every once in a while, he scratched something on the legal pad he kept balanced on his lap. If he noticed the *rap, rap, rap* of her impatient tapping, he didn't acknowledge it. As far as she could tell, he was lost in thought. She had already finished the few contracts and legal permits that needed to be done that day. It had taken her less than two hours. She could step out for a manicure and a donut, and he wouldn't even notice she was gone. If she didn't already feel guilty about conning her way onto the payroll, she might have done it; but he was paying her to be here, so this was where she would stay. Even if the potent mix of boredom and impatience killed her.

She itched to look at her phone and check the time again. They had been sitting in silence for what felt like years. The inactivity was making her antsy. She'd never been one to sit still for long periods of time, and once she started law school, any hope of sitting still had flown out the window. The fast-paced environment was a perfect fit for her. She was always studying, working, writing, or studying some more. She made law review her first semester, and she reveled in the accomplishment, adding the pressure and commitments to her daily schedule without missing a beat. All of her professors commented on her drive and focus, and she took every compliment as a sure sign that she was doing the right thing.

She secured a research assistant position with one of her professors in her second year. As the months went on, she slept less and less, using every extra hour to study more, write another article, accept another extra task. She got an internship with the city attorney during her third year and spent the summer after graduation studying like mad for not only the Massachusetts bar exam but also the California exam as well. Two days after taking the test in Boston, she boarded a plane and flew to San Francisco to take the California exam. She hadn't told her dad she was coming back to the West Coast. She hadn't wanted to see anyone; she just wanted to take the test and get out of the state. She passed both exams on her first try and started work at O'Brien, Shae, and Collins the following week.

She had jumped into the sixty-hour work week at the firm without complaint. Go, go, go. There was always something to do, always a task to be done, and she was fine with that. She liked being busy. She thrived on the hectic pace, the high expectations, the mind-numbing exhaustion at the end of every day that helped her sleep. If she worked hard enough and long enough, she was too tired for nightmares. In those blissful hours of oblivion, she wouldn't hear the scrape of metal, the crash of broken glass, or her sister's screams. It was when she stopped moving, when she stopped running and working and pushing herself, that the memories stirred. It was in the quiet, empty moments that the past came calling. In the stillness, Megan's face haunted her.

So, the longer Chris sat in his contemplative silence, staring at the blank whiteboards, the more restless she became. The past crept up on her, slithering through the quiet like a snake getting ready to strike. She needed to get moving; she needed to do something; she needed a distraction—and her new employer wasn't helping at all.

She drummed her fingers with more force. How was staring at a wall working? Shouldn't they be filming something or interviewing someone? She was willing to do anything except sit in the tiny office surrounded by walls that felt like they were closing in on her.

Every molecule of her body wanted to throw something at him. She uncrossed her legs and re-crossed them with the other leg on top. She could have written three briefs and yelled at an intern in the time he had spent staring off into nothingness. If this was what the film industry looked like, she was glad she had chosen law school. She took a deep breath and tried to not sigh as she exhaled. Lily was always telling her to slow down, to stop running, to be patient. Maybe if she closed her eyes, she could live in the moment, like the late-night, self-help gurus advised. She glanced at Chris, but he was still staring at the wall, so she closed her eyes and waited for the peace those $19.99 motivational tapes promised.

She gave it about ten seconds, but it wasn't peace that was waiting in the blackness behind her closed eyes. She only found annoyance at this waste of time. Irritation that she had to sit in this makeshift office waiting for a movie director to get ready to work so she could find the man who killed her sister. Anger that he was walking around, free to live, maybe get married, and work, free to enjoy all the things he had stolen from Megan. Anger turned to rage, and she opened her eyes, afraid of the darkness that was inside her and what it was turning into.

Chris was watching her. When had he focused those soft blue eyes on her? She turned the anger boiling inside of her toward him. She didn't want him staring at her. It left her feeling exposed, as if he saw something no one else did. She sat up straighter, daring him to question her, hoping for a fight, for a chance to vent the bitterness that threatened to choke her. Sharp words leapt to her tongue, ammunition locked and loaded and ready to fire at the slightest provocation. If he said one word—

"Tacos," he said.

The anger dissipated, chased away by confusion, and her defenses deflated. "Tacos?" She repeated, certain she must not have heard him correctly.

Chris nodded. The matching rolling chair Noah had found in some corner of the mission skidded away as he stood. "We've been at this long enough. It's time to refuel. I vote for tacos." He grabbed his phone off the desk and stuffed it into the side pocket of his cargo pants.

"At this?" she sputtered, her feet hitting the floor with a loud click of high heels. "At what? We haven't done anything. You stared at the wall for two hours, while I twiddled my thumbs. You call that working?"

He looked at her like she had lost her mind. "This is definitely working. I can't just pick up the camera and start shooting. I need a plan. This," he gestured to the blank whiteboard, "is the planning phase. I'm getting the shots lined up in my head, clarifying the story I want to tell, honing in on the right details. It's about the mood, the atmosphere." He reached for a postcard that was lying on the desk and then used a magnet to stick it one of the whiteboards. The colorful downtown skyline stared back at her. "I'm trying to figure out how to use Los Angeles as a character in this film." He reached his arms over his head and stretched like he'd just finished a marathon when the only thing she'd seen him accomplish all morning was sticking a postcard to a whiteboard.

"LA is not a character," she said, as if explaining the concept of geography to a confused child, which she was starting to think he was. "It's a city." She had no idea what to make of him. She'd seen his movies; she knew he was talented; but she was starting to worry about his mental state.

He laughed. "Come on, Kate. You know this place is more than just another city. It's more than atmosphere or background. It's a living, pulsing personality. LA, Hollywood, all of this—it's definitely a character."

She scoffed. "The villain probably."

Chris shrugged. "Sometimes." He looked at the few notes he'd scribbled on the legal pad. "It's got a dark side, right? The stuff that doesn't make the postcards and the tourist ads."

Crunching metal and shattering glass echoed in her mind. Yes, it had a dark side. She lived it, breathed it; even three thousand miles away, the shadows of it followed her. "And your film is going to expose it? Shine a light on all the dirty secrets of Hollywood Boulevard?"

"Not all of it." The intensity in his eyes stunned her. While she had been bored out of her mind that morning, Chris had been crafting something, sharpening his vision for the film, and she had missed it. There was depth, like the deepest part of the ocean, behind his eyes. Once again, she had underestimated him. While she had seen only a blank whiteboard, he had been envisioning a narrative full of color, vibrancy, and passion. "Just the one corner God has given me."

And there it was. She bent down to pick up her purse, so he wouldn't see her roll her eyes. *God.* Of course, he thought God was behind this documentary. She resisted the urge to tell him the truth. It was a naïve dream. A fantasy. God didn't call people to make movies or write books or go to law school. He created the Earth, set it spinning in motion, and then split, leaving His creation to figure things out on their own. There wasn't a plan or a Divine scheme at work. It was all coincidence and bad luck, and anyone with an ounce of common sense could see that. She admired what he was doing, and she wanted to be supportive, so she kept her opinions to herself. But in the grand scheme of things, how much of a difference could one small documentary make? Especially when the director spent most of the morning doing nothing but thinking.

"So, what do you say?" he asked. "Tacos and then back to work?" He crossed the small room and stood in front of her, his hand reaching for hers.

Kate ignored his outstretched hand and stood, looping her purse strap over her shoulder. She'd be amazed if they ever actually started filming this thing. "Sure."

Chris followed her to the open door. "I've got a special place in mind. How does Venice sound?"

She stumbled on her next step. A wild collage of images flew through her head. Private jet. St. Mark's Square. Gondolas in the canals. A million crazy thoughts fought for her attention. Ben had taken Lily to a movie premiere for their first date, complete with a red carpet and paparazzi and celebrity superstars. A trip to Italy would put that to shame.

Excitement shifted to anxiety. Was it a date? Did she want to go on a date with Chris? She adjusted her purse as she stalled for time.

She wasn't interested in him—she couldn't be—and yet her heart was arguing with her about that. He was passionate and handsome, and she liked talking to him, but he was only a friend. Going from friend to more than a friend was too big. It was a huge decision; it might mess everything up. She had too much riding on this. "Italy?" she squeaked.

His forehead scrunched as he looked at her. "Beach. Venice Beach. I know a guy down there who makes the best fish tacos." He laughed as they walked into the hallway and he shut the door behind them. "Italy? Man, Kate, how long have you been in Boston?"

He was still laughing as he led the way to the parking lot. The heat of a blush crept up her cheeks. She had been on the East Coast for too long. Clearly, her California credibility was in serious jeopardy.

*****

Even in late January, Venice Beach was a bustling hub of tourist activity. Street performers stretched as far as she could see. Mimes, balancing acts, break dancers, and electric violinists lined the small street that had long ago been closed to cars. Tourists and locals mingled in the wide-open space. There were singers, artists, magicians, and acrobats all vying for the attention and spare change of the people walking by. Music and laughter echoed from every direction. In the distance, waves rolled against the sand with a gentle rhythm, bringing the tang of salt and seaweed to mix with the smell of hot pretzels and cotton candy. It was a kaleidoscope of humanity with an energy that vibrated through the crowd. It was everything that made LA unique— a mix of color, energy, and activity that shouldn't go together, and yet it did, flowing with the same ease and endlessness of the ocean that thrummed a few steps away. Dreamers, business people, surfers, families, yelling children, and slowly meandering elderly couples, all mixing together in the winter sunshine and salty breeze.

Quirky shops and t-shirts vendors lined the east side of the street, and endless miles of beach stretched into the distance on the west. Bicyclists in wetsuits steered their bikes with one hand while they held their surfboards with the other. Chris and Kate passed souvenir shops selling keychains and miniature personalized license plates along with beach towels and sunglasses. Every block looked like a photo on a postcard stamped with the words, "Wish you were here."

Kate generally avoided tourist attractions, preferring to frequent quieter, less well-known places, but Chris didn't seem to share her aversion to crowds. Without missing a step, he walked past the family photo ops, the selfie-sticks, and the tourists on wobbly, rented Segways darting across the sidewalk. The noise and confusion were too familiar, too much a part of her past. It was loud and congested, and so completely LA that she wanted to leave as quickly as possible.

She swallowed her growing irritation as they passed a street performer doing some sort of interpretive dance with a hula hoop and a puppy. She closed her eyes, trying to shut out her memories, the days she had spent on this same boardwalk, the shops she had visited, the sound of Megan's laughter as she tried on the oversized hats and cheap sunglasses from the small shops. A fragrance rushed by, a wisp of Megan's favorite perfume, and she turned, drawn by the scent, searching for a face she knew she wouldn't see, stepping into the center of the road.

Strong arms wrapped around her waist and pulled her back. Chris held her against his chest as he turned, whisking her from the path from a fast-moving roller skater in neon shorts. The smooth slip of the wheels rushed past as she gasped, inhaling the spice and sea that surrounded her.

"Are you okay?" Chris asked, his hands clasped in front of her, enveloping her in warmth and safety, wrapping her in a protection she had never felt before.

She nodded, knowing she needed to step away, to put some distance between them, to retreat into the cold isolation she was used to. "I'm fine. Thank you. I just—" His sunglasses covered his eyes as he watched her, but she could picture their intensity. She felt the scrutiny, and vulnerability washed over her. "I'm fine," she said again and stepped away, out of the circle of his arms, away from the broad plane of his chest and the tanned comfort of his hands. She smoothed her jacket and avoided looking at him. "Thanks for the rescue."

"Anytime," he said, and she tried not to read into that one word, tried not to imagine what it would be like to have a rescuer, to have someone ready to slay dragons for her. It was a foolish thought, and she didn't have time for it.

Chris led her further down the street, and when he stopped at a food cart, she almost threw her hands up in defeat. He'd talked her into tacos. They'd spent forty-five minutes in traffic and had to park almost a mile away. She'd fought through the crowds in her designer heels, had been almost run over by a roller skater and for what? A food cart?

A thousand sarcastic comments rose to her lips. She was choosing which one to fling at him when he turned around. The grin on his face froze the words in her throat. A salty sea breeze tossed his hair, and the sun glinted in the blue of his eyes. Wearing khaki cargo pants and a long-sleeve athletic shirt with a surf foundation logo on the chest, he fit in perfectly with the sun-kissed sand and vacation atmosphere, like he had been made for bonfires and beaches.

She tugged on her black blazer, aware that she was as out of place here as he would have been arguing a case in a stuffy courtroom. When she'd left home, she had wanted to cut Los Angeles out of her heart, banish it to the trash pile of childish memories, like a toy she once loved and then gave away. She'd done it far better than she'd anticipated. She barely remembered the girl she'd once been. The beach parties and amusement park trips. The endless days of sunshine and palm trees, the Santa Ana winds that blew through with vengeful terror every October. Her life had been defined by where she was born. It was in every cell of her being, right up until the day she left for Boston and never looked back. She'd traded crowded freeways and warm winters for snow and brick buildings. She told herself she didn't miss it. She didn't miss the color, the vibrancy, the energy. She didn't miss the smell of sunscreen and salt or the way the sky burned red and gold as the sun sank into the sea. If she said it enough, maybe she would believe it.

Chris passed her two white cups with plastic lids and paper straws. She held them while he carried a brown box filled with tacos wrapped in wax paper. Salsa and spice wafted from the box and made her stomach growl. They crossed the sidewalk and headed for the beach. As she left the paved road, her heels sank into the sand. Holding one cup in her hand and cradling the other against her chest, she kicked off her shoes and used her free hand to scoop them up. They dangled from her fingers as she took unsteady steps across the chilly, winter beach.

Sand squished between her toes. Cold and gritty and soft, it seeped over her pink-painted toenails and caressed the soles of her feet. A pang of longing spiked in her heart. How long had it been since she'd felt sand beneath her feet? If she had gone back to Boston when she was supposed to, she would be spending the day fighting through snow to get to work, walking through the sleet and icy wind, her nose runny and red, the wind making her eyes water, and the piercing cold freezing the tears on her eyelashes. Instead, she was walking on the beach under a winter sun to have lunch with a famous director and his favorite fish tacos. She may have been having a career crisis, but at least she was warm.

Chris led them to one of the large swing sets that dotted the beach near the edge of the sidewalk. He sat in one of the swings and waited, a challenging smirk on his stubble-covered face. Kate rolled her eyes, and he laughed. Every minute of the past six years protested—every workaholic habit she had developed, every instinct that screamed at her to keep moving, to keep busy, told her not to do it. Sitting on a swing on the beach in the middle of the day was the most un-Kate-like thing she could think of, and yet, Chris sat there patiently, the swing swaying slightly as he waited for her to join him.

Her stomach rumbled again. With an exaggerated sigh, she dropped onto the swing next to him. She wasn't giving in; she was just hungry, and he was holding the food. She set her shoes neatly in the sand and passed him one of the sodas. When he held the box of tacos to her, she selected the one that looked like it had the least amount of grease on the paper. This whole thing was ridiculous. She would eat, but then she would insist that they get back to work. The sooner they got started on this film, the sooner she would get her hands on the information she needed. She kept her face stern and serious to prove she wasn't getting swept up in his taco adventure nonsense. The last time she had been adventurous and impulsive, Megan had died. She had learned her lesson.

Someone laughed along the water's edge, and Kate followed the sound. She remembered playing in the waves on the beaches that were further north. It was the same water, the same sea that she had grown up with. It was all the same, but nothing was the same. For six years, those waves had been touching the sand, and she had ignored it, tried to forget it, to tear every memory of it from her heart, and yet it had kept on. The ocean hadn't disappeared; she had.

He set the box on his lap and grabbed his own taco. "Trust me, Kate," he said with a boyish grin. "It was worth the drive."

She forced a smile on her face, thinking that unless this taco was made of gold, there was no way it was worth a forty-five-minute drive on the 10 West freeway that took her straight into every memory she wanted to forget. She unwrapped the taco, inhaling the pungent aroma of cilantro and onion, and took a bite.

She was wrong.

It was totally worth it.

Chapter Six

KATE THOUGHT HE WAS CRAZY.

He probably was.

Sitting on a swing, eating tacos, while he had a film to make was probably not the best idea. Kate made it clear that she disapproved, but he desperately needed to get out of that tiny office. The more time they had spent together that morning—her flaming hair dancing in the corner of his eye, her irritated sighs echoing in his ears—the less he could concentrate. He had started that morning planning the film, but by the time he made his escape, he was planning ways to make Kate laugh. She was magnetic, drawing his attention until he couldn't focus on anything except the rhythm of her breathing and the deepening scowl on her forehead.

She definitely thought he was nuts.

The empty corkboard he spent the morning staring at would eventually be a storyboard. The whiteboards would keep track of the filming schedule, locations, and the post-production elements. He was plotting the scenes in his head, crafting the documentary on paper before he put it on film. It was his usual process. He never wanted to waste time on set by trying to figure out the next shot while the cast and crew were waiting around. He prided himself on his careful planning and scheduling, but the closer Kate was, the more that process flew right out of his mind. He'd needed to get out of the office just to catch his breath. The tacos were a happy bonus.

She swayed slightly on the swing beside him, sipping her soda as she stared at the water. He might be wrong, but he was pretty sure she needed to catch her breath, too. Ben's warnings rose to the surface of his thoughts. He sensed a fragility in her, a tenderness beneath the severe suits and piercing looks that came from tragedy. If she was a character in one of his films, he would know every detail of her life, every secret, every shattered dream, every twist and turn that led her to this place. But this wasn't a movie, and he wasn't working from a script. He didn't know her backstory or what caused her to be so serious. Lily had shared stories of their college days, and he couldn't imagine the straight-laced woman next to him was the same woman who convinced Lily to sneak into the Hollywood Bowl with her and sing boy band songs from the darkened stage until the security guard chased them out. Somewhere between the Hollywood Bowl and Boston, Kate's story had changed.

The question was why. If he was directing the movie of her life, what would cause such a drastic turn? He twisted the swing so he could face her, dragging his feet through the sand, as a thousand stories leapt to life in his imagination. Who was Kate Sullivan?

She turned her head, her eyebrows raised in question. "What?" she asked. "Is there salsa on my face?" She didn't wait for him to answer but started patting her mouth with a napkin.

"No," he said. "I was just thinking about who I would cast you to play in a movie."

Her hand froze, and she blinked at him. Confusion danced in those big, green eyes, and he was secretly pleased to have thrown her off her game. Maybe she needed a few more curveballs in her life. Maybe he could be the one to throw them.

"Me?" she sputtered. "In a movie?"

"Well, I'm not saying you should give up your day job. In fact," he added quickly, "please don't. I think I'm going to need a good lawyer. But let's say you walked into an audition—who would I see you playing?"

"And?" she asked, her voice losing that clipped, professional tone he was used to. She sounded more relaxed, more at ease, and he was thrilled with the change. Maybe this was the woman he had been long-ing to know, the laughing girl buried beneath the suits and sarcasm. "What did you decide?"

He lifted his soda to his lips and took a long drink as he pretended to consider her, enjoying the way she stared back at him with undisguised expectation. The wind caught her hair and pulled the long waves over her shoulder. There was no stress, none of the tension that usually kept her so distant. He'd interrupted her work-first mentality and introduced something completely new. He liked being the one to disrupt her train of thought and shake her out of her routine. He tilted his head as he continued to look at her, drawing out the question, enjoying, perhaps a little too much, her undivided attention. "Maybe an international spy," he said. "The sharp suits and briefcase are a cover for your real work tracking down rogue agents bent on starting World War III."

She wrinkled her nose, and he longed to reach across the short distance that separated them and touch her cheek. "I'm not sure I'm super spy material. I'm not great at following orders."

He nodded, filing that information away. "Then how about a tena-cious journalist who uncovers a government conspiracy and has to run for her life?"

She pointed at her fancy high heel shoes on the sand. "I'm not much of a runner."

"That does complicate the whole running-for-your-life plot." He wadded up the last of the taco wrappers and tossed it in the takeaway box. He set the box by his feet, nestling it in the sand so it wouldn't blow away.

Across the beach, a family was building a sand castle. Beyond them, a couple lounged in folding chairs. The man was asleep, while a woman—Chris assumed it was his wife—read a book next to him. When the wind picked up and tossed the edge of his beach towel over his legs, his wife reached over and smoothed it back down. The man didn't even stir.

Inches away, Kate waited. Impatient, busy Kate. She watched him with an intensity he'd become so familiar with, as if every moment was important to her. She didn't want to waste a second and had very little tolerance for those who did. His mind spun as images sped past. Kate was strong and capable, but underneath it all, she had a soft heart. She might not want to show it, but he'd seen the way she protected Lily and the way she stood up for Hannah. Kate would never fade into the background. There was nothing subtle or subdued about her. She was color and movement, like a Van Gogh in a room of black and white photographs. People noticed her, and she knew how to use that to her advantage.

He snapped his fingers. "I've got it," he said. "You're a warrior queen, who leads her people to freedom."

She laughed, and the sound set a flurry of butterflies winging through his stomach. He'd heard her laugh before, but he'd never been the one to make her laugh. It was as if he'd won an award, and her laugh was the prize.

"I like that one," she said and sat up straighter in the swing, trying on her newly acquired royal title. "'Queen Kate' definitely has a nice ring to it."

Her eyes sparkled when she laughed, and he wondered what had happened to make the joy in her life so rare. He wouldn't ask; it wasn't his business. Not yet. As she turned away, the lightness of her smile changed, replaced by the haunted and distant expression he was used to seeing, as if she suddenly realized she wasn't supposed to be laughing. It was like something precious had been stolen, a gift he had barely glimpsed suddenly snatched away. She looked out at the sand and sea, the beach towels and people, like she was looking at foreign land.

"Do you miss all this?" he asked. "I know it's not snow and baked beans, but it's got some perks."

She pushed her feet against the sand and rocked the swing back and forth. She was quiet for so long, he wasn't sure she was going to answer. "Sometimes." The word was hushed, as if it escaped before she could stop it, a whisper of longing she couldn't control. He held his breath, hoping she would continue but afraid the smallest movement might frighten her back into her professional armor. "I left because I needed a change, but I have to admit, I forgot how special this place can be. It's . . . " She paused, then turned her face to his. "You were right; this place is a character. It has a heartbeat all its own."

Down by the water's edge, a seagull hopped across the wet sand, and a little girl chased it. Her mom followed close behind as the girl toddled after the bird, her hands reaching out and her laughter louder than the waves that rolled along the sand. Palm trees waved in the gentle breeze, and music drifted from behind them. Chris had been all over the world, and he'd never found another place like this. Even with the traffic and smog and earthquakes, *special* was the right word for this city.

Kate turned to look at him. "My sister and I used to love the beach. When I got my driver's license, we'd go almost every weekend. I even talked her into skipping school a few times so we could go to Zuma or Malibu. My dad would have killed us if he ever found out." She shook her head as Chris soaked up every word. "I was always the one causing trouble, dragging her into my adventures and schemes. Megan—" The word cracked under the weight of her memories. "Megan went along with it because she loved me."

"Megan sounds like a good sister. My little sister liked to tattle on me." He laughed. "I'd love to meet Megan someday."

Kate turned away and looked back across the waves. "Megan died six years ago."

He sucked in a breath. In the distance, white caps danced on the waves, leisurely rolling to the shore. He tried to imagine losing his own sister, the hole that would leave in his life. Even with her living so far away and busy with her own life, he would feel that loss every day. "I'm so sorry, Kate. I didn't know."

She shrugged. "I don't talk about it much. It's hard, knowing she's gone and I'm . . . not." She straightened her shoulders, pulling the armor back on, shielding herself once again. "I actually haven't been to the beach since she died. It's weird being here without her, like I'm doing something wrong."

Chris set his soda next to the box of crumpled wrappers on the sand and reached for her hand. "I'm glad you're here."

He met her gaze, searching for hesitation, waiting for her to pull away, but she didn't move. His fingers held hers loosely, giving her the freedom to move, the chance to withdraw. Her skin was soft against his, like silk sweeping against this palm. He wanted to pull her closer, to hold her tighter, to sit under the winter sun with her until the sadness in her eyes vanished.

The shrill ring of her cell phone intruded, a warning bell that rang too late. If he hadn't hesitated, if he'd moved quicker, maybe neither of them would have even heard the phone. Kate blinked like she had stepped out of a fog. Chris stuffed his hands in his pockets as she pulled her purse from the sand and dug inside it. The phone was still ringing when she looked at the caller ID. She pressed her lips together as the number flashed across the screen. With a decisive tap, she sent it to voicemail.

She dropped the phone in her lap and rubbed her eyes. Chris was about to ask if she was all right when her phone beeped again. She sighed and looked at the text message, her back stiff and her shoulders tensed for a fight.

He stepped away to give her some privacy. The sudden change in her demeanor hit him like a rogue wave. It only took a second for the vulnerable girl on the beach to disappear. She was distant and wary once again. He would have given anything to chase the worry from her face, to ease whatever burden she was carrying.

She stood and reached for her shoes. "Sorry to cut our lunch break short, but I need to go." Curt and to the point, her crisp, business tone was as cold as the winter waves. She brushed the wrinkles from her suit and pulled on the sleeves to straighten them.

Chris nodded and bent to pick up the box of trash. "Is everything all right?"

She shrugged as if there wasn't an easy answer to that question. "It's my dad. He asked me to come over as soon as possible. He said it's important."

If he remembered correctly, Kate had grown up in the San Fernando Valley, a land of suburbs and bedroom communities up north that were far from the smog and congestion of Los Angeles but close enough to commute to work.

"No problem," he said. "Let's go."

They walked back across the sand to the sidewalk. Kate stopped and set her shoes on the ground. "If you drop me at the mission, I'll grab my car and let you get back to work. I can catch up with you and your staring at the walls tomorrow."

He held her elbow to keep her from falling as she bent over to brush the sand from the soles of her feet. "That's a terrible idea." She glanced up at him as she slipped her shoes on, a protest already forming on her lips, but he kept talking before she could launch into her argument. "That's forty-five minutes of back tracking to the mission, and you'd still have another hour drive after that to get up north. It makes more sense for me to drive you."

She straightened, three inches taller in her fancy shoes, and pulled her arm from his grasp. "You don't have to do that. You've got work waiting for you. Besides, I don't know what my dad has in mind, and you don't want to end up stuck at my dad's house all day, do you?"

Actually, he did. He wanted to sit in traffic with her, and he wanted to sit in Detective Sullivan's house while they talked. He wanted to see where she grew up and look at the school pictures that he was willing to bet were hung on the walls of the house. He wanted to know who she was, where she came from, and what had driven her to leave.

She turned and briskly headed back to his car. He tossed the taco box in the trash and jogged to catch up with her. Kate had left him behind on the beach as soon as she looked at that text message. No discussion, no room for a change in her plans. Her mind was made up, and she was moving ahead with it. At the pace she was setting, he had about five minutes of walking to the car to convince her to change her mind.

"It's not a problem. Plus . . . " He searched for a reason that would sway her. He needed logic and efficiency—that was a language she understood. "I need to talk to your dad, anyway. He's got the leads from the club. It'll give me a place to start researching, and it might even give me some ideas for how to structure the film."

Kate stopped abruptly, and he stumbled to avoid crashing into her. The crowd moved past them, parting and passing like a river that never stopped flowing as the two of them were rooted like rocks in its path. Chris stood in front of her, waiting for her decision. Her green eyes darted from side to side, and he imagined her thoughts were bouncing around just as quickly. She was adding up the pros and cons, calculating the cost, debating both sides in her head. He was certain she wouldn't appreciate it if he told her she looked adorable when she argued with herself, so he kept quiet.

"All right," she said with unwavering finality, as if the jury had reached its verdict and all that was left was the sentencing. She lifted her chin, her gaze meeting his, and his heart did a little leap in his chest. "If you don't mind the drive, that would be a big help. Thank you."

Chris grinned. It was a small victory, but he'd take it. "I don't mind at all."

He walked beside her as they went back to his car. His step was easy and casual, not at all like the euphoria of a man who had just managed to convince the woman of his dreams to spend the rest of the day with him. He should have won an Academy Award for that performance.

Chapter Seven

KATE STOOD ON THE SIDEWALK outside her father's house in the early afternoon light. It was the neighborhood she had grown up in, the same street where she and Megan had ridden bikes and set up a lemonade stand every summer. A quiet community where people moved when they wanted to get away from the city, but still be close enough to work downtown or take field trips to the museums. It had everything her parents wanted for their kids—a good school district, a place where they could play outside and make friends. It was distant from her dad's work on the police force and far away from the death and destruction he witnessed.

At the end of the cul-de-sac, a mom watched her two children race their tricycles in circles. Ribbons dangled from the handles, and laughter drifted up the street. It wasn't the first time Kate had been back to the house since she arrived in Los Angeles, but it hadn't gotten any easier. The house she'd grown up in felt as foreign to her now as the streets of Hollywood. Too many years and too many memories had gone by. The gray stucco, two-story house had white shutters and empty window boxes, and the roof was fading from years of exposure under the southern California sun. Her dad's nondescript blue sedan was parked in the inclined driveway.

Chris waited beside her as she stood on the concrete walk that led to the front door. When she was growing up, the walkway had been lined with colorful flowers. She and Megan had helped their mom plant the flowers every spring. One year, it had been marigolds; another year, they had planted geraniums. She remembered going to the nursery and looking at all the bright flowers spread out in endless lines of color. Those trips usually ended in a squabble between her and Megan as they argued about which flowers to plant that year. And yet, somehow, her mom had always managed to find a compromise; and by the time the three of them were digging up the ground beside the walkway, they were all happy and laughing again.

The ground at her feet was now bare and empty, covered with a blanket of faded mulch that needed to be changed. She was surprised to find that she was grateful for Chris' presence. She hadn't wanted him to come with her. She preferred to deal with her family drama on her own. She didn't want to share that part of her life with anyone. She couldn't believe she had talked about Megan with him. Not even she and Lily talked about Megan anymore, but somehow, this man had managed to pull those memories out of her. It was unnerving.

But now, standing in front of her dad's house, stalling and searching for reasons to run away, she was actually relieved Chris was there. He'd kept up a steady stream of small talk as they'd left the frenetic pace of downtown behind and climbed into the sleepy, bedroom communities north of Los Angeles. When she drove these roads by herself, each mile raised her anxiety like a vise of regret that tightened around her chest until she could barely breathe. She hated this drive, hated going back to her past and all the reminders of her mistakes.

Chris and his soothing presence had made it easier. He was relaxed and calm, and that put her at ease. Whenever she started to freak out, he made a joke or asked a question, and she forgot to be nervous. It was as if he could read her mind, sensing when she needed to be distracted. Of course, she knew that wasn't true because if he could read her mind, he never would have let her join his production company. He was obviously good with people, sensing their moods and knowing how to interact with them. Kate wasn't sure how she felt about that. She didn't want to be so easily understood. The more people she was close to, the more chances she had for getting hurt.

She glanced at Chris and wondered if she had made a huge mistake bringing him here. It was a side of her life she didn't let people see. And yet, here he was, patiently waiting outside her dad's house for her to go knock on the door. It was the fact that he was so quiet and patient as he stood next to her that spurred her to action. If she had been alone, she would have continued to stall and stand on that spot on the cracked concrete, thinking of reasons why she should leave. Not today, though. Not with Chris waiting and watching her every move. She refused to look weak in front of him, refused to admit the yawning cavern of emptiness that filled her heart, the fear that kept her from knocking on the door. It was pride that propelled her forward and pride that made her ball her hands into fists to keep them from shaking.

Her heels clicked on the concrete as she walked resolutely to the front door and knocked. She'd faced off against some of the most powerful attorneys on the East Coast; she could face her own father.

The door swung open, and her dad stepped out onto the porch. He pulled her into a hug, wrapping her in the familiar scent of his aftershave. It was the same one he'd worn her entire life, and the smell of it brought back every Christmas and Father's Day when she had given him a bottle of it and he'd pretended to be surprised. She tried to remember the last time she had sent him a bottle, but she couldn't. It had been too long. The thought of her dad buying his own aftershave was unexpectedly sad. "Kate, I'm so glad you're here."

She hugged him back, allowing the warmth of his embrace to chase the chill of anxiety away. Her dad had always been her rock, her biggest fan, and her strongest defender. After Megan died, everything fell apart, and they only had each other to cling to. Megan was gone and a few months later, her mom was gone, too. The strain of her sister's death had broken their family to pieces. Her mom's grief turned to alcoholism, and that addiction eventually drove her away. She left them, disappearing right when Kate had needed her most.

She still remembered sitting in the dorm room she had shared with Lily at UCLA when her dad called and told her the news. Her mom was gone. She'd packed up her clothes, scribbled a note, and vanished. She hadn't even said goodbye. Kate had driven home immediately, refusing to believe her mother would abandon her; but as soon as she had stepped through the door, she'd known it was true. The house radiated emptiness and sorrow. First Megan, then her mom. Kate and her dad sat at the kitchen table, absorbing the silence and the loss, neither of them knowing at the time that Kate would be the next one to leave. Had her dad sat at that same table when she left for Harvard, alone in the house, abandoned by everyone he had ever loved? The thought churned in her stomach, a guilt she couldn't assuage and didn't know how to atone for.

"Hi, Dad," she mumbled into his shoulder, fighting to keep the past at bay, to keep the regret from paralyzing her. She pushed the thoughts away, drawing the familiar camouflage of strength around herself and easing into the detachment she had relied on for years.

Her dad let go and stepped back to look at her. "You are so thin. Are you getting enough to eat? Do you need money?"

She laughed. "I'm fine, Dad. In fact, I was eating tacos with Chris when you called."

Her dad's gaze settled on Chris. She groaned as years of police experience were suddenly focused on the director. Her dad was far more perceptive and observant than most people. It was the same look he had given every boy who'd ever shown up to take her on a date. That suspicious, vaguely threatening, dad look that he had perfected.

Chris didn't seem disturbed by the look. "Detective Sullivan, it's nice to see you again." He extended his hand, and her dad shook it firmly. If her dad did that guy thing where he squeezed hard to prove a point, Chris didn't flinch.

"You, too, Chris." Her dad glanced between the two of them, no doubt trying to gauge their relationship, and she was happy they didn't have anything to hide. "Come on in," he said, stepping aside as she and Chris crossed the threshold into her childhood home.

The house hadn't changed at all. After losing Megan and her mom, she had tried to run from all of her memories. She'd changed everything, so there was nothing left to remind her of what she'd lost. Her dad, on the other hand, had frozen his surroundings in time, as if he'd captured the last days their family had been together and preserved it in this house. Photos of her and Megan hung on the walls, the same photos she'd walked past every morning on her way out the door. He'd added framed photos of her graduations from UCLA and Harvard and one of Ben and Lily's wedding, but it was Megan's face that caught her attention. Megan, forever young. Megan grinning with her crooked pigtails in a school photo. Megan posing in a ballet recital. Megan at eighteen standing on the beach for her senior photos, smiling into the camera with no idea that less than a year later, she would be gone.

Kate turned away. That wasn't how she remembered Megan. All those beautiful photos were gone, erased from her mind, replaced by the one image that was burned into her brain. The last memory she had of her little sister was the last breath she took. It was the memory that never faded, the image of Megan that had replaced all of the others. She couldn't think of Megan without seeing that night, without seeing the moment she died. There was no escaping it.

"Are you okay?" Chris' hand was warm on the small of her back, a touch that broke though the ice she built up around herself. He was here. Why was he here? Why was he in this house? She wanted to ask him to leave, to shut him out before he saw too much, before he caught a glimpse of who she really was. The image she had so carefully crafted during her years in Boston wouldn't hold up here, not in this house, not surrounded by all these reminders of her past. But it was too late. She had let him in, and she was afraid she might never be able to shut that door again.

She stepped forward, pulling away from his touch and the protection it promised. "I'm fine." She turned and followed her dad into the kitchen. Chris' footsteps echoed behind her. Her worlds were colliding. The professional and reserved woman she had become was face to face with the wild and reckless girl she had been. It was a crash she wasn't prepared to deal with. She needed to find out why her dad called her here and get out as quickly as possible. She could always come back later, have a longer conversation with him at another time when Chris wasn't there to witness it.

Her dad poured thick, black coffee from his old drip coffeemaker into three mugs. As she and Chris sat at the table, he brought the mugs over and set them on the table. He went back for cream and sugar and added them to the table. He sat across from her in his usual seat. It was the same place he had been sitting when she came rushing back from college after he told her about her mom. The same place he had been sitting when she told him she was leaving for Harvard. She had been scolded, comforted, and guided at this table. She had thrown temper tantrums and cried her eyes out at this table. It had been the heart of their home. How many nights had Kate sat here while her mom made dinner and her dad concentrated on files he had brought home from work? When dinner was ready, her mom would make him put all the papers away. Everything stopped when they sat down to dinner, a family of four. Then it was three, then two, until finally it was just her dad left alone in an empty kitchen.

Her dad ignored the cream and sugar and took a sip of his black coffee. "I'm sorry for the emergency call, but something's happened, and I need to talk to you about it. It couldn't wait." Her dad had aged in the years she'd been gone. He was still fit—in fighting shape, as he'd call it—but his dark brown hair had faded to gray, and wrinkles lined the corners of his eyes. She saw a pair of glasses poking out from the breast pocket of his shirt, and she wondered if he was supposed to be wearing them. It was information she should know. She was the only one left to take care of him, watch out for him. She should know if he needed glasses, or if he was drinking too much coffee, or if his cholesterol was too high. But she didn't know those things. She didn't know anything about his life. She had been too busy trying to forget hers.

Her heart ached when she thought about what the past few years had been like for him, alone in this house while she was in Boston. He had his work on the police force, and she knew he loved it, but what had he done after work in the long hours between his shifts? He drove home to an empty house every night, surrounded by photos of the women he loved. The women who had left him.

She sipped her coffee; the strong, black brew was bitter on her tongue. She hadn't called as much as she should have. There'd always been a good reason. She was studying; she was working; she was busy. How many days had gone by when she could have called or texted, but she didn't? She'd been so determined to leave all of this behind that she'd ignored the one person who had been there for her. He'd never complained about it, and somehow that made it worse.

It was one more thing she had lost. One more thing she laid at the feet of the man who had shattered her family when he drove his car into hers. One more thing she would make him pay for.

She set the mug down and folded her hands. "What is going on, Dad?"

He cleared his throat and scratched his head, hesitating as he glanced at Chris.

Chris pushed his chair back, and the wooden legs squeaked against the tile floor. "If you don't mind, I've got a couple of phone calls I should make." He put his hand on her shoulder, a touch that caught her breath, like a shaft of sunlight cutting through a block of ice. He was strong and reassuring, like a mountain that never moved. Circumstances may swirl out of control, but that mountain remained standing. She didn't even realize he had become such a fixed point in her life, a compass that kept pointing her north. "I'll be out front if you need me. Sir." He nodded at her dad and slipped from the kitchen, leaving his coffee untouched on the table.

Her eyes followed him, imaging the path he walked through the living room, hearing the front door open and close. Perceptive and polite, it was quintessential Chris.

Her dad seemed to agree. "He's a good man. I like him." Kate blinked at her dad's pronouncement. She couldn't remember him saying that about any boy she had dated. Apparently, everyone—even a hardened police detective and overprotective father—liked Chris. "I'm glad to see you with him."

Kate shook her head. "It's not like that, Dad. We're working together on his new film. It's just a job. That's all." But she couldn't stop her gaze from drifting to the door he had walked through, part of her wishing he'd come back, but she didn't know why. "All right," she said as she took another sip of the brutally strong coffee. "You got me here. What's so bad that I had to race all the way up here?"

Even with Chris gone, her dad still stalled. Worry spiked in her gut. Was he sick? Fear rose, cold and unforgiving. Was she going to lose him, too? Anger quickly followed, warming her with its familiar fire. It was her favorite defense mechanism, a habit she refused to break. Anger was her comfort, her constant companion. It kept her strong. She tightened her grip on the coffee mug as thousands of worst-case scenarios trampled through her imagination. What more bad news could hit her family? Hadn't she and her dad been through enough? It was more proof that there was no one looking out for them, no one she could count on.

"Katie." He used the nickname he reserved for special occasions, and her stomach plummeted. It was the same name he used in the hospital when he sat by her bed and told her Megan was gone. Dread clawed its way up her throat. She held herself still, tensing for the blow that was coming, worrying she would shatter like glass hitting the floor. "It's about your mom."

Relief washed through her. He wasn't sick, and he wasn't dying. She exhaled and let her shoulders relax. She'd written her mom off years ago. There was nothing he could say about her mom that would hurt her, not anymore. She didn't see how anything about her mom would constitute an emergency. Footsteps echoed in the living room, and Kate swiveled in her chair, expecting to see Chris, wondering if he'd forgotten to take his phone with him. Giddy with relief that her dad was all right, she prepared to mock Chris for his forgetfulness.

"Your mom is here."

Her dad's words had barely registered as the world around her faded into the background and she struggled to breathe. It wasn't Chris who entered the kitchen. It was as if she was living in slow motion, like she was trapped in a thick web, unable to move, unable to flee. No. It wasn't possible.

A woman stood in the doorway of the kitchen. She was older and thinner than Kate remembered. Her hair was shorter, cut in a bob that framed her face. She was tan, and Kate remembered her dad telling her once that her mother had family in Arizona. Is that where she had been all these years?

Her mom smiled—a tentative, hesitant smile—as tears shone in her eyes. She clasped her hands in front of her stomach, and Kate noticed the pale pink polish on her nails, the wedding ring on her finger. The same ring in every family photo. The same ring Kate had tried on when her mom washed dishes. "Hi, sweetie."

Her mother's voice yanked her back to the present like a rubber band that snapped. How many times had she heard those words? Stumbling downstairs for breakfast or running through the front door after school. In the carpool pick-up lane or on the phone in her dorm room. When she was laying in the hospital bed and crying in her bedroom. Then the words were gone, and for six years, there had been only silence. The past came rushing back in a blur of resentment and a swift wave of anger.

Her mother had come home.

Chapter Eight

CHRIS ENDED THE PHONE CALL with the equipment rental company and leaned against the side of his car. At the end of the street, the kids were still playing and racing in circles. The sun was starting its slow descent, and the afternoon breeze had picked up. He ran the numbers in his head. The cost of the camera he wanted was a bit more than he had planned, but he was still under budget, which was good. Between the money Ben invested and the significant withdrawal he'd made from his investments, he should have enough to film, edit, and score the documentary. He was going to have to trust God for the marketing and advertising campaign.

He tapped his cell phone against his leg. It was the distribution that had him worried. If he couldn't get the film into theaters, it wouldn't matter how good it was. People couldn't see it if it wasn't playing anywhere. He needed to get the film onto screens, and to do that, he needed a distributor. He didn't have a plan, and there wasn't much he could do without a finished film, so he shuffled that issue to the bottom of his "things to be worried about" list.

He was adding the pick-up date he'd scheduled with the rental company into the reminder app on his phone when the front door to the Sullivan house slammed behind him. He turned and braced for impact.

Kate stormed down the concrete walk, her high heels clicking like machine gun fire. She strode to the car, her face hard and her jaw clenched. He'd seen her mad before; he'd even seen her stand her ground against a dangerous criminal, but nothing like this. He raced around the car to open the passenger door before she could rip it off.

"Bad news?" he asked, knowing full well that whatever had happened in the house was worse than she had expected.

She aimed her gaze at him, and his breath caught. Pools of pain and unshed tears sparkled in her eyes. She crossed her arms over her chest like it was the only thing holding her together. He stepped forward and took her in his arms, pulling her against his chest and cradling her head on his shoulder. She stiffened in his arms as if she would pull away, but he held her tightly, running his hand over her back. Whispered prayers fell from his lips and tumbled into her hair. Resistance fled, and she sagged in his arms. Her jagged breathing rasped against his chest, and his heart ached. Confident, brash Kate, the woman who could reduce a man to a puddle with one look, cried like her world was ending.

They stood on the sidewalk in the shadow of her father's house until her breathing evened out. She stepped back and ran her hands over her face, scrubbing away the tears. "I'm sorry."

"For what?" Chris touched her cheek and caught a stray tear. He wiped it away with his thumb as the breeze caught her hair and tangled it around his fingers. If he took a step closer, he could kiss every tear from her face. The thought raced through his body, and his hand stilled against her cheek.

Kate shook her head. "For this," she said waving her hands at herself. "I just . . . " She stopped as if she didn't trust herself to say anymore, and the raw vulnerability he saw made him want to pull her against him again and never let her go. Kate wasn't invincible, and for the first time, she was letting him see it. It was like being entrusted with a precious jewel, and he knew he could blow it with one careless word. "Can we go?" she asked, her voice ragged from the tears she had shed.

"Absolutely." He stepped back and held the car door open for her, his heart pulsing in a wild gallop. Kate needed him.

She put one foot in the car and stopped, a curse flying from her lips. "I left my purse in the house."

"Don't worry," he said. "I'll get it." She nodded weakly, sinking into the passenger seat, and the defeat in her shoulders wrecked him.

He closed the car door and walked back to the house. Detective Sullivan opened the front door before he finished knocking. "Is she okay?" His face was tense and sad as he looked over Chris' shoulder, searching for his daughter, hoping for information Chris didn't have. Was Kate okay? Definitely not, but judging by the weary sorrow that lined Detective Sullivan's eyes, neither was he.

Chris struggled for words. "She's upset." That sounded like the biggest understatement he'd ever made, but Detective Sullivan didn't press for more. Whatever had happened in the kitchen after he left had devastated them both. It was as if an earthquake had rattled through the house, upending everything and shattering their fragile relationship. "Kate left her purse here. I told her I'd get it."

An older woman came to the door. Detective Sullivan stepped to the side, and she stood next to him. He recognized her from a few of the photos he'd seen on the walls. She had the same green eyes and square chin as Kate. In the photos, she and her daughters all had the same bright smile. Kate's mother. She held out Kate's black bag. "Here it is," she said. It wasn't sadness in her voice but resignation, as if she knew she had lost the battle before it even began.

"Thank you," he said as he took the purse and tucked it against his side.

She smiled faintly and walked away, her back hunched and her head low, as if she carried a weight that had become too much to bear.

Chris looked at Detective Sullivan. The hardened police officer sighed and shook his head. "Take care of my Katie," he said, and the unvarnished emotion of the words cut into Chris. "This isn't going to be easy on her. Or any of us."

He didn't know what to say or do. It was like watching an accident happen right in front of his eyes and being helpless to stop it. "I will."

Detective Sullivan nodded, and Chris turned away. He knew the detective was watching, keeping the door open, hoping his daughter would come back; but Kate sat in the passenger seat, her eyes staring straight ahead, refusing to acknowledge him.

Chris opened the driver's side door and got in. He passed Kate's purse to her, and she took it with a mumbled thanks. Her jaw was rigid as he started the car. As they drove away, Chris glanced in the rearview mirror. Detective Sullivan stood in the open door, waiting.

Kate never looked back.

*****

They drove in silence as Chris headed south, back into the hustle and bustle of LA. He didn't want to push, but he felt the tension in the car, the tenuous grip Kate had on her emotions. He told Detective Sullivan he would take care of her, but he wasn't sure how. Maybe he should take her straight to Lily and let her do the best friend thing.

Kate leaned against the passenger door and stared out the window at the passing cars while he drove and prayed. The radio played in the background, but neither of them paid any attention to it. Kate was lost in thought, closing off more with every mile, retreating into a place he wasn't sure he could reach.

As the sun dipped below the horizon, an idea formed. He could have run it past Kate, but he decided surprise might be the best tactic. They passed the junction to the 101 freeway that would have taken them back to Hollywood, and Kate sat up. She turned to Chris. "Where are we going?"

Chris shrugged. He might be making a huge mistake. Kate probably hated the fact that he'd seen her cry. She probably wanted to go back to the mission, get her car, and drive as fast as she could straight to the airport and hop on a plane back to Boston. He wasn't ready to let that happen. So, in the miles of silence, he'd hatched a plan.

"You've had a rotten day," he said, and she snorted. "I happen to have a foolproof cure for rotten days. It is absolutely, one hundred percent effective." He glanced at her. Shadows swathed the car, and she sank into the darkness. For once, she refused to fight or argue. That willingness to surrender was more worrisome than anything else. "Are you up for it?" he challenged, hoping for a spark, some remnant of the fire he was used to, but she was quiet.

"Does it involve a large amount of alcohol?" she asked. Her expression was tired and hollow, like she'd been emptied out and nothing remained but the shell.

"Nope."

She turned her gaze back to the window. "Then it doesn't sound very effective."

He reached over and took her hand. It was small and cold in his, and he folded his fingers over hers, wrapping her hand tightly. She sucked in a breath, but she didn't pull away. He squeezed until she looked at him. "Trust me, Kate."

He saw the conflict in her eyes, the indecision and doubt. Trust did not come easily to her. He sensed the deep capacity for love and loyalty within her; he'd seen it in the fierce protectiveness she showed her friends. She would fight to the last breath for the people she cared about. He'd seen her stand up for her best friend, going toe to toe with a movie star to defend Lily. He'd watched her march up to a knife-wielding man to protect Hannah. Kate was bold and brave, and at that moment, she desperately needed someone who was willing to fight for her. He wanted to be that person—if she would let him.

He kept his eyes on the road and her hand in his as he waited.

"All right, I trust you." It was little more than a whisper, barely louder than the heater that hummed in the car, but it was enough.

Chapter Nine

KATE WALKED THROUGH THE SMALL courtyard behind Chris. A collection of pretty townhouses surrounded the well-maintained common area. Flower beds still bloomed in the winter air, and the palm trees were tall and green. The sound of ocean waves and the tang of salt told her they were near the beach. Kate peeked through the gaps in the buildings and caught a glimpse of white foam sparkling on the inky ocean. The dark, evening sky matched her mood. Dull, black, and starless.

She was exhausted, and what she really wanted to do was to go back to Ben and Lily's house, crawl into the comfy guest bed, bury herself under a fluffy blanket, and never leave. She didn't know why she agreed to Chris' rotten-day antidote plan. There was nothing that could fix the mess of this day. She should have pulled herself together and insisted that he take her right back to the mission, so she could have had her breakdown in private. Instead, she'd dissolved into a crying mess right in front of him.

The memory of how he'd pulled her into his arms rushed through her with a tingle of excitement that she tried to ignore. This was Chris. She couldn't dwell on his strong arms or his hand on hers or the way he had held her like she was someone special. That was too complicated. There were too many things that could go wrong. She would get through this one night, and that would be the end of it.

She had been distracted and foolish to agree to come here with him, but after the shock of seeing her mom again after almost six years, she didn't know what to do. Her whole world had been turned inside out, and she didn't know which side was up anymore. She couldn't stay in that house, not for one second, with her mother. The woman who had walked away, packed up, and left without even saying goodbye had suddenly reappeared, showing up like she would be welcome, like all would be forgiven. The fact that her dad would even let her in the house was ridiculous. That he had been a part of it, asking her to come to the house without telling her why, crushed her heart with such force, she was amazed it was still beating.

Of course, he didn't want to warn her about her mom being there. He knew she never would have come. That he would be a part of the ambush, springing it on her like some twisted surprise party, made her want to scream. He was the one person she thought would understand, the one person she thought was on her side. Her mother had abandoned him, too. Had he forgiven her? Let bygones be bygones? It was impossible. Her mother didn't deserve forgiveness.

She didn't care if her mother had come to apologize. Words wouldn't make up for what she had done. Words didn't matter. Would words bring back all the years she had lost? Would an apology make up for the damage she had caused? No. It was too late for apologies or phony tears. That bridge had been burned a long time ago, and Kate had no interest in rebuilding it. As far as she was concerned, her mom could go right back to wherever she had been for the past six years. She hadn't been there when Kate needed her, and she certainly didn't need her now.

Sitting in Chris' car when he went to get her purse, she had no idea what to do or where to go. She thought about going back to Boston.

Forget about Megan and the accident, forget about Los Angeles and her family. She wanted to run away, to get as far away as possible from her parents. She wanted to go back to the city where she had tried to start over, but she didn't have a job there anymore, and she had canceled the lease on her apartment. There was nothing for her in Boston anymore. There was nothing for her anywhere. She wanted to run and never stop, but she didn't have anywhere to go. She could have said no to Chris' plan and gone back to Ben and Lily's house, but Lily would have taken one look at her and wanted to talk. Lily was her best friend, and she loved her, but she wasn't in the mood for encouragement or prayer or support.

So, she had ended up in a small complex of townhouses in Santa Monica with Chris. He had been so kind to her, holding her when she dissolved into a weepy mess, ignoring the sob-induced hiccups and incessant sniffling. The truth of the matter was that she hadn't wanted to be alone. She didn't want to be tough and strong anymore. She had been unprepared for the shock of seeing her mother, and as much as she hated to admit it, she didn't want to deal with it on her own. It wasn't her finest moment, and she wouldn't have blamed Chris if he had dumped her at her car and sped off into the night. Nobody wanted to walk into that much family drama.

She didn't want to think about what he thought of her—or what she looked like. She probably had mascara streaks covering her face and snot crusting on her nose. Honestly, she was too tired to care. She was empty and exhausted, and more than anything, she wanted to forget.

Chris had let go of her hand when they left the freeway and started driving down the narrow, two-lane roads. When they parked, she wondered if he was going to try to hold her hand again, and she wondered if she should let him. Instead, he led them to a corner townhouse with a leaded glass door. She stood behind him as he sifted through the keys in his hand.

"Where are we?" Kate asked.

Chris glanced over his shoulder as he answered. "My place."

Nerves tingled in her stomach as he unlocked the door and pushed it open. He'd brought her to his house. Implication and anticipation warred within her. She scrambled to find the logical thing to do, the common-sense choice. Should she stay? Should she go? Was she about to do something incredibly stupid?

Chris flipped on the lights and waited. "Are you coming?"

She was about to object. Her mushy brain was formulating an excuse when he smiled. "It's okay, Kate. I promise."

How she longed for a promise she could believe in. She followed him inside, willing to go anywhere that didn't require her to think, work, or pretend like everything was fine.

As he led the way, she looked at his house. It wasn't flashy or overdone; in fact, it was barely decorated. No movie posters on the walls or flashy colors. The entryway had an oak table with an orderly collection of shoes sitting underneath. Chris kicked off his shoes and slid them under the table. As Kate slipped off her shoes, she looked at a stack of unopened mail piled next to a basket where he tossed his keys. No fancy chandeliers or expensive furniture. It was quiet and humble, like the man who lived there.

She wasn't sure if this was exactly what she had expected from Chris or if she just hadn't thought about it before. Part of her had assumed he would live in a big house like Ben, enjoying the perks of Hollywood life, set apart and distant from everyone else. Maybe a personal chef or at least a big garage with a bunch of fancy cars. It was unexpectedly comforting to have been wrong. Chris was the same man here that he was in the office—simple and unpretentious. What would it be like to be that honest? Guilt pricked her conscience, and she pushed it away. She was too tired to examine the mistakes she had made—the mistakes she was continuing to make.

She followed him into the living room. The tile floor was cold against her bare feet. The living room was large and open with a wall of windows that faced the ocean. Whitecaps rolled in the distance. "Oh, wow," she whispered and crossed to the glass doors.

Chris smiled and slid the door open. A chilly breeze hit her—salt and sand and memories. She stepped out onto the wooden deck and breathed deeply. Two large surfboards were propped against the wall to her left, and a massive grill sat to her right. Black wicker chairs with thick, blue cushions faced the sea, and a short staircase led to the beach. No wonder he picked this place. She could have walked down the stairs and been at the water's edge in less than a minute. The temptation was strong, the pull of the tide and the lullaby of the waves. Soon the moon would be high, its light reflecting on the shifting surface. She knew what it felt like to swim in the moonlight, to dive into the quiet immensity of the ocean at night.

"This is what sold me on the place," Chris said as he stood beside her, his long hair caught up in the breeze. He tucked it behind his ears. "I couldn't say no to having the beach for my backyard. The place needs a lot of work, which we all know I am incapable of doing myself, but it was worth it."

"It's amazing." Kate looked at the view, longing and loneliness dancing in her heart. She had given up so much trying to escape her past, and after all those years, she ended up right back here, at the edge of a southern California beach in the moonlight.

"Do you want to walk on the beach?" Chris asked.

She shook her head. She wasn't ready. Not yet. A trip to the beach at night, a drive down a canyon road—that was what had started her on this path—one bad decision that had changed everything. She couldn't face it. Going to the beach was the last thing she had promised Megan, and they never made it. She couldn't go on her own. Not when Megan's memory still haunted her, still echoed in a tangle of broken glass and screaming tires.

Chris didn't insist or ask why. He went back into the house, and she followed him into the kitchen. The appliances were outdated, and the small, square tiles that covered the counter tops spoke of the age of the house. But everything was clean, almost sparse. Kate had never been a neat-and-tidy kind of girl. Her office at the firm had been organized and clean, but that was because it had been expected. No one wanted to hire a disorganized lawyer. Like everything else in her life, it had been about keeping up appearances. Her apartment in Boston was another story. It had usually been a mess, simply because she didn't have the time or the desire to keep it clean. She knew where everything was, and she didn't entertain enough people to require her to keep it respectable-looking. She was the only one who saw it, and it didn't bother her.

Chris opened the refrigerator and peered inside. From behind him, Kate saw that his food selection ranged from leftover Chinese food to a variety of half-empty condiment jars. "Water? Coffee? Soda?" he asked.

"Water would be great, thanks."

He passed her a bottle of water and grabbed one for himself. "Step one of my Rotten Day cure. Pizza." He pulled a frozen pizza out of the freezer. Based on the stack of pizza boxes in the freezer, Kate guessed it was one of his go-to meals. Not that she had any room to judge him. Her culinary skills were limited to making breakfast and reservations. At least now she knew why he showed up at Ben and Lily's house for dinner so often. Without Lily's cooking over the past few months, they both might have starved.

As he turned on the oven to preheat and unwrapped the pizza, she looked at the photos on his fridge. There were several photos of a young boy and a baby girl. In one, the boy was wearing a giraffe costume. In another, the little girl had a big pink bow on her head and a onesie that said, "My uncle loves me." There was also a family photo taken somewhere in snow-covered mountains. Chris and two older people she assumed were his parents and a young woman. Girlfriend? Sister? Ex-wife? She had no idea. She looked at the photo and realized how little she knew about him. She had always thought of him as Ben's friend. The guy who tagged along, the best man at the wedding. In all the time they'd spent together, she'd never bothered to ask about him, and yet, there she was, in his house by the beach, while he made her pizza. In focusing all her energy on finding Megan's killer, she had overlooked so much.

"Are these your parents?" she asked, pointing at the photo.

Chris nodded. "Yep. That was four or five years ago. We spent Christmas in Tahoe. That's my little sister, right before she met the man she ended up marrying. They live in Michigan, and my parents moved out there to be close to the grandbabies. The California sun was no match for the pull of baby snuggles and dirty diapers." He laughed as he slid the pizza into the oven. "But I don't mind sending them our weather reports every winter. I'm pretty sure they're snowed in right now."

He led the way out of the kitchen and into the living room. His chocolate brown sofa was squishy and soft and so comfortable, she thought she could fall asleep on it. Once they were seated, he turned to her. "Ready for step two?"

Apprehension raced through her. His nearness was . . . she searched for the right word. Unsettling. It ignited nerves and excitement she thought were dead. It wasn't like she'd never been on a date or had a boyfriend; she'd had plenty, but most of them had ended in disappointment or disaster. She just hadn't been on a date for a really long time. The last time she'd thought about a relationship was when she'd foolishly thrown herself at Noah, and he'd turned her down.

The townhouse was suddenly too warm. She felt the heat of it in her face. She should have gone back to Ben and Lily's house. She should have gone back to Boston. She was about to get up and leave, call a cab to take her back to the mission and put some distance between her and Chris, when he gently touched her hand.

"It's going to be okay, Kate." Peace enveloped her. She wanted to believe him. She wanted to trust him. He passed her a blanket, and she snuggled under it while he grabbed a remote control from the coffee table in front of the sofa.

A large, flat screen television mounted to the wall across the room sparked to life. He may not have updated his kitchen appliances, but the television was state-of-the-art. Chris scrolled through the menu and pulled up a black-and-white movie she'd never heard of. She narrowed her eyes at the screen. She had expected him to play one of his movies, something he'd made, something with his name on it. In her experience, men were quick to brag about themselves, always trying to impress with their achievements. She had learned to play the same game, flaunting her victories and her accomplishments to keep pace with them, to feel like she was a part of that world.

Piano music filled the room as Charlie Chaplain waddled across the screen swinging a cane. "This is step two?" she asked, unable to keep the disbelief from her voice. "Charlie Chaplain?"

Chris looked scandalized, as if she had just insulted his childhood hero. "Don't underestimate Charlie Chaplin. This guy was a genius. He wasn't just the star of his movies. He was the writer, director, even the composer. He completely changed film-making. I took an entire class on his films in graduate school."

Kate nodded with all the solemnity she could muster. "Was that class before or after Explosions 101 and Tactics for Effective Alien Invasions?"

Chris laughed and wagged his water bottle at her. "Hey, Explosions 101 is paying for our documentary."

A tickle fluttered in her veins when he said "our documentary." He had given her a place when she didn't have one, included her in his dream, shared his deepest hope with her. She didn't deserve it. If he ever found out her real motivations, he'd never forgive her, and she wouldn't blame him.

She watched the flickering scene, lulled into comfort by the piano music and the lack of conversation. Her world was all about words. Arguing legal precedents, searching for loopholes in contracts, debating the meaning and ramifications of a single word. It was exhausting.

Heaviness gripped her heart. Two words from her father had sent her entire world crashing down. *She's here.*

She tried to focus on the movie, but her mind kept going back to her father's house. Was her mother still there? Had he let her stay? After everything she had done to them, the pain she had caused, was he going to let her move back and pretend like nothing happened? She didn't know if she wanted to call her dad and yell at him or never speak to him again.

The timer on the oven beeped, and Chris went back to the kitchen. Kate didn't want to think about it anymore, but she couldn't stop. All of the carefully constructed walls she had built, the boxes she had used to ignore her pain and her memories—it was all gone, blown to smithereens by her mother's reappearance. What was she supposed to do now?

Chris reappeared at her side and handed her a plate with two slices of pepperoni pizza. "Step three of my feel-better cure is to stop thinking about the thing that made your day rotten until after ice cream."

She looked up at him, his tousled hair and broad chest, his golden skin and blue eyes. He hadn't asked any questions. He hadn't demanded to know the details of her family drama. He'd brought her here and made her dinner like it was the most natural thing in the world. No one had ever treated her so gently. Most people she knew were happy to capitalize on her strength and confidence. They expected her to have it all together, to push through and get things done. Chris was willing to take care of her without even being asked. In this house, with this man, she could be vulnerable; she could be sad; she could be a hot mess; and he didn't mind. He accepted her in the midst of the chaos, instead of demanding that she get her act together first.

From somewhere in the back of her mind, from the recesses of her heart, she heard the whisper of a word. *Grace.* Grace was a concept used by people who refused to take responsibility for their actions, an excuse for failure. She wasn't interested in that kind of easy road. In her world, people got what they deserved.

Kate took the plate and tried to smile, silencing the echo. "There's going to be ice cream?" she asked, struggling to get the words past the dryness in her throat.

"Of course, there's ice cream," he said. "I'm not a savage." He sat next to her with his own plate and closed his eyes in prayer.

She watched him, oddly comforted by his willingness to pray over frozen pizza. His faith was so ingrained in his life, in everything he did, that not even pizza was too little to pray about. She had never felt that way about God. Even living with Lily, she never accepted the idea that God cared about the small details of her life. Growing up, she always thought He was more of a big-picture God. She'd been convinced that as long as she took care of the day-to-day details of her life, as long as she was a generally good person and tried to do the right thing, God would be there for the big stuff. She had believed that if she was ever really in need, He would show up with lightning bolts and power, but when that time came, He wasn't there. If He didn't show up when her sister was dying, why would He care about pizza?

Even though it didn't make sense to her, she appreciated that Chris believed. He might be wrong, but at least he was sincere. It was something she could count on, one of those immovable mountain things that gave her topsy-turvy world a center.

Chris opened his eyes and looked at her, and she swallowed, embarrassed that he'd caught her staring at him. "Do you want to talk about it?"

"What?" she asked.

"Whatever happened back at the house."

She shook her head, feeling guilty for not wanting to open up to him, to explain the entire tragic backstory, but she wasn't ready. "I'm sorry. I'm not being very much fun."

"You don't have to be fun or put on a brave face or pretend like everything is okay." He reached across the distance between them and covered her hand with his. "Just be you; that's all I want."

His hand slipped away, and he pushed play on the remote control. As Charlie Chaplin danced on the screen, Kate longed to take Chris' hand, to hold it close, but she refused. She didn't have anything to offer him, nothing to bring to the table. She didn't deserve his goodness, and he deserved much more than the broken woman she had become. She left destruction in her wake everywhere she went, and she didn't want him to be the next casualty.

Chapter Ten

IT WAS AFTER NINE THE next morning when Kate emerged from the guest room at Ben and Lily's house. She had snuck in after midnight and tiptoed down the hallway to her bedroom like a teenager sneaking in after curfew. Creeping down the hallway, she told herself she didn't have to sneak. She hadn't done anything wrong. She was a grown woman who could stay out until midnight if she wanted to. She was just being polite by not waking up her friends as she walked silently down the dark hall using her cell phone for a light. She was being thoughtful—and not at all evasive. Plus, there hadn't been anything to discuss at midnight. It wasn't like she had been on a date.

As she left the guestroom, she checked both ways, but the hallway was quiet and empty. Ben and Lily were both probably up and gone. She hadn't deliberately planned to miss seeing them, but it was a fortunate coincidence that she had more time to think through what had happened yesterday. Pizza, movies, and ice cream with anyone else would have qualified as a date in her book. But not with Chris. Obviously not with Chris.

Chris was different.

He was funny and sweet, and he had taken care of her when seeing her mother again had nearly destroyed her. He hadn't asked about it; he didn't press; he'd simply been there for her in a way no one else ever had. In her experience, dinner and a movie at a guy's apartment usually came with expectations. Last night had been surprisingly expectation-free. After three black-and-white movies, that she had to admit she enjoyed, and a bowl of cookie dough ice cream, Chris had driven her back to her car at the mission.

The drive through the deserted streets had been so different from their drive back from her dad's house. She felt lighter, as if the stress and worry had lifted. She had assumed it was because she was too tired to think about the decisions she needed to make, the drama she would have to face, but maybe it had been something more. Being with Chris had made her burden less heavy. He hadn't solved her problems; she hadn't even explained all her problems, but knowing he was there had been exactly what she needed. It didn't make sense. All he'd done was sit on the sofa and reheat a frozen pizza.

And yet when they had pulled into the mission parking lot, she was sad the night was over. Noah had met them there with a sleepy and suspicious look on his face as he unlocked the gate so Kate could get her car. She hadn't missed the pointed look Noah had given Chris, but Chris hadn't said a word. He walked her to her car and gave her a quick hug, then waited in the parking lot until she drove away. She drove the winding roads back to Ben and Lily's house under a silver moon with images of Charlie Chaplain playing through her mind, and for the first night in years, she'd fallen asleep with a smile on her face.

She walked toward the kitchen and frowned as she thought about the interrogation Noah had most definitely given Chris after she left. What would he say? What did Noah think happened? What did Chris think about last night? Did he think she was an emotional wreck? She wouldn't blame him after he witnessed her spectacular meltdown outside her dad's house. When she'd used the restroom at his place, she'd looked in the mirror and gasped. Her blotchy face and red eyes hadn't been a pretty sight. He must think she was a mess. He was right.

She reached for her cell phone to text him but stopped. What was she going to say? *Thanks for the pizza. Sorry I cried on your shirt and ate all of your ice cream.* She stared at the phone, her thumb tapping on the screen. When was the last time she worried about what a man thought of her? She didn't like the feeling, so she shoved her phone back in her pocket. There would be no texting and no acknowledgement of her breakdown. Nothing happened that couldn't be forgotten. She would go back to the office and act like everything was exactly the same as it had been before. Nothing had changed. She wouldn't mention it; he wouldn't mention it; and they would all move on.

She entered the sun-dappled kitchen and punched the buttons on the coffee maker. She needed to stop thinking about ice cream and Charlie Chaplain movies and focus on why she was here. This was about justice. Romance was not part of the plan. Chris was a distraction that needed to be controlled.

"Long night?"

Kate jumped, her hand gripping her chest like she'd had a heart attack. Lily sat in one of the oversized chairs in the living room that faced the panorama windows. Her Bible was open on the small table beside her, along with a coffee cup and an empty plate. A teasing smile played on her lips, and Kate knew that Noah had tattled on her. The rat. He'd probably texted Lily before he'd even left the mission parking lot. "I thought you already left for work."

"And miss this story? I think not." Lily pointed to the other chair. "Grab your coffee, get a cinnamon roll, and fill me in."

Kate sighed. As her coffee mug filled, she added a fresh cinnamon roll to a plate. She went to the large living room and set the mug and plate on the coffee table before sitting in the chair opposite Lily.

Her friend looked radiant in an oversized sweater, her hair pulled back in a ponytail so the kids at the church's preschool wouldn't be able to yank on it. Lily was curled up in the chair, comfortable and cozy in the house she had made her own. Little touches of Lily decorated the space. Pretty flower arrangements had appeared after they returned from their honeymoon. Framed posters of Ben's movies still hung on the walls, but now there were framed Scripture verses as well. Where the house had once been austere—tastefully but impersonally decorated by a professional designer Ben's agent had hired—now it felt like a home. Married life agreed with Lily, and Kate was happy for her. True, she had been skeptical of Ben at first, downright hostile to him at times, but she was glad she had been wrong. She was significantly less glad about the knowing look on Lily's face.

She might as well get it over with. "Yes, I was with Chris last night. No," she added quickly when Lily's smile got a little too big. "It wasn't a date or anything romantic. My dad dropped a bombshell on me yesterday, and Chris was the one stuck picking up the pieces. That's all."

She bit into the ooey-gooey goodness of the still-warm cinnamon roll and remembered that Lily's cooking was one of the reasons she loved her.

Lily's smile faded. "What bombshell?"

Kate took a sip of her coffee and wished she'd used a bigger mug. There wasn't enough caffeine in her system for this conversation. "My mom is back in town. She was at my dad's house when I got there." The cinnamon roll tasted like sawdust, and she put it back on the plate. "I was sitting in the kitchen, talking to my dad, and then there she was . . . walking in like it was still her home." She wiped her hands on a napkin and concentrated on folding it into a neat rectangle. "Let's just say, I didn't handle it well. Chris and I were . . . " She hesitated, wondering how much she could explain; tacos and swings and the beach seemed so far away. "We were working when my dad texted. Chris drove me to my dad's place, so he was there when it all went down."

Chris may not have understood the significance of her mom being at the house, but Lily would get it. Lily had been with her when she got the call from her dad all those years ago. Lily had coached and dragged her through the rest of that semester, refusing to let her drop out, forcing her to keep going when she wanted to give up. Lily had seen the destruction her mother's leaving had caused. Lily would understand why she couldn't forgive her.

"Well, that's . . . " Lily paused, searching for the right word. "Unexpected. What did she say?"

Kate shook her head. "Nothing. I got up and left. I don't want to hear anything she has to say."

"But your dad—"

Kate dropped the napkin on the table. "My dad was wrong. He should be just as mad at her as I am. She left him, too." Anger rose as fresh as it was the day her mother left. Time hadn't healed this wound; if anything, it had made it worse. Years had gone by, years without her mother, years her mother had thrown away. It was too late now. Her mother could stay gone for all she cared.

Lily held her coffee cup between her hands, her eyes glancing to the open Bible. Kate bristled. She wasn't in the mood for a lecture about Jesus or forgiveness or honoring your parents. If her mom wanted honor, she should have acted like a mother instead of running away. How do you honor someone who broke your heart?

"That must have been a huge shock. I'm so sorry, Kate."

Relief washed through her. She wasn't ready to stop being mad. It wrapped around her like armor. Anger kept her going, anger kept her strong. If she stopped being angry, the people who wronged her would get away with it. Forgiveness made people weak, and she was done being weak. "Chris had the misfortune of seeing me fall apart. He drove me to his place, where we ate pizza and watched old movies. That's it."

Lily raised her eyebrows as she peered at Kate over the rim of her coffee mug. "That's it?"

Was that it? Kate stood and walked to the big windows that overlooked the Hollywood Hills. A thick marine layer hovered over the skyline, obscuring the skyscrapers and blanketing the horizon in gray. "I'm not looking for a relationship."

"Sometimes, that's exactly when you find one." Lily laughed. "Do you think I was looking for a relationship when a movie star jumped into my car at the airport? God's timing doesn't always line up with our timing."

"I'm not interested in God's timing," Kate snapped, and instantly regretted it. Lily didn't deserve her irritation. She crossed back to the chairs and sat down. "I'm sorry, Lily. I just have too much going on right now. I'm thrilled that God worked things out for you and Ben, but that was different. Me and Chris—we don't make sense. He's sweet and kind—"

"And handsome," Lily interrupted.

Kate stuttered, her train of thought derailed by a memory of Chris' broad shoulders and stubble-covered face. "Yes, he's handsome, but

I'm a mess." The truth slipped out before she could stop it. She was a confused, angry, sad mess. Blue eyes and ice cream couldn't change that.

"Maybe," Lily said. "But you're God's mess, and He has a plan for you. It's time you start believing that."

Kate wanted to argue. She had fact after fact to throw at Lily, to prove that God didn't care. She could construct a winning legal case proving that there wasn't a plan and that she didn't need Him, but Lily was so convinced of her faith, so trusting, that she couldn't do it. She knew how much Lily's faith meant to her, and she couldn't bring herself to snuff it out. If Lily found comfort and purpose in believing in God—and that was fine—but Kate knew better. "I'll try," she said, and that was as much as she was willing to concede. She stood, ready to end the conversation, ready to go back to her plan to forget about everything except Megan.

Lily hugged her, and for a moment, it was like they were back in their dorm room. It had always been the two of them. Holding on to each other when struggles and heartbreak hit. Lily had Ben now, but Kate was grateful she still had a place in her life. She hadn't been a great friend these past few years, and she wanted to make up for it.

"I will be praying for you," Lily said. "And for your mom and dad." She pulled back and looked at her, her brown eyes twinkling as the sun broke through the haze. "And for Chris. In fact, I think I should plan a dinner party. Just a small one. Me, Ben, you, Chris—"

"No." Kate held up her hand and stopped Lily's planning. "No matchmaking."

Disappointment stole the smile from Lily's face. "But—"

"You do realize that every couple you've ever tried to set up has been a terrible failure, right?"

"That's not true." Lily pursed her lips, and her forehead wrinkled. "Well, it's a little true, although Emma and Cho definitely would have worked out if he hadn't driven over her foot on their first date, so technically, that wasn't my fault." She tapped her finger against her lips as she tried to think of a successful couple she had set up, but having been her friend for nearly a decade, Kate knew Lily's schemes had never once ended in a happily ever after.

She shook her head as she picked up her half-empty plate and stacked it with Lily's. Lily took both coffee mugs and followed Kate to the kitchen, continuing to claim her talent as a matchmaker. "And just because a few other couples have had their differences, that doesn't mean you and Chris won't work out."

Kate put the plates in the deep sink and turned around, leaning against the counter as she looked at her friend. "Lily, I don't know what's going to happen. Honestly, I don't even know how I'm going to get through today. I just . . . " She swallowed hard. "I don't want to hurt Chris." The confession was costly. People around her got hurt. Megan, her dad, Hannah. Kate wasn't a bearer of sunshine and happiness. Tragedy, sorrow, and pain followed her everywhere she went. She didn't want that for Chris, even if . . .

She paused. Even if a part of her wanted something more.

Lily set the coffee mugs on the granite island. "Chris is a big boy. If he's willing to take a chance, let him. You deserve to be happy, to be with a man who loves you and knows how special you are. Don't end something before it begins just because you're scared."

Tears pricked Kate's eyes, and she turned back to the sink. Warm water spilled over her hands as she focused on scrubbing the plates. How could she be happy when Megan was dead? When her father had spent years alone in an empty house? She couldn't be happy, not until she made the person responsible for all of it pay.

Chapter Eleven

"IF YOU POINT THAT CAMERA at me one more time, I will hit you with my granola bar."

Kate had put up with Chris and his new camera for an hour before she threatened him with bodily harm. He thought that was a pretty good sign. A few weeks ago, that granola bar would have been flying at his head within the first five minutes. He had been walking around the small office filming her from every angle, having her stop and pose, look this way, look that way while he changed lenses, zoomed in and out. Twice, he tripped over a box and nearly fell.

Lights, tripods, a shoulder mount for the camera, batteries, microphones, and recording equipment littered the office. Kate had shifted the boxes around in an attempt to keep the office tidy and to give them room to walk around, but the piles of equipment left only one small path between the desk and the door. Once everything was unpacked and stored in cases, there would be a bit more room. When he had started organizing the shoot, he hadn't anticipated having Kate with him, so he had planned everything for a crew of one. Which was probably for the best. He stifled a laugh as he tried to imagine Kate in designer high heels and slick business suit holding a bulky, overhead boom mic in the middle of downtown LA while he was shooting. He doubted she would be enthusiastic about the idea. It was probably just as well that he had opted for a high-quality shotgun mic that attached to the camera instead.

He lowered the camera. "I'm just trying everything out, so we're all set to start filming. You do want me to start filming, right?"

She sighed heavily, and he had to work hard not to grin at the exasperation in her tone. Something had changed since their pizza-and-a-movie night last week. It was subtle, and he couldn't label it, but Kate was softer. She was laughing more, and her patience with his creative process had been steadily increasing. She'd even started offering insights on the storyboard, and he was amazed at her perception. She wasn't a part of the movie industry, and her perspective was fresh and new, untainted by years in the business. Once he had explained his system to Kate, she had quickly gotten the hang of it. She'd even pointed out a few ways to make it more efficient. She looked at the project with innocence. There wasn't an agenda or an undercurrent of selfishness. Where Tessa had been willing to use and exploit him for her own purposes, Kate looked at the film with an eye to making it better and supporting his vision. It was a good feeling having a partner he could trust.

"I don't think you appreciate the significance of the moment, Kate." He set the camera back in its heavy-duty protective case. It was a state-of-the-art handheld camera that he would be able to manage by himself while he filmed. He didn't have access to a soundstage, scaffolding, camera dolly, or crew, so his gear needed to be as compact as possible. It reminded him of the cameras he had used in high school when he coerced his friends into making films in his backyard and around the neighborhood. Except this one was much more advanced—and much more expensive. This camera was going to be the tool he used to make the film that would define him, one way or the other.

He'd always loved movies. Some of his earliest memories were of going to the movie theater with his family, the swell of excitement he felt when the lights dimmed and the music surrounded him on every side. The sticky butter on his fingers from the popcorn and the crazy sugar combination of soda and candy. He lost himself in those films, and when he was old enough to start figuring out how movies were made, he knew exactly what he wanted to do for the rest of his life.

He spent hours writing scripts and filming them. His friends, neighbors, and anyone else who happened to stop by were all cast in his movies. There was *The Curse of the Minivan*, featuring his mom's car, *The High School Detective Series* starring his best friend as a nerdy student who solved crimes between classes, and the one and only musical he'd ever attempted in *Maple Avenue Revue*. Some of his fondest memories were of those days, the freedom he felt in filming whatever he wanted, writing outlandish and ridiculous scripts and making them happen. He spent hours on his laptop learning how to edit footage and add special effects. He staged screenings in his living room complete with fresh popcorn and candy and his family as a captive audience.

His parents had been supportive, even if his mom had continued sliding business school brochures under his bedroom door until the day he left for college. He was sure he was going to succeed in film school. It was his dream, and he had no doubts about it. He'd been stunned to walk into class that first day and realize how much he still had to learn, but he loved it. The first time he saw his name on a big screen was during his senior year. His student project had won an award and was screened at a small film festival. Sitting in the front row, Chris watched his name appear in the opening credits. It didn't matter how many times it had happened since then; that first one would always be the one that meant the most. It was proof that he'd made it. His dreams were coming true. He was a director—it said so on the big screen.

He was hired as an assistant director right after graduation. It was a low-budget movie that went straight to DVD, but it was a start. He rented a tiny apartment with three roommates in Studio City. One was an aspiring actor; the other two were musicians. The apartment was messy and loud, but it was cheap. He lived on pasta and take-out as he worked his way up, paying his dues, making connections, getting jobs on larger and larger films, and building his credits. He was the second assistant director on his first major studio film when he and Ben met. Ben had been working as a stuntman, jumping off buildings and getting tossed through windows, when he was discovered by a powerful agent who set him on a path to leading man status. The two up-and-comers became fast friends. They worked well together, understood each other, and became a winning combination. Their careers rose together—Ben as an actor, Chris as a director. In fact, one of the scripts Chris had turned down would have been a perfect Johnston/Prescott vehicle. Lots of action, danger, and explosions.

After all these years, after massive soundstages, exotic locations, huge crews, and production staff, he was right back where he started—an idea and a camera. He wanted to believe that camera was a symbol of moving on, of following God's leading into new territory, even if in the back of his mind, he was worried it might be a symbol of an end to the career he loved.

"And I don't think you appreciate the significance of my aim with a granola bar."

Chris laughed and crossed to the desk. He sat on the edge, his leg brushing hers as he looked at her. She had the threatening granola bar in her hand and a stack of papers on the desk in front of her. It was something about permits and insurance, and for the hundredth time since he'd hired her, he was grateful for all the paperwork she took care of. He was pretty sure it was more than she had signed on for, but she never complained. If it had been up to him to handle all of the legal details, he would be weeks behind where they were. Kate and her efficiency and legal skills had been a blessing in more ways than he could count.

She was still wearing dress pants and fancy shoes, but her sharp blazer had been replaced by a bulky sweater. He considered that progress. He might be able to turn this boardroom lawyer into a movie nerd after all. "You wouldn't do that. You like me too much to hurt me."

The words jumped out before he had a chance to think them through. Kate's eyes widened as the subtext hit them both. Too soon, Chris. Too soon. They hadn't reached that plot point yet. He wanted to take the words back, but it was too late. His mind scrambled for a way to soothe the awkwardness, but Noah chose that moment to make it worse.

"Don't count on it," Noah said. "Kate thinks bodily injury is a sign of affection."

A fierce blush stained Kate's cheeks, and his stomach dropped. He stood and turned, shielding Kate from Noah's view. "Spoken like a man who's been hit with his fair share of flying granola bars."

Noah shrugged. "You're not wrong." He leaned against the door frame and crossed his ankles. "You're both coming tonight, right?"

"To celebrate the birth of the most obnoxious brother in the world?" Kate asked, her voice strong and taunting. Chris didn't need to look at her to know the blush was gone. Kate always rose to face a challenge. "Of course."

"You, too, right, Chris?"

"I'll be there."

"And are you two coming together?" Noah asked, the mischief in his voice enough to make Chris' stomach drop again. "Birthday parties make great dates."

The granola bar whisked through the air and smacked into the wall next to Noah's head. "Go away, Noah," Kate said. "Or I'm taking your present back."

Noah laughed and disappeared down the hallway.

Chris walked to the door and shut it. "You know," he said, as he bent to pick up the weaponized granola bar. "Noah's right. It does make more sense for us to go to the party together."

Kate narrowed her eyes as she stared at him. "The house is, like, two blocks away. I think we can walk."

"Exactly. We can walk together." He stood on the opposite side of the desk and watched the inscrutable expression on her face—her courtroom face, he called it. The practiced emotionless expression she used when she didn't want to give anything away. "What do you say, Kate? Want to go to a party with me?"

She hesitated, the calculations running through her mind as surely as if she had been adding up a list of expenses. "Okay," she said.

"Shake on it?" He extended his right hand, holding the granola bar in his other hand, out of her reach. She put her hand in his. "It's a date," he said.

"No, it's not." She laughed. "It's a walk."

He tightened his fingers, enfolding her delicate hand in his. "Every great story has to start somewhere."

Kate's mouth dropped open.

Speechless.

He had rendered the unflappable Kate speechless.

He let go of her hand and picked up the camera.

A good director knew when to end a scene.

Chapter Twelve

SHE READ THE INSURANCE REQUIREMENTS from the city for the third time. The letters were all in the right order, but she couldn't make sense of the words. Her thoughts were scattered, jumping from Chris to Charlie Chaplain and back to Chris again. What was it about him that made him stick in her brain? She'd known him for months, but it was as if she'd never seen him before, not really. He was like a shadow that suddenly stepped into the light. He wasn't a vague presence in the background anymore. He was real and defined, and she couldn't stop thinking about him.

"Get it together, Sullivan." She shook the papers and squinted, determined to keep Chris from her mind for the two minutes it would take to read this section.

The contract language was straightforward. It was the details that were difficult. Hollywood and film industry were new to her. She couldn't effectively negotiate the best deal if she didn't understand the hidden agendas and the secret deals that went on behind closed doors. There were profit splits, financial risk assumption, and a bunch of other legal terms that took all the magic right out of movie-making. There was as much drama behind the scenes as there was on the big screen, and she wanted to get it right.

Chris was planning to premiere the documentary at a film festival with the hope of lining up a nationwide distribution deal after the screening, so she wanted to be ready. There was nothing worse in a negotiation than walking into a meeting unprepared. Whatever deal they were offered, she wanted to be able to counter it immediately. She only had a few months to become an expert on the film industry. She had been up late the night before researching distribution deals, licensing rights, and intellectual property until her eyes burned. It felt like being in law school again as she tried to learn everything she could about movies and where the money went. She knew Chris had a lot riding on this film, and she wanted to help him. A week ago, she told Lily she would keep their relationship strictly business. She couldn't be his girlfriend, but she could be his lawyer. She would do everything she could to find him the best distributor for his film. That would be a better deal than her broken, empty heart, anyway.

Blowing out a long breath, she sat back in the chair. The words on the page were starting to blur, and she longed for a simple, hostile takeover bid to negotiate. That would have been easier than navigating the backrooms of Hollywood.

"Katie?"

She looked up. Her dad was standing in the doorway holding a box. He was dressed in black pants and a gray dress shirt with a matching sport coat. Growing up, Kate had called it "detective chic." His badge was clipped to his belt, and she knew his pistol was holstered on his left side next to his ribs. How many times as a little girl had she hugged him and brushed against the cold metal and leather under his coat? It was a constant reminder of how dangerous his job was.

He looked tired and uncertain, as if he wasn't sure if he should come in. That was her fault. The list of voicemails on her phone and the text messages she hadn't replied to pricked at her conscience. She hadn't trusted herself to call him; she was afraid of what she'd say, so she'd decided not to say anything, to sweep it under the rug and pretend that none of it existed. Her mother coming home, her dad being a part of it, even Megan—she pushed it all aside because it hurt too much to think about. It was an effective coping mechanism when she was on the other side of the country, but it was a lot more difficult when her dad lived only an hour away.

He walked into the office and stood on the opposite side of the desk. His sport coat was open, and he was wearing a blue tie she had sent him for Christmas while she was in law school. "This box was delivered to my house, but it's addressed to you. From your law firm." A question hovered in the air between them.

Kate stood and looked at the return address. O'Brien, Shae, and Collins. She had given them her dad's name and address as an emergency contact. Apparently, they had gotten tired of waiting for her to come back and collect her things. She ran her hand over the clear packing tape that held the cardboard box together. Her framed law degree, a few reference books, and her favorite coffee mug were no doubt inside. Maybe a scarf she had kept in a drawer for when the weather took an unexpected turn and the glass jar of peppermints that sat on the corner of her desk. There wouldn't be much else in the small box. She'd never gotten the hang of decorating her office. It was just a place she worked. There wasn't much sense in bringing in a bunch of distractions and knickknacks. She had only wanted her computer, coffee, and a stack of work to keep her busy.

"Kate, is there something going on? What happened at the firm?" Her dad watched her, his sharp eyes reading her expression. He was an excellent detective; there wasn't any point in lying to him.

She tapped the top of the cardboard box, the remnants of her corporate law career. She might as well get it over with.

"I'm not with the firm anymore." Embarrassment settled like a stone in her throat. She had made her choice, and she accepted the consequences; but telling her dad that she had been fired, admitting that she had failed, was harder than she thought it would be. "They let me go when I didn't go back to Boston."

Let go. A pleasant euphemism for being fired. Three years of law school, two years at the firm, and all she had to show for it was a cardboard box and a black spot on her resume. Doubt wormed its way through her thoughts, but she ignored it. Everything she had given up, everything she had lost was the price it cost to find the man responsible for Megan's death. When she found him and made him pay for what he'd done, it would all be worth it. It had to be.

Her dad crossed his arms, and she instinctively bristled. It was his interrogation stance. He hated when she called it that; but growing up as the daughter of a police officer, she knew what it meant. She stood up straight and faced him. "It's fine, Dad. I've already got a new job."

He sighed and rubbed his hand over his face. "It's not that. Why didn't you tell me? If you wanted to stay in LA, you could have lived with me. You could have come home." His voice rumbled with emotion, and it reached the loneliness in her heart, the longing for the years they had lost, the years her mother had stolen from them.

Resentment seethed within her. "Your house seems a little full at the moment." Tension crackled in the air. She wanted to regret her words, but she didn't.

They stared at each other across the desk. Kate waited for his response, hoping he had an explanation, wanting him to say that he'd taken her side, that he'd told her mother to go back to wherever she'd been hiding, that he hadn't forgiven her. "Your mom . . . " He began, his gaze dropping to the floor, and she knew she didn't want to hear the rest.

"My mom abandoned us, remember?" Kate snapped her words like a whip. "Remember you and I crying at the kitchen table? Megan was gone; then Mom was, too. She packed up and left, leaving us holding the shattered pieces of our family. She didn't even say goodbye." Tears pricked at her eyes, and she dug up more anger to keep them from falling. She wasn't sad; she wasn't hurt; she was furious. "How could you let her come back? After all these years, you just opened the door like nothing had happened. How could you?" Anger threatened to consume her; cruel words danced on her tongue anxious to leap out. She was holding a match to the last bridge in her family, and with one more word, she could watch it burn. She clamped her mouth shut, knowing she was teetering on the edge of destruction, desperate to keep the full fury she was feeling from breaking free.

Her dad's shoulders were slumped and heavy, like a prize fighter who had been knocked down and was struggling to stand. "Katie, I have loved your mom for thirty years. Aside from you and your sister, she's the only woman I have ever loved. She saw me at my worst and stood by me. I can't do any less for her."

Kate shook her head. "No. I saw you at your worst. She left when it got bad. I stayed." She sucked in a breath as her conscience called her out. She hadn't stayed. Not really. She left as soon as she could, the same way her mother had.

Kate straightened her spine. None of that mattered. "You can forgive her if you want, but I don't want anything to do with her."

Years of sorrow etched deep grooves across his face. He looked at her, raw sadness in his eyes, and she winced at the loss she felt. Growing up, he'd always been the one she could to turn to, the man who gave her strength and told her to keep going. That was gone. She had thrown it away, chosen her anger over him, and she didn't know how to take it back.

"I love you, Katie. Your mom does, too." Her dad walked round the desk and put his arm around her shoulder. She stiffened, but he pulled her close and kissed her head.

Kate didn't reply. There was nothing left to say. He'd chosen her mom over her. He was willing to forgive the unforgiveable. She wasn't interested in forgiveness. She wanted justice.

He stepped away. "When you're ready, I will be here for you," he said. He took a step, then stopped and reached into his pocket to pull out an envelope. "Will you give this to Chris please?"

She nodded and took the envelope. Her dad turned and walked to the door. Placing his hand on the doorframe, he paused. "You know, we all grieved for Megan differently. Maybe none of us got it right."

He left, and Kate sank into the chair, tossing the envelope from her dad on the desk. She didn't want to look at the open door, and she didn't want to open the box of her former life in Boston. She dropped it on the floor. There was nothing in that box she wanted. Picking up the papers she had been working on, she tapped them against the desk and straightened the pile. She sorted her pens and moved the stapler. When the desk was neat and orderly, she took a deep breath. Her life might be falling apart, but this she could control. Work. She would focus on work.

Footsteps resounded in the hallway, and she looked up, a part of her dreading the thought of seeing her dad again and an equally big part of her hoping that it was him. She didn't want to leave things on a bad note with him, but she didn't know how to fix it.

Chris popped his head around the corner. "I just saw your dad leave. Everything okay?"

She propped her elbows on the desk and rubbed her temples. "Got anymore Charlie Chaplain movies?"

He shook his head. "I don't know if Charlie can help us this time." He stepped into the office and set the camera case on the floor. Dropping into the chair across from her, he grinned. "This looks like it might call for explosions. Lots of explosions."

Kate nodded. Explosions were just what she needed. "I'll bring the pizza."

"It's a date." He rushed on before she could disagree again and say it wasn't a date. "But not tonight. Tonight, we are going to a birthday party. Ready to go?" He grinned and offered her his hand.

She slipped her hand into her lap. "I just need a few minutes to put some of these papers away." It was too much to think about. Too many thoughts swirled in her head. She needed a moment. She needed a second to catch her breath, to get her bearings, to focus on what was important, but how could she do that when Chris was sitting there in his stubble-covered handsomeness?

Chris stood and patted his pockets as if searching for his keys. "No problem. We're the last ones here. Hannah left with Lily a while ago to set up for the party and gave me the keys. I'll start locking up, and we'll head out when you're done." He went to the door, then stopped abruptly. "Hey, did your dad drop off anything for me?" he asked.

Kate blinked, her mind fighting through the fog of her disconnected thoughts. "What?"

"I was hoping he came by to give me that list of names from the club, but he left before I could ask him about it. Did he have it?"

The heat in her veins turned to ice, and her heart hammered in her chest. She glanced at the envelope sitting on the desk. That must be the list. Sweat slicked her hands, and lightheadedness washed over her. That was what she had been waiting for. It was right there, at her fingertips.

"Kate?"

Her gaze leapt to Chris. He was standing by the door, waiting for her response.

If she gave it to him, there was no guarantee she'd get easy access to it again. What if he decided not to use it? What if he tossed it before she had a chance to see it? The seconds ticked away as she weighed her options.

"No," she said quickly, a bright smile on her face and a knot in her stomach. "He came by to give me this box that was sent to his house by mistake. That was it."

Regret twisted her insides. She had never outright lied in court. She had never been blatantly dishonest in a negotiation. She had spun the truth for her clients, put the facts in the best light, but she'd never been a liar.

Until now.

Chris smiled and pulled a keyring from his pocket. "Okay. I'll be back in a few."

She nodded, the taste of her deception bitter on her tongue. Chris left, and she forced herself to walk calmly across the office to close the door behind him. She waited, counting to ten to be sure he wasn't coming back. She went back to the desk, condemnation and conviction dogging her every step. None of it mattered. Nothing mattered except Megan. She grabbed the envelope and tore it open.

It was a list of names.

She read through the names, her breath ragged and uneven.

Somewhere on that list was the man had who killed her sister.

Chapter Thirteen

KATE SAT ON THE LOVESEAT beside Chris. She took one look at Lily and knew it had been planned. By the time she and Chris got to the Shaw house, every other seat in the family room had been taken. Pastor Evan was in his ancient recliner. Lily, Ben, and Hannah were on the sofa, and Noah was on the floor at Hannah's feet. The Shaw family room was full, but the small loveseat had been left conspicuously empty. Lily was playing matchmaker, and she had enlisted help. Only Pastor Evan seemed to be oblivious to the not-so subtle machinations at work.

"What's next?" Noah demanded. His hands were extended, and he was opening and closing them like a toddler who wanted another cookie. He was surrounded by shredded wrapping paper and had a tidy pile of presents stacked beside him. "Pay your tribute to the birthday boy," he declared.

Lily smacked Noah on the head. "Oh, sorry, Hannah," she said. "I guess smacking the obnoxious out of him is your job now."

Noah reached for Hannah's hand and kissed her palm. "Hannah would never do that. She's a sweet and gentle lady, unlike my bratty, little sister."

"Hey, now," Ben said. "That's my wife you're talking about."

Ben wrapped his arm around Lily and pulled her against his side, while Lily stuck her tongue out at Noah.

It was everything Kate loved about this family. The love, laughter, and warmth. She had always been welcome here, always been included. She had lost guest status at the Shaw house during her first year of college when Pastor Evan's wife, Amy, told her to make herself at home and meant it. She knew where the extra towels were and how to jiggle the off-kilter back door so it locked properly, and she knew she was safe.

She had spent countless nights in this house. After Megan had died and her mother left, this little yellow house in Hollywood had become her home. When she needed to do laundry or when she was desperate for a home-cooked meal, this was where she came. It wasn't to her dad's house filled with sorrow and emptiness. It was here, sitting around the kitchen table while Amy stirred pasta sauce or rolled out pie dough that Kate talked through the drama in her life. Amy had stepped in as a surrogate mother when her own mother had disappeared. She had offered motherly advice on dating and class choices, and it had been Amy Shaw who had proofread her essay for her law school applications.

Amy had given her everything she craved in a mother. She listened to Kate's dreams; she made her hot chocolate when a boy broke her heart; and when Megan died, Amy hadn't run away. She had stood up in the face of tragedy and given Kate the strength she needed to do the same.

Kate called Evan and Amy her bonus parents. When Amy died from cancer only four years after Megan, it was like losing her mother all over again. It was one of the few times Kate had flown back from Boston—to attend Amy's funeral. Kate had talked to Amy over the years that she fought breast cancer. From the first diagnosis, through chemotherapy and radiation, and during that glimpse of hope when she went into remission. Then only six months later, the cancer came back. It grew so quickly and aggressively that Kate only got to talk to Amy once before she was gone. Her voice had been weak and quiet but filled with the joy and contentment Kate had come to associate with Amy Shaw. Even in the face of death, she had been filled with peace, the same peace she had tried to share with Kate, but Kate never understood it. Kate had stood with Lily and Noah at the railing of the small boat as Evan scattered his wife's ashes in the Pacific, and she had cried for the woman who had stayed, the mother who hadn't given up on her. She flew back to Boston feeling unmoored and motherless and once again trapped in a world of death and loss.

Hannah reached for a small box on the coffee table. "I'm next, Birthday Boy."

Noah took the box and kissed her cheek. "Thank you, sweetheart." He unwrapped the ribbon with far more care than he had shown for any other gift, and Kate couldn't help but feel a little squishy inside at the love they shared. The squishy warmth was quickly replaced by the chill of guilt when she thought about how close she had come to destroying their relationship. She had meant well. She was trying to protect the Shaw family, but she had been wrong. It was one more mistake she had made, one more foolish decision to add to her collection.

Noah dug through the tissue paper and removed a small, glass bottle filled with dirt. He pursed his lips as he studied it. "I feel like this is a test. Am I going to get in trouble if I don't know what this is?"

Hannah rested her hand on his shoulder, and he turned to face her. "That's a little bit of dirt from the canyon where we had our first date. That's where I went when I was thinking of running away. It's where I was standing when I decided to stay, when I knew I could face anything as long as I was with you."

There was a collective sigh as Hannah's words filled the room. Tears stung Kate's eyes, and she wiped them away. Chris put his arm around her shoulders. His warmth drew her in, and she wanted to sink against his side. No one was looking at her; every eye was focused on Noah and Hannah, so she let herself disappear into the moment. In the comfort of this house and with Chris by her side, a spike of longing she had never known before sprang to life. It was a whisper of what Amy had tried to give her, a peace that washed over her, a quiet that set her anxious mind to rest and pieced her broken heart back together. It was tempting, a tantalizing promise of what could be, a hint of the life she could have if she was willing to let go of the past.

Noah clutched the bottle in his hand and stood. He swept Hannah into his arms. "This is the best dirt in the world. And you, Future Mrs. Shaw, are the best woman in the world." He kissed her loudly on the top of her head. "No offense to Mrs. Prescott or the Future Mrs. Johnston."

Kate sucked in a breath and sat up straight. Lily looked at her with a twinkle in her eye, and Ben grinned at Chris. Distracted. She had gotten distracted. Chris and his stupid stubble and stupid smile, his stupid sweetness and stupid hand on her shoulder. Heat filled her cheeks, and she started to stand up, ready to run, but Chris gripped her shoulder. "Don't leave. Wait for it," he whispered, his voice a low rumble only she could hear.

"Wait for what?" Kate whispered.

The air whooshed out of Noah's lungs as Hannah elbowed him in the ribs. "Why are the women in my life always hitting me?"

Everyone laughed as Noah rubbed his wounded side. Kate exhaled in relief as the attention shifted. Chris seemed content to keep his arm around her shoulder, and she was content to stay. "See?" He spoke the words low and intimate, hiding them under the laughter from the others. "Your friends have your back." Chris put his hand beneath her chin, tilting her head up. "And so do I. I'm on your side, Kate."

His eyes were blue depths that swallowed her whole. Chris. Chris was all she could see. Her stomach flipped, torn between excitement and terror, and unable to make a decision. Was this a mistake? A huge disaster? Or was it . . . something else.

Her eyes darted to her purse on the table behind him. If Chris knew what she had done with the list her dad had given her, he wouldn't be on her side anymore. If she could just finish this, find the man who had killed Megan and end it, then she could be free. She would be free from the past, free to move on. She only hoped Chris would still be there when it was all over.

Chapter Fourteen

CHRIS WOKE UP EXCITED IN the mornings. Not just because of the film, but because of Kate. He had expected to make this movie alone, but Kate had come alongside him like a partner—a sometimes cranky and impatient partner and an always distracting and beautiful partner, but a partner nonetheless. It was something he hadn't known that he wanted, and yet, there she was. She still wore business attire most of the time, but she'd traded her high heels for more practical flats. He was pretty sure it was only a matter of time before she showed up for work in jeans and a sweatshirt. He was secretly hoping for that day.

Both Kate and filming exhilarated him. He loved the fast pace of filming and the always changing shooting schedule. Every day was different. On Monday, they were in downtown Hollywood; on Tuesday, they were in the San Fernando Valley. For him, it was exciting and fun. He had never been cut out for a regular nine-to-five job. This was his element. He thrived on the thrill of spontaneity.

It was driving Kate crazy.

From what he had seen, she liked routines and knowing exactly what was coming next. This project had very little of that. The times he set for the schedule were approximates; but in Kate's opinion, once they were written down, they were set in stone. When traffic caused a delay or when they had to find an alternate location and it set them back a few hours, her impatient foot-tapping started. He'd also discovered that she was not a fan of early mornings, so his suggestion that they get some sunrise footage had not gone over well. Fortunately, Lily tipped him off that Kate had a weakness for peppermint mochas, and he'd come armed with caffeine. She may have needed the jolt of coffee to wake up, but all he'd needed was the sight of her in the golden-hour light of the rising sun.

Chris checked his watch. He'd arrived at the Los Angeles Manna Center early. He and Kate planned to meet at the Center instead of at the Hollywood Mission to save them both about thirty minutes of traffic, since they were coming from different directions. Usually, they met at the mission and traveled to the locations together. They had spent hours in his car. He'd never been grateful for LA traffic before, but the gridlock and construction gave him extra hours with Kate. He brought coffee; she brought snacks. They fought over the music. He preferred worship radio. She wanted rock. In the end, they settled on a classical channel. They filled the time talking and sharing stories. Kate asked interesting questions about the movie industry and film-making, and he was excited to talk about his years in film school with her. That led to talk about her years at UCLA with Lily and then law school, the cases she'd handled, and the corporations she'd worked with. They went to lunch at small, out-of-the-way spots or grabbed something to go on their way to another location. For two people who weren't dating, they were doing a pretty good job of looking like they were. Chris thought about pointing that out, but he didn't want to scare her away. Knowing Kate, she'd start driving her own car everywhere just to avoid the conversation.

Kate was keeping him on his toes without even meaning to. At Noah's party, she had leaned against him, content with this closeness, but she absolutely refused to use the word *date*. She didn't mind his flirting; she bantered with him, but then she would pull back, as if she suddenly realized what she was doing. She was like the slow build of a drama—the steadily rising stakes, the building tension. Kate was a movie waiting to be made, a song aching to be played. She was the inspiration of a poem just before the first word was written.

He stepped out of the car, laughing at his own romantic musings. This was not something he could tell Ben and definitely not Noah. The morning was crisp and chilly with a bite to the air. His breath puffed in front of him as he pulled his camera equipment out of the trunk and slung the audio bag over his shoulder. He checked his phone for a text from Kate. Nothing. He shoved his phone in the back pocket of his jeans and closed his eyes. Things with Kate would either end really well or in total catastrophe. There was no middle ground with her.

He slammed the car trunk, the sound echoing in the early morning stillness. The Manna Center sat on a hill high above downtown. Tall, mature trees lined the edge of the parking lot, and high shrubs obscured the chain link fence that surrounded the center. Colorful benches dotted the grass beneath the trees, but at this hour, he was the only one outside. Adjusting the heavy equipment, he headed to the front door of the expansive complex.

The Manna Center was a collection of buildings that were all older than he was by about a hundred years. It had originally been built as a convent. For decades, the Sisters of Mercy had watched over Hollywood from the convent on the hill. As the Los Angeles area grew, the sprawling city had encroached, and development moved closer every year;

but the convent had remained, a stubborn remnant of what the area had looked like before Hollywood had taken over.

As the years went by, the community of the Sisters of Mercy shrank, and the cost of upkeep for the large collection of buildings became too much. When rumors started that the Sisters were going to sell, real estate developers had jumped at the chance to buy the large piece of land. The convent and its years of history had been marked for destruction, another casualty of urbanization. Condo developers, strip mall builders, and private investors were in a bidding war for the property, but the Sisters had turned everyone down.

Until his friend Jonathan made an outrageous offer.

Pastor Jonathan Lopez offered the Sisters one dollar and his promise that the convent and the surrounding buildings would not be torn down. He pledged to restore the buildings and use them to serve the community and carry on the work the Sisters of Mercy had done for a hundred years. They accepted his offer, and the Los Angeles Manna Center was born.

For over a decade, Jonathan and his small team had been a beacon of hope and help to the community. The Manna Center had dorms for men and women, an addiction recovery program, transitional housing for teens aging out of foster care, and a program for human trafficking survivors. The renovation work on the center was an ongoing project. As soon as a bedroom was refurbished, Jonathan brought in someone who needed it. The waiting list for housing at the center seemed endless. There was always a need, and Jonathan did his best to meet those needs. He devoted time to feeding the hungry on Skid Row and putting together backpacks full of school supplies for kids every autumn, and last Chris heard, he was working on building a transitional home for homeless veterans.

Chris admired the work his friend was doing, and he wanted to showcase it in the documentary. People needed to see not just the tragedy and horror of what was going on, but also the hope that men and women like Jonathan were bringing. It was one thing to focus on the bad news, to show what evil looked like, but providing a glimpse of goodness—that was what would give the film hope, and that was what he wanted to accomplish.

He climbed the cement steps to the front door and juggled the equipment in his arms so he could push the buzzer. When the light above the door handle turned green, he opened the door and stepped into a welcome embrace of humming, heated air. A receptionist sat behind the counter surrounded by a plexiglass wall. She smiled as she greeted him and asked for his I.D. He set his gear on the floor, so he could find his wallet. Once he had signed in, she passed him a visitor's badge but kept his driver's license filed in a box behind her wide reception desk.

Chris was about to ask her to call Jonathan's office when he heard his friend's voice behind him. "What, no entourage? I thought you were some big deal movie director now." Chris laughed as he shook Jonathan's hand.

But a handshake wouldn't do. Jonathan pulled him in for a hug and clapped him on the back with the strength of a UFC fighter. He stepped back and shook his head at the receptionist. "Can you believe this guy, Lenore? He doesn't even have an assistant."

"Here," Chris said, passing him the camera case. "Hold this."

Jonathan hold the heavy case with one hand, his bicep flexing. "Okay."

Chris smiled at Lenore, who was watching from behind her plexiglass shield. "Now I have an assistant."

Jonathan's deep laugh echoed in the lobby. He was a few inches shorter than Chris, but he was all muscle. Chris followed as Jonathan led him out of the lobby and down a short corridor. The Manna Center was Jonathan's ministry, a project built by his prayers, hard work, and sweat. Chris was certain Jonathan had done most of the work on the building himself. Even while he was busy running the programs and serving as the center's pastor, Jonathan still picked up a hammer or fixed the plumbing when the need arose.

They had met years before when Chris was fresh out of film school and working on low-budget movies. Chris had been on a location shoot in downtown Los Angeles, and when he went for a quick lunch break, he'd bumped into an energetic man passing out fliers for a youth service at the Manna Center. That chance meeting had started a friendship between Chris and Jonathan that had lasted for years. When Chris told him about the documentary and asked for his participation, Jonathan hadn't hesitated. If there was anyone who was an expert on the dark side of Hollywood, it was Jonathan.

As they headed to the cafeteria where Chris would set up to film, Jonathan filled him in on the work the Manna Center had been doing.

"We've doubled the number of people getting meals at our food kitchen every day. We had a couple of stars from the local teams step up with donations, and that has been huge. Our recovery program received a grant, and that enabled us to add a few more beds to the residential program. They were filled before the ink dried on the check. I've got plans for the next grant, too. The application is sitting on my desk." He sighed. "Seriously, the paperwork is the hardest part of this place."

His words flowed like a waterfall, tumbling out with the same force of nature. Jonathan was passionate about his work, and he was always searching for new ways to tell people about God. He grew up not far from where the Manna Center now stood. His father had disappeared, and his mother had worked three jobs to provide for him and his siblings. By the time he was thirteen, he was involved in a notorious street gang in Los Angeles. He lived through years of violence and illegal activities before his mother's prayers caught up with him and he came face to face with Jesus. His life had changed that day, and ever since, he had been committed to reaching out to men and women who were suffering on the streets of his hometown.

"I don't know how you do it all." Chris shook his head, barely keeping up with the conversation. He would never complain about his to-do list ever again.

"God, man. It's all God." Jonathan slapped him on the back again, and Chris wondered if he was going to be bruised by the time the day was over. "You know that. It's the same with your movie. Give God the reins, and then hold on. God's looking for people willing to do the work. All you gotta do is say yes."

He led them to a quiet corner of the large cafeteria. The room was dim, and the light from the windows high in the ceiling didn't reach the spot where they would film, so Chris started setting up the portable lights he'd brought with him.

"I haven't seen you around much," Jonathan said as he sat on a stool and watched Chris work.

"I've been attending the Hollywood Mission. Pastor Evan gave me a room over there to use as a temporary office for the production company."

Jonathan nodded. "I know Evan Shaw. He's a good man. He and his wife brought a lot of love to that neighborhood."

Chris nodded. He'd never met Amy Shaw, but he saw the legacy of her influence everywhere at the mission. Evan still wore his wedding ring, and Chris didn't think he'd ever take it off. Amy was the love of his life, and not even death could change that.

He flipped on the studio lights. Jonathan blinked and shielded his eyes with his hands until Chris reduced the brightness. "Thanks for doing this," Chris said as he dug in his backpack for the legal pad he used for notes. "I'm going to turn the camera on, and we'll have a simple conversation. I'll ask questions, and you can go anywhere you want with the answers. Just be you. I promise I'll make you look good."

Jonathan laughed. "That's the last thing I'm worried about," he said, but Chris noticed he straightened his Manna Center polo shirt and brushed some lint off his jeans. "How do I look?"

Chris set the camera on a tripod and peered through the lens. "Annoyingly handsome," he said and decided to change the lens for a tighter shot. "You should be married with five kids running around by now."

Jonathan shrugged. "I've got thirty-four kids living under my roof right now. I don't have time for anymore." He sat still as Chris moved the camera a few feet to the right. "Besides, you don't have any room to talk. Where are your wife and kids?"

Chris busied himself with the microphone, keeping his back to his friend as he positioned it on the camera. He wanted to get married. He'd always assumed that was part of God's plan for his life, but as the years had gone by, he'd started to wonder. Then he met Kate. She wasn't anything like the woman he thought he would marry. She was stubborn and independent, and as far as he could tell, she wasn't interested in God, church, or ministry. She was all hard edges and prickly thorns, but beneath that, there was a softness and a vulnerability he adored. He'd watched her laugh hysterically at slapstick comedy and get teary-eyed over a happy ending. She put on a tough front, but it was covering a deep hurt. The question was whether she would let him, or anyone, close enough to see the vulnerability beneath the tough exterior. Did she even want anyone to try, or was she content with her defenses?

Jonathan's cell phone rang, and he stepped away to answer it, leaving Chris with his equipment and his unanswered questions. Everyone told him she needed time and space, and yet the more time he spent with her, the more he became convinced that she didn't need distance at all. She needed someone who was willing to brave the thorns, who was willing to risk her temper.

A heavy hand slapped his back, and he turned to Jonathan. "You don't, by any chance, have a red-headed lawyer, do you?"

Kate.

Chapter Fifteen

KATE WAS STILL REELING FROM the interrogation she went through just to get in the building. That receptionist could put most courtroom bailiffs to shame. If Jonathan hadn't come to rescue her, Kate was pretty sure she would have ended up on her rear end at the bottom of the steps.

"Glad you made it," Chris said and reached for her. Instinctively, Kate shook his hand. Chris laughed and perfunctorily returned the handshake before taking the visitor pass from her other hand and clipping it to her jacket.

The receptionist behind the plexiglass snickered, and hot embarrassment drenched Kate. What was wrong with her? She blamed a late night researching social media profiles from the list of names her dad had given her and a too-early-in-the-morning alarm . . . that she had snoozed three times.

"Thank you, Lenore," Chris said, then leaned in close to Kate. The heat of his cheek leapt across the space between them as he whispered, "There's coffee in the kitchen. Lots of coffee."

Chris led her to the cafeteria. He pointed her toward the kitchen and then crossed to the camera set up. Coffee. She needed coffee and a second to catch her breath. Maybe then her muddled brain would start working again. "Oh, wait," she called. When Chris turned back to her, she handed him a folded sheet of paper. "This is for you. It's the list of names from Norma Jean's."

Sweat coated her hand as she held it out to him. She'd used the copier in Ben's home office to make a copy of the list. She had the original, and she was making notes on it as she dug through the online records of each name on the list. So far, her late-night searches hadn't turned up anything. She was going to have to switch to physically tracking these men down, so she could identify them.

But Chris didn't need to know that. She gave him the information from her dad. She wasn't hiding it from him. She turned over the evidence just like a discovery process in court. She simply didn't give him all the details of her copy or what she was doing with it. That was how she rationalized it.

If only her sweaty hands and the pit of guilt in her stomach agreed.

"This is great," Chris said as he scanned the list. "Thank you." He refolded it and stuffed it in his bag.

See, the devil on her shoulder whispered, *if you had given him the original, you would never have even seen it.* She wasn't exactly lying to him, but she wasn't being forthright either; and she didn't like that. After everything Chris had done, and as close—she swallowed hard on the word—as close as they were becoming, she knew it wasn't right, but there wasn't any way around it. She owed it to Megan.

Kate, her coffee, and her guilty conscience sat quietly on one of the vinyl-topped metal stools behind the camera. She watched as Chris interviewed Jonathan. Jonathan was animated and passionate as he shared his story and what led him to start the Manna Center. The interview went all over the place, from the streets of LA to the boardrooms of major corporations. The scope of the need hit Kate in a way she had never experienced before. There was so much she didn't know, so much she chosen to ignore in her quest to find Megan's killer.

She was on her third cup of coffee when Jonathan introduced them to a young girl named Graciella, who agreed to be interviewed for the film. Chris stood behind the tripod, his glance switching between the viewfinder and the girl sitting in front of the camera. Jonathan Lopez sat beside Kate as they watched Chris conduct the interview. Graciella was nineteen, and she'd been staying at the Manna Center for almost a year. Police had found her when they conducted a raid on a house near downtown. Graciella, along with four other girls, had been found locked in a closet. As she told Chris her story, Kate didn't know if she should scream or cry or both.

Graciella was slim, with large, brown eyes and long, dark hair that fell halfway down her back. Kate looked at her and thought she should have been in school, or running on the beach, or laughing with her friends at the mall. Instead, she told them a story of such evil that Kate could barely breathe. She faced the camera, her voice quiet and halting as she shared the nightmare she had lived through.

Graciella was from a small town in Central Mexico. Her family didn't have electricity or running water. They lived in a one-room house with a dirt floor. The only school was miles away in a larger town, and Graciella's parents hadn't been able to afford the required school supplies for their children. While her parents worked, Graciella helped care for her younger brother and sisters.

One day, a group of men arrived in her village. For months, the men came bringing food for the families who lived there and toys for the children. They stopped by once or twice a month, and whenever they showed up, Graciella received a treat. American candy, clothes, and food she had never seen before. On and on it went until one the day, the men told the village parents that they could get the girls jobs in the United States. They said they knew employers that wanted hard-working girls and that once they had jobs, they would be able to send money home or even bring the rest of the family to the United States.

Graciella had been sixteen and desperate for a chance to help her family. She begged her parents to let her go to America. Her mom had hesitated, not wanting to lose her oldest child, but her dad reminded her of how kind the men had been. Surely, they would take care of Graciella. In the end, Graciella and two other girls left with the men. They drove for hours, not stopping to rest or eat, but Graciella and her friends had been excited and eager for the new adventure.

Two days later, they reached Tijuana, and everything changed.

The girls were passed on to different men. These were not the men who had brought candy and toys to the village. They were hard men, angry and intimidating. When one of her friends started to cry and said she wanted to go home, one of them men slapped her. Cold fear had gripped Graciella as the men forced them into the back of a box truck and locked the rolling, metal door behind them.

It was hot and stuffy, like there wasn't enough air in the dark confines of the space. The truck bumped and bounced as if they were driving through dirt and not on paved roads. Graciella felt sick—panic and motion sickness churned in her stomach—and she cried in the hot darkness of the truck. She and her friends clung to each other, sweat sticking to their skin, her throat aching with thirst until she thought she would die in the sweltering blackness.

When the truck finally stopped and the back rolled open, the cold night air rushed across her, and for a moment, she was thankful, grateful that the worst was over.

But the worst was just beginning.

Graciella and her friends were thrown into the dark pit of human trafficking. She was separated from her friends, beaten, and raped. Her days became a terror, each one worse than the day before. She was moved from city to city, up and down the West Coast. She never knew where she was. She couldn't read the signs written in English. They drugged her to keep her quiet, trapping her in a world of fog and confusion. Months passed in a blur of pain and hopelessness until suddenly, the closet door was thrown open, and she stared into the bright flashlight of a police officer.

She had been found in Los Angeles, only a few miles from where Kate was sitting. The police brought in a social worker, and the social worker had contacted Jonathan. He had just launched the program for survivors of human trafficking two months earlier, and Graciella became the third young woman to enter the program. She had been living at the Manna Center ever since.

A potent mix of anger and sorrow melded within Kate as she thought about everything this young girl had endured, and she had been only minutes away. Graciella was the same age Megan had been when she died. They deserved a chance to grow up, and they had both been robbed. Kate turned to the wall as if she could see through the thick cinder blocks and into the city below. What was happening in those streets? Who else was suffering in silence? What evil was going on while people drove past on their way to work or school?

It was too much.

Kate stood and walked away. She wanted to keep walking. She wanted to walk to the door, get into her car, and drive away. She wanted to escape the reality that was staring her in the face, but where could she go?

Graciella had been suffering right down the hill, in the middle of one of the biggest cities in the world, surrounded by people who never saw her. Megan had died on a road to the beach. There was nowhere could she go where evil wouldn't follow. It didn't matter how far she went; there was no safe place. Evil was everywhere, and that seemed like a pretty solid case against a supposedly all-powerful and all-loving God. If He wasn't willing to protect young girls like Megan and Graciella, what was He doing?

She left the quiet of the cafeteria and leaned against the cool plaster wall in the hallway. She hoped the men who had hurt Graciella paid. Using her phone, she made notes on Graciella's story. She could find the arrest records, follow up with the prosecutor's office, and see what had happened to the men. She couldn't believe the sophistication of their enterprise. Moving the girls, trading them between syndicates. It was organized crime like she had never seen before, and it was happening right under her nose, in big cities and small towns all across America. It had to be stopped. It had to be dragged into the light. She finally got what made Chris so passionate about this film. He couldn't keep silent about this, and neither could she.

"It's quite a story, isn't it?" Jonathan slipped from the cafeteria and closed the door behind him, his face lined with concern.

Kate shook her head. "I've never heard anything so awful. What she's been through . . . " Her throat constricted, and she paused. She tried to breathe, but the air got stuck, as if her body was so full of anger that there wasn't enough room for oxygen. Graciella has gotten away, but how many other girls and boys were still suffering? Who was going to help them? Where was God?

"How can you serve a God Who lets that happen?" The words flew out before she could stop them.

Jonathan braced one foot against the wall behind him and leaned back. He didn't seem offended by her question. He didn't even look shocked. She was sure Chris would have been hurt if he'd heard her ask it. Lily would have been full of sympathy and Bible verses, and Pastor Evan would have compassion and understanding, but Kate wasn't interested in any of that. She didn't want clichés. She wanted the truth. This man had seen the worst of Los Angeles. He'd seen hunger and violence and abuse. He'd seen every evil humanity could do, and yet he still believed. She wanted to know why. Why believe in a God Who stood aside and let that happen? It would be better if there was no God at all than to believe in a God Who didn't care when people suffered.

Jonathan hooked his thumbs in the belt loops of his jeans, as if he was getting ready to discuss last night's football game. He was calm and relaxed, like he dealt with questions about God and the universe every day. "God isn't the one who hurt Graciella," he said simply. "God is the One Who rescued her."

Kate snorted. "She probably would have preferred if He'd stopped it from happening in the first place, don't you think? Isn't He God? Can't He do anything He wants?" Kate used her cross-examination voice, leading the witness into the trap of her making.

"Yes," he said, seemingly unaware of what was coming.

"Then why didn't He use His power to prevent it?" The trap was sprung. Kate crossed her arms, daring him to contradict her, daring him to defend a defenseless God. God could have stopped it. He didn't. Therefore, God was as guilty as the men who had taken Graciella. God could have stopped the man who killed Megan, but He didn't. That made God guilty, too.

Jonathan nodded. "That's a great question." Kate waited for his response, marshalling her counter arguments. "Honestly, I don't know."

Kate stared at the pastor. Wasn't this his job? Wasn't he supposed to know this stuff? "That isn't an answer."

Jonathan shrugged, unphased by her questions or her annoyance. "Would you like me to tell you that God has a plan? That His ways are perfect? That God is God, and I am not?" He crossed his arms over his chest. "All of that is true, but you don't strike me as the type of person who wants platitudes or clichés. You're a lawyer, right?" Kate nodded and braced herself for a lawyer joke. "Then you know that facts aren't always what they seem. Surely, you've noticed that a prosecutor and a defense attorney can take the same fact and spin it to their advantage."

He wasn't wrong. She'd done that plenty of times herself. She was doing it right now. "Yes," she conceded. "Lawyers have a great skill for using facts for their advantage."

"Most people see evil in this world and use it to 'prove' that either God doesn't exist or that He doesn't care. What if instead of using it as evidence against God, we used it as evidence to show His love?"

Kate shook her head. "That makes no sense."

"Sure, it does. If the world is full of evil, if people hurt each other every day, if girls like Graciella suffer, surely God would be justified in wiping us out, striking down every single one of us. Instead, He made a way for us to return to Him. Instead of condemning the world, He sent His own Son to redeem it. When faced with evil, God didn't run. He offered forgiveness."

And there it was. That magic word. *Forgiveness.* The constant refrain of Christianity. Forgive and forget and all that nonsense. What good was forgiveness? Graciella needed justice. Megan needed justice. Forgiveness didn't fix anything; it just let the bad guys off the hook.

"Listen, Kate." Jonathan was blunt, and she liked that about him. He didn't sugarcoat his faith, and he didn't try to make it sound perfect. "The simple truth is I don't know what God is thinking. He is, in fact, God, and I am not." He winked as she rolled her eyes. "But I do know this," he said as he stepped away from the wall and stood beside her. "I trust in the character of God. What He does may not make sense, but I know Who He is, and that is what's important."

Kate pinched her bridge of her nose. It was too early in the morning for theological debates.

Jonathan laughed and touched her shoulder. "I will say one more thing, and then I'll get you another cup of coffee. Deal?" When she nodded, he stood right in front of her, his deep brown eyes meeting hers. "Think about Chris. He gave you an address and told you to meet him here. You woke up this morning, got dressed, and drove to a place you'd never been before because he told you to. Why would you do that? Why would you drive all the way here just because Chris said so?"

Kate shrugged. "Because I work for him and it's my job to go where he tells me to go."

"And you trusted the address he gave you was the right one. Why?"

"Because he'd been here before. Because it was his plan. Why would he send me to the wrong place if he wanted me to be here?"

"And if, on your way here, someone hit your car, would that be Chris' fault?"

"Of course not."

"Even though he was the one who told you to come here? He was the one who gave you the directions. Are you sure it isn't his fault?"

Kate bit her lip. She didn't like where this was going.

Jonathan's gaze bore into her, and she saw compassion there. "God is in control, but He gave us free will; and sometimes, people use that free will poorly. They make stupid decisions. They hurt other people. They ignore God's leading and go their own way. People get hurt; people die; and it's not fair."

Kate swallowed hard. Tears stung her eyes, and she pinched her thumb and forefinger together to keep the tears from falling. She would not cry. She would not crumble.

"But, Kate." Jonathan's voice was warm and deep. "We aren't alone in it. God is there; even in the worst situations, God is with us. There are plenty of times when I don't understand what's happening, when I get mad at God, or when I want things to be different; but when that happens, I go back to what I know about the character of God. He is loving. He is good. He is patient. He is forgiving. And He is always with me. I may not know why I'm at a certain address, but I can trust that God is already there."

Dragging in a breath, she latched on to one thing he said. "You get mad at God?"

"More times than I like to admit." Jonathan turned back to the cafeteria, and she followed him. "But God isn't afraid of our anger. He wants us to bring it to Him. He can handle it. In fact, when we bring it to Him, He takes it away and gives us peace instead."

She winced when he said anger. How much had he seen when he looked at her? Was her anger so obvious? He talked about peace, but she didn't know what that would feel like. She couldn't remember what it was like to not be angry. If she stopped being angry, what would she have left?

Jonathan held the door to the cafeteria open, and she walked through. Chris had finished the interview and was talking in low tones with Graciella. When Kate walked in, he looked at her. He smiled, and she missed a step.

Maybe she would have something left after all.

Chapter Sixteen

"YOU CAN'T USE THE NAMES of the men Graciella mentioned." Kate shifted in the Adirondack chair on Chris' deck so she could face him. "You don't have proof."

They had been debating including that part of her interview in the film for almost half an hour. Chris pounded his hand on the arm of his chair. "We have her statement."

"It's her word against theirs." Kate kept her voice calm, rational. "This is what you're paying me to do—protect the film and your company from legal liabilities." She raised her eyebrows, waiting for him to agree. He refused.

"But, Kate, it's important."

"It's a liability. Do you want to get sued?"

They had been working on editing the footage from the Manna Center all day. Once Chris had finished interviewing Jonathan and Graciella, they drove straight back to his house. Anticipation and excitement had captivated him, and Kate could barely keep up with him as he sped along the freeway. That had been seven hours ago. Seven hours of staring at a computer screen watching the footage over and over again. Kate's eyes were exhausted and dry, but she couldn't bring herself to leave. There was something powerful about the work they were doing. An indescribable tremor rippled in the air, and she wanted to be a part of it.

They had moved from his living room to the back deck when dinner had been delivered. Empty Thai food containers littered the small table between the chairs as the sun began to set over the ocean.

Chris narrowed his eyes at her, and she braced for another argument. She may not know much about cameras and editing, but she knew the law. Graciella had told them stories of the men she met during her time with the traffickers. Names, professions, descriptions. Chris wanted to use it all. He wanted to tell the stories, to drag all the secrets and all the lies into the light. He was willing to risk everything, but she wouldn't let him throw it all away. Not when she could protect him.

"Fine." Chris said, and it was the closest thing to a pout she had ever seen on him. "But it's not fair."

"Life's not fair," Kate countered.

Chris scrolled through the footage he had uploaded to his laptop. He marked certain spots in the film, using tick marks and time stamps, scratching notes on the paper he kept by his side. He moved sections of the footage, highlighting some and cutting it, then stitching together the gaps in precise detail.

"Between the stories these girls are sharing and your lawsuit rules, we might not even need to use the list of names from the club." Chris rubbed his hands over his eyes. "I like keeping the focus on the women, telling their stories."

Kate fidgeted before she could stop herself. Taking a deep breath, she forced her body to be still. "Sure," she nodded, guilt churning with the curry in her stomach until she thought she might be sick. Chris deserved better.

That realization was worse than the guilt. She didn't deserve him. The mistakes she'd made, the foolish things she'd done—they disqualified her from a relationship with Chris. She would never measure up, never be good enough, never be worthy of his love. She should walk away now. She had what she needed. That list was the only reason she signed on to this project. She should quit and stop seeing him. She should leave before he discovered the truth. Chris deserved a chance to be happy, and that was one thing she could never do. She could never make him happy. And yet . . .

She stayed. Every day, she stayed.

She glanced at Chris, at the passion on his face, the strength of his heart. He was so committed, so determined to make a difference. She wanted to be there for it. She wanted to be there for him.

He cued up a new version of the interview and pushed the empty dinner boxes out of the way, so he could set the computer on the table in front of them. Kate thought the interview would be less powerful, less emotional than it had been when she watched it in person. Instead, it was even more gripping than she remembered. Chris had framed Graciella beautifully—the way the light rested on her, the slightly off-center position of the camera—it made her look young, but also determined. She faced the camera with unflinching honesty, and she spoke without reservation. It was raw and vulnerable, and it felt even more intimate than it had that morning.

Chris had used the camera to make the interview personal. It was as if Graciella was talking right to her, reaching through the screen and pleading with Kate to hear, to see, to know what she had endured. Even though she knew the story, had heard it directly from Graciella, seeing it on film touched a chord in her heart, and the cry that resulted couldn't be undone.

When the footage ended, Chris shifted in his chair to look at her. "So," he asked, "What do you think?"

Kate struggled for the right word. "It's . . . amazing."

"Really?"

She wanted to laugh at the boyish excitement in his voice. She wondered how he could even ask that. How could he not see what he had created? The scene was incredible. "Yes, really. It's powerful and beautiful and . . . " She waved her hands at her face. "I knew what was coming, and you still made me cry."

Chris leapt to his feet with a whoop of victory. He lifted his hand for a high-five and when she smacked his hand, his clasped her fingers and pulled her out of the chair and into his arms. Electricity sizzled on her skin as she leaned into him. She rested against his chest and breathed in the spice of his aftershave and the salty breeze that clung to his hair. Warmth washed over her as he wrapped his arms around her. He was strong and steady, and the beat of his heart drummed beneath her own. She made no move to pull away. She could stand there in his arms and let the minutes tick past and never miss them.

Her phone buzzed on the glass table, and she blinked away the fog of the moment, the daze of his arms.

Chris stepped back, and she missed him immediately. The empty air between them was cold and lonely, but she didn't trust herself to reach for him again. She was already too affected by him. Distance was what she needed.

She glanced at the text message on her phone.

"Are you late for a big date?" Chris asked.

"What? No." She picked up her phone. "I haven't been on a date in months."

"Really? What exactly have we been doing then?" He bent to collect the discarded Thai food boxes, and she was sure she heard hurt in his simple response.

"Chris, I didn't mean us. This thing we have—it's complicated. It's—" Her phone buzzed again.

"It's fine." He took the boxes into the house, and Kate knew it was anything but fine.

Why did she always mess things up? Why was life so complicated?

She followed him into the kitchen, anxious to explain, but not knowing why she should. "The text is from Noah. He's asking about the wedding."

With less than three months before Hannah and Noah's wedding, the preparations were in full swing. Kate had tried to excuse herself as much as possible when Lily and Hannah got together. After all, Hannah had been the one who helped Lily plan her wedding. Kate had stayed in Boston until the last possible second, stalling even on her best friend's wedding because of the memories she didn't want to face. It was only right that she let Hannah and Lily share this wedding, too. They had a bond Kate wasn't a part of, and even though it hurt, she accepted it because she had brought it on herself.

Chris washed his hands and dried them on a kitchen towel. If he was relieved by her admission, he didn't show it. "When are you planning to head up north?" The wedding was in Hannah's hometown, and the whole Shaw family was going to be there.

Kate hesitated. She hadn't planned on going to the wedding. She figured she was the last person Hannah would want there.

Truthfully, she'd been shocked when Hannah had given her the invitation. If the situation had been reversed—if Hannah had tried to sabotage her relationship—Kate probably never would have spoken to her again, let alone invited her to the very wedding she nearly destroyed. She would have held a grudge and enjoyed every minute of it.

She'd almost ruined everything for Hannah and Noah. Kate may have thought she was being protective, but really, she had been jealous. Jealous that Hannah was going to get to be a part of the Shaw family, that Hannah was Lily's friend, and that she'd been there when Kate hadn't. She'd been petty and judgmental, and she hated herself for it. She should have told them sooner that she wouldn't be there, but she could never find the right way to say it. Lily was going to be disappointed in her. And Noah . . .

Noah had been a good friend to her. He hadn't brought up any of the things she'd said about Hannah, and he didn't treat her any differently now than he had before she made a stupid scene with him; but still, she didn't know if she could face them on their wedding day. Sitting in the church, watching them say their vows, knowing that she had nearly destroyed it—the guilt would eat her alive. They may act like everything was fine, but how could either of them forgive her for what she'd done?

Chris leaned against the dishwasher and crossed his arms over his chest. "The initial filming will be done, and we'll be on to scoring, final edits, and all that. It's going to be busy, but I was thinking of driving up the day before and heading back home the day after the wedding. You can catch a ride with me." He looked at her, and warmth spread down her back and all the way to her toes. "If you want."

Kate squeezed her fingers together, her nervous habit kicking in. "No. That's okay."

"Oh." Chris dropped his head and stared at the floor.

Kate crossed her arms, irritated that she had to explain herself. This wasn't any of his business, anyway. What did it matter to him if she stayed home and ate ice cream to avoid thinking about Noah and Hannah getting married and all of her closest friends being there without her? "I'm not going to the wedding." There. She said it.

Heavy silence descended on the room. He raised his eyes and looked at her. His intense gaze made her uncomfortable, like he was seeing more than she wanted him to. "What do you mean, you aren't going?"

She straightened her shoulders, feigning a confidence she didn't feel, and lifted her chin. Lesson one she had learned in law school, if you didn't have a good answer, use bravado to win the case. Evidence was best, but style worked, too. She'd made her decision, and she would have to live with it, but she didn't see why she had to justify it to him. "I haven't been a very good friend to Hannah. I wasn't exactly nice to her when I came back to LA for Lily's wedding, and I said some stupid stuff to Noah. I highly doubt they want me there on their special day."

Chris crossed his ankles as they faced off across the kitchen. "If they didn't want you there, they wouldn't have invited you."

She ran her hands through her hair. He didn't get it. Of course, Chris—Mr. Perfect, Mr. Mature, Mr. Always Does the Right Thing—wouldn't understand. "Look, I would feel awful if I went. I messed up, and I don't deserve to be there."

Chris walked to where she stood and plucked her phone from her hand. "People mess up, Kate. It happens. We forgive each other.

Hannah and Noah want you there. The only person holding on to the past is you."

She wanted to argue with him, but she didn't have a good response. Yes, she was holding on to the past because that's where her mistake was. She had to carry it around with her. She didn't expect anyone else to forget what she'd done. What right did she have to act like it didn't matter? Actions had consequences; that was a simple law of life. There weren't any takebacks or do-overs.

"Kate." He held her phone up and wiggled it in front of her face. "You can either text Noah and tell him you're getting a ride up north with me, or I can call Lily and tell her you're planning on skipping her brother's wedding. It's up to you."

Irritation rose within her. He was making this difficult. And yet, her heart skipped and tripped when she thought she might actually be welcome at the wedding. What if Hannah really had forgiven her? What if she could move on from one of the biggest mistakes of her life? Was it possible to let go of the past? To start over?

"You're not playing fair," she said.

He laughed. "I wasn't trying to be fair." He took her hand and ran his thumb over her knuckles. "You're being too hard on yourself. Noah and Hannah are your friends. They care about you, and they want you to be there with them. Don't let guilt rob you of that."

She had reasons for not going. She had reasons for keeping herself closed off, but the blue of his eyes and the feel of his hand made her forget what those reasons were. She had spent years keeping herself insulated, protected from the pain and betrayal of life. The tougher she was, the stronger she was, the less anyone could hurt her. She was fine on her own. She liked being independent and not needing anyone. Was it lonely? Sure, but lonely was better than broken.

Chris waited, his hand holding hers. He was the voice that kept calling her back from the tiny cave she'd built for herself. He was the one who kept reaching out for her, the one who made certain she wasn't alone. Everyone else would have let her off the hook and let her slide back into the shadows, but not Chris. He held her hand like he didn't plan on letting go, and for the first time in years, she didn't want to be alone.

"Fine," she said. "I'll go." Chris smiled, and she itched to trace the curve of his lips, to touch the stubble on his face, to feel the line of his jaw. "But you're driving."

A grin spread across his lips. "It's a date."

She shook her head. "No, it's not."

Chapter Seventeen

CHRIS PULLED THE THICK HEADPHONES off his ears and nodded to the sound engineer. The music for the documentary was right on schedule. He had hired a composer he worked with on two of his past studio films, and he was thrilled with the progress so far. She had an excellent grasp on the feeling and atmosphere he wanted. The theme was touching, with a mournful quality that almost ached. She was working on the build now, a swell of hope to end the film. He gave her a thumbs up from his seat inside the booth. On the other side of the soundproofed glass, seated behind a grand piano, the composer smiled and bowed.

Chris closed his eyes and imagined the music with a full orchestra. Music brought so much emotion to a film. He knew the exact feel and background he wanted for every scene. Once the shooting and editing were done, he'd go into post-production and work on the final details, all those little things that an audience might not even notice but that enhanced the movie. The music, sound effects, narration—a thousand different things that all worked together. It was a lot to think about, and it was easy to get overwhelmed. It was a good thing he had Kate there to make lists and keep him on track.

Kate.

Chris was tempted to text her, to send her a snippet of the music, even though she had already heard it. He was looking for an excuse, a reason to reach out, to hear her voice and see her face. He stood abruptly and almost knocked the chair over. He needed a distraction before Kate became the distraction. He decided to grab a cup of coffee and clear his head so he could focus on something other than the lawyer waiting for him at his office.

As the composer went back to work on the melody, Chris made some notes on the clipboard she'd left for him and clapped the engineer on the back. Excitement followed him, a giddy tingle of hope he was afraid to grasp, as he left the booth and went to the coffee room across the hall. It was all coming together. The weeks of planning, the early mornings, the hours and hours of video that would never be used—piece by piece, the film was taking shape. It was actually going to happen. This film would get made. What had started out as a whisper in his soul was becoming a reality, and it was so close now, he could almost touch it.

He remembered the night the idea for the documentary had come to him. For months, he had been dissatisfied, believing there was something more he should be doing, something that would have an impact. He'd prayed for guidance, an open door, or at least an arrow pointing him in the right direction. That arrow came just a few days after they rescued Hannah from Norma Jean's. She was safely back with Noah, but the story she had shared stuck with him. He'd never really thought about it before—that there were women and men trapped in an industry that used them and discarded them. He couldn't sleep that night, so he'd picked up his Bible instead.

Sitting in his bed, he opened the worn and marked-up book, and Proverbs 31:8 leapt off the page. "Speak up for those who cannot speak for themselves." In that moment, he'd felt a leading, a direction so strong he didn't know what to do with it. How? How could he speak up for those trapped in human trafficking? What did he have to offer? He wasn't a politician or a police officer. He didn't have a talk show or a huge non-profit organization. What good was one voice against so great an injustice? Surely, there were other people more qualified and more effective. Other people who could do more and make a bigger difference.

The Scripture reverberated in his mind, a persistent call he couldn't ignore. "Speak up."

There was only one thing he knew how to do. Make movies. The certainty of his decision had filled him with calm, but that calm was quickly followed by something close to panic as he considered what it might cost him. He'd never thought of himself a coward before, but in the dark of that night, he realized how much his career meant to him and how much he didn't want to lose it. He was proud of what he had accomplished. He loved his job. Was he ready to put it on the line because of a nudge from God?

He stepped into the small break room in the music studio. Flyers covered the bulletin board advertising musicians for hire, concerts, and art shows. A single-serve coffee maker sat on a long counter with a sign asking for a dollar per cup. He tossed a dollar bill in the glass jar and dug through the variety of coffee flavors. The smell of caramel rose as the coffee maker popped and gurgled.

The truth was he might have given up on the film already if it wasn't for Kate. Without her, he would have been bogged down in paperwork. Whether she knew it or not, she was a huge part of this film. She showed up every day and went to work. When he might have stayed lost in his thoughts, obsessed with planning and hesitating about moving forward, her foot-tapping and watch-checking kept him moving forward. She wrote contracts and tracked the legalities, but she also carried equipment. She adjusted lights, scouted locations, and kept notes. She organized story cards and pointed out things he'd forgotten. He thought he could make this film by himself, but he'd needed Kate every step of the way.

As hot coffee filled the Styrofoam cup, he thanked God for the progress on the film and for sending Kate into his life. She was confusing and frustrating, and most of the time he didn't know what she was thinking or what he was supposed to do. She kept him off balance, like a merry-go-round that never stopped; but even with the all the spinning, he knew he wanted her with him. He couldn't have picked a better partner on the film if he had tried. She was everything he needed, and if she wasn't ready for anything beyond their not-a-date relationship, he would wait. He had been waiting for over a year, tongue-tied and foolish around her, paralyzed by his own attraction and ready to give up, when she waltzed into his office with fire and flash and gave herself a job. God certainly did work in mysterious ways. He had no idea what was going to happen with Kate, or the film, but he was more certain than ever that God was up to something on both fronts.

Grabbing his coffee, he was about to head back to the sound booth when Ed Caine stepped into the room. Ed was one of the executives at the movie studio that had produced the last film he made with Ben. He was middle-aged and balding, charismatic and charming, with a gregarious personality that made everyone feel like a friend. He was a business man through and through, from his tailored, navy sport coat and blue, silk tie to the shine on his black leather shoes. Ed had been a staunch supporter while Chris was at the studio. He was friendly and upfront, qualities Chris admired in business relationships.

Ed smiled when he saw him. "Just the man I was looking for. I was hoping to run into you." He extended his hand, and when Chris shook it, he grasped it firmly. "A little birdie told me you'd been down here working on a secret project."

Hollywood was a small world. Chris should have anticipated that word about his film was going to get out, especially once he started using some of the well-known artists in the industry. He was a little surprised by Ed's appearance at the recording studio, though. He didn't have anything to hide, but he wasn't quite ready to go public with it yet. "It's not a secret, Ed. Just a side project I've been wanting to make."

"Without any studio backing?" Ed leaned against the doorframe, effectively blocking Chris' exit. "Is it a full-length feature?"

Chris shook his head. He debated whether he should tell the executive about it. He'd always tried to be honest in his business dealings, and he'd never been one to play games; but this film was close to his heart, and he felt protective of it. Thanks to Tessa and the debacle that followed their relationship, he knew what it felt like to have a film ripped out from underneath him. At least this time around, he had a partner he could trust.

He sipped his coffee as he stalled. The truth was, it wasn't really his project at all. It was God's film, and God had nothing to hide. "It's a documentary on human trafficking."

The executive looked thoughtful, his lips pursed as he looked at Chris. "Interesting. A hard-hitting documentary on a pressing crisis from one of Hollywood's best directors. That's got human interest story written all over it." Ed's eyes shifted from side to side, and Chris could see him running calculations in his mind. He'd been in enough meetings in studio board rooms to know when the profit-loss margin was being debated. "Do you have a distribution deal yet? Marketing campaign? Media endorsements?"

So, that's what this supposedly chance meeting was about. Ed was hoping to partner on the film's distribution. He offered a quick, silent prayer for wisdom. He had said from the beginning that he would trust God for how the film would get out and be seen. The rest of the documentary was coming together; maybe God was making a way and putting it on a fast-track. Maybe Ed was the opportunity he had been praying for. Maybe Ed was the piece he had been missing. Excitement coursed through him as he tried to keep his face neutral. He didn't want to jump to conclusions, and he didn't want to move too quickly. It wouldn't take much for him to travel a hundred miles per hour away from God's plan.

"Not yet," he replied as casually as he could. "I'm planning to premiere it at the New Mexico Film Festival and see what happens after that." If the premiere went well, he should be able to secure distribution for the film without any studio involvement. It was risky, but it could work.

Ed nodded. "Sure, sure. But," he said as he stepped closer, "what if we could get the distribution squared away before the premiere and give you a wide release instead? A few hundred screens nationwide to start, a nice press build-up. Take all the uncertainty away and let you focus on finishing the film. What would you say to that?"

His head was swimming. Could it really be this easy? Without distribution, no one would see the film. It could be an incredible movie, but without screen time, it would languish in his computer and never see the light of day. He didn't think God had called him to make the movie without a plan for it to have an impact. He was tempted to say yes, ready to shake on it and go celebrate, but he held back. He was walking a delicate line. "If you want to send the paperwork over, I'll have my partners take a look at it." God. Ben. Kate. A trio of excellent partners.

Ed shook his hand again. "That sounds fair. I'd love to work with you again, Chris. You're a talented director, and I'm excited to see this film of yours."

After a quick exchange of business cards and another round of hand shaking, Ed walked away whistling. Chris stood in the small break room and prayed. He asked for discernment. He asked for guidance, and He thanked God for what he was doing. Then he pulled out his phone. He didn't have to think twice about who to call first. With a smile on his face, he dialed Kate's number.

Chapter Eighteen

KATE KNOCKED ON THE OPEN door to the church's office. Noah wasn't there, but Hannah was seated at the desk they shared. At Kate's knock, she looked up from the computer and smiled. Her hair was pulled up in a messy bun, and she was wearing one of Noah's sweatshirts. It was huge on her, and she'd rolled the sleeves up over her wrists. A pang of regret at the sweetness of it twisted Kate's heart. The innocence of such a simple gesture was something she had never experienced. She'd never cared about a man enough to borrow his clothes.

"Hi, Kate, what's up?"

Kate considered coming back another time. She could deal with Noah; she knew how to navigate that. They had history and years of friendship and a heavy dose of sarcasm. She still wasn't sure what to make of Hannah.

But she was already there. She could handle a little bit of small talk, and after everything Chris had said to her about letting go of the past, this would be a chance for her to give it a try. She lifted the stack of papers she was carrying. "Is it okay if I use the copier?"

"Of course." Hannah pointed at the large copy machine in the corner. "It's a little finicky at times. Let me know if it starts acting up. I know where to hit it so it cooperates."

Kate put the papers on the top tray and punched in the number of copies. As the machine started to hum and spit out papers, Hannah went back to adding numbers on a calculator. Kate waited, her finger tapping on the copier. She should say something. She shouldn't just stand there and ignore Hannah.

She waited until Hannah was finished with the calculator before speaking. "So, how are the wedding plans going?"

Hannah rolled her eyes and groaned. "There are so many details. My mom is doing a lot of the work, but she's constantly sending me photos and suggestions and asking me to make decisions." She rested her head on her hand. "I understand now why Lily was such a nervous wreck at times planning her wedding."

"Lily was a wreck?" She tried to imagine what Lily had been like during the months leading up to the wedding. Calm, level-headed Lily turning into a freaked-out bride? Kate tried to picture it, but she couldn't. She didn't know what it was like because she hadn't been there. While she had been focused on contracts and negotiations, her best friend had been planning a wedding and learning how to walk again. Kate hadn't come back to Los Angeles until a week before the big day. Hannah was the one who had been there through it all, and Kate had made her feel bad about it. Guilt nibbled at her conscience. It was one more thing she had messed up, one more thing she had failed at.

Hannah laughed. "Not exactly a wreck, but she was thoroughly stressed out. I totally get it now." She came out from behind the desk and joined Kate by the copy machine. "Noah and I are heading up to my parents' place this weekend to make some final decisions on wedding stuff."

"I hope it goes well." Kate checked the number of copies left to go. She had time. She should apologize for all the things she had said and done. The doubts she had tried to plant in Noah's mind about

Hannah, her distrust. Kate had been so sure she was right, but she had been wrong about everything. If Chris was here, that is what he would tell her she should do, and she wanted to be that person, the person Chris saw in her.

"Hannah, I—" She cleared her throat, trying to find the words. "I wasn't very kind to you when I first came back from Boston. You were a good friend to Lily; you are the perfect woman for Noah; and I was wrong to treat you the way I did. I'm sorry."

Hannah looked stunned. Her mouth dropped open as she blinked at Kate. "Thank you." She pulled Kate into a tight hug. "I know you were just trying to protect Noah and Lily. I would have done the same thing."

Kate stepped back, at a loss for words. That was it? No anger, no recrimination? Like Graciella, Hannah had been through terrible things. She had escaped and turned her life around. It didn't make any sense how she could stand there, full of faith and joy when she carried the scars of her past. It was as if the things that had been done to her and the things she had done didn't matter anymore. Kate wanted to ask her about it, but she didn't know if she had the right. In all fairness, she was part of the trauma of Hannah's past. She had inflicted some of the scars. She hadn't given her the benefit of the doubt. She had been skeptical, snarky, and downright mean at times, and look what it had gotten her. Hannah was happy, engaged, and in love with a great guy, while she was . . .

Kate looked at the copies piling up in the tray. She was like those papers, a copy of the woman she'd been before Megan's death, before her mother left, before she'd allowed anger and bitterness to take over. Every day, she woke up and put on one of those facsimiles, trying to pretend that nothing had changed, when deep down, everything was different. She didn't even know where the original was anymore. Most days, she felt like a copy of a copy, like she was fading more with each passing day. Eventually, there wouldn't be anything left.

She swallowed an irrational panic that crept up her throat as she thought of the list in her purse. The day she faded away completely might be closer than she thought. She was clinging to the hope that finding the man who was driving the other car would fix everything, that somehow when she got justice for Megan, her life would snap back to what it had been before. It was the only way out of the pit her life had become.

And yet, there was Hannah, standing in front of her with a smile on her face and a pencil sticking out of her bun. Hannah, who had been to the darkest places and had come back from it. Lincoln, the man who had abused her, was in jail. Maybe she could move on because the man who ruined her life had been caught. That was what Kate was hoping for, that somehow justice would make it all right in the end, but she worried even that wouldn't be enough to pull her back from the brink of the abyss she was standing on.

"How do you do it?" The words slipped out before Kate could stop them, escaping from her thoughts and rushing out her lips.

A wrinkle creased Hannah's forehead as her eyebrows squished together in confusion. The scar she had gotten the night Noah found her pinched above her eye, and Kate looked at the strip of pale skin. Hannah wore a reminder of her past every day, and yet it didn't seem to bother her.

"How do I do what?" she asked. "The wedding planning?"

The copier swished and slid, the light gliding from side to side under the cover while the smell of hot ink wafted to her nose. She'd unintentionally given Kate a way out. She could deflect the conversation, steer it another direction, and move on. She didn't really want to know the answer, did she? She'd been around the Shaws and Hannah enough to know what her answer would be. Just like Chris, Hannah would point to God, and Kate was tired of hearing that response. She wanted something she could hold on to, something real—not a feeling or a childish fantasy and definitely not some Old Man in the sky Who wanted her to behave but ignored her when she needed Him most.

She stacked the papers on the copier, tapping them into a neat pile, the last page slightly lighter than the original. Fading away. She was fading away bit by bit. She looked at Hannah, the woman she had misjudged, who had proven to be far stronger and far more compassionate than she was, and she decided to ask the question that had been bothering her for months.

"How did you get past the hurt? After everything you went through, everything Lincoln did to you, how can you stand here and smile like it's all okay?" Kate's chest constricted, and tightness stuck in her lungs like a weight. "Where did you put all the pain?"

Hannah exhaled with a short huff, as if the question had knocked the air out of her lungs, and Kate immediately regretted asking it. "I'm sorry. I shouldn't have said anything. It's none of my business."

"No, Kate, it's fine. It's a good question. I just wasn't expecting it." She twisted her hands together, the shiny pink of her fingernail polish disappearing as she folded her hands into a tight ball. "When Noah found me, when he saved my life, I was a mess. I felt like I was marked, like everyone could see that I was a lost cause. I was sure I was beyond forgiveness. I didn't think anyone could ever love me, could ever see past the mistakes I'd made, the things that had been done to me. It turns out I was wrong."

"Noah," Kate said, remembering the way he said Hannah's name, the way he smiled when she walked in the room, and the way his eyes followed her. Even when Kate hadn't been willing to trust Hannah, she'd seen the way Noah looked at her. She had seen it and known it was too late for her, too late for anyone else. Noah was in love. He hadn't cared about Hannah's past; he only cared about her.

"Noah is amazing, and I love him, but he wasn't the one who changed everything. Just don't tell him I said that." Hannah laughed and shook her head. "It was Jesus."

Kate sighed. It was exactly what she didn't want to hear. She nodded once, like she'd heard enough and turned to go. She should have known. It always came back to God. She thought Hannah would have had a better answer. After everything she had been through—all of the times she had prayed for help and it didn't come, all of the pain she had endured—she still believed. Kate wanted to give her all the reasons why it didn't make sense, but she couldn't argue with the peace and joy Hannah radiated. Fear coiled in her stomach as Kate looked at her own life. Maybe it was her. Maybe there was something much more broken inside of her. It wasn't that she didn't believe in God. She knew Him, and she didn't trust Him.

"Wait." Hannah reached for her arm and touched her elbow. "You asked me where I put the pain . . . When I couldn't carry it anymore, when it was too heavy for me, I took it to the cross, and I left it there." Silence weighed on the room, a hush that Kate could feel. "I stood in this church one Sunday morning, feeling like I could never go home, like I was too far gone and there wasn't any hope for me. Guilt and regret and shame were eating me up inside. I didn't feel like me anymore, but I didn't know who I was. I couldn't see any way past it, like nothing would ever change and I would feel that sad and empty forever. And the worst part was, I was okay with that. I didn't expect anything better."

She took a deep breath, and tears glittered in her eyes. "Then I heard Pastor Evan pray, and it was like God was speaking to me personally, reminding me that He loved me and that He wanted me to come home. When I showed Him all of the pain and the emptiness inside me, He took it. It was like I had been carrying a hundred pounds on my back, and then suddenly, someone else showed up and carried it for me. Jesus took it all—all the hurt, all the mistakes, all the shame—and it was gone."

Hannah sniffed and wiped her eyes with the sleeve of her sweatshirt. It sounded so easy—to pass the burden on to someone else, to let someone else carry it—but that was exactly the problem Kate had with it. It was too easy. Nothing was that simple. "I'm happy for you, Hannah. I don't know how you can just let it all go. I couldn't do it."

In the years since Megan's death, she hadn't done it. She hadn't tried, and she wasn't going to start now. She had perfected the art of unforgiveness. Maybe Hannah could forgive and forget, but not her. She wanted to make sure the people who had hurt her paid for what they did. None of those people had come to her and apologized. No one had admitted the wrongs they'd done. She would hold on to her anger and bitterness until those people deserved her forgiveness. She wasn't about to forgive someone who hadn't earned it and let them off the hook. If she did, that would make whatever they did to her okay, like it didn't matter. She wouldn't dishonor Megan's memory by forgiving the man who'd killed her. Megan deserved more.

She switched the copier off and grabbed the original papers. "Thanks," she said and crossed the office to the door.

"Kate." Hannah followed her.

Kate turned, impatience building in her nerves. She didn't need to hear any more. She didn't need preaching or advice; she needed someone to help her track this man down and close that chapter in her life. Once she had taken care of everything God overlooked, maybe then she would be willing to listen to Him. But by that time, what would she need Him for?

Hannah tugged on Noah's sweatshirt. "I don't want you to think that it was easy for me. It wasn't, but God makes all things possible."

"Some things are too big to forgive. Even for God." Kate stepped into the hallway, eager to escape the conversation. She had no interest in a God Who would forgive the man who killed her sister. Where was the justice in that?

"Hang on, Kate; there's one more thing." She sighed and waited for Hannah to catch up to her in the hallway. "I'm sorry to ask this, but with Noah and I going up north next week, there won't be anyone here to help set up for Sunday service. Would you be willing to come by and give Lily and Evan a hand that morning?"

She wanted to say no, but how could she and not sound like a terrible person? So, she stuck "facsimile Kate" on her face and smiled. "Sure. I can do that." She didn't say anything about staying for the service. She would set up, do her good deed, and leave.

That was all she could offer God.

Chapter Nineteen

SUNDAY MORNING ROLLED AROUND, AND Kate resisted the urge to hit the snooze button on her alarm. She was turning over a new leaf. She had apologized to Hannah, and that simple act had made her feel so much lighter, she decided to try to do more of the Christian-type things Chris and Lily kept talking about. So, even though she really, really wanted to snuggle back under the covers, she swung her legs out of the bed before she could change her mind. Today would be a fresh start. She would help at the church, and who knows, she might even stay for the service.

But first, coffee.

She had been up until after midnight digging through information on the men on her father's list. Nothing, nothing, and more nothing. When she finally gave up for the night, frustration and impatience kept her awake as she lay in bed. It was like the man had vanished. A passing glance and then he was gone, just like the night of the accident. He was slipping through her fingers, disappearing into the shadows, and she wanted to scream at the unfairness of it all. She took a deep breath as she got dressed. She had to focus on one thing at a time. First church, then back to her search.

Lily was thrilled she was coming to church, and she had been only mildly disappointed when Kate said that she would take a separate car to the mission. Riding with Ben and Lily would have meant sitting in the backseat while Lily dropped hints about Chris. Kate wasn't ready for that conversation. She needed more time to think it through. She had made too many mistakes jumping into relationships too quickly, and Chris wasn't like the other men she had dated. Not that they were dating, she quickly chided herself. They were . . . what? She didn't have a word for what Chris meant to her. He was beyond labels and categories, and that stumped her. She was used to neat columns and quick judgments, but Chris was elusive. He kept her guessing and, though she didn't want to admit it, that was incredibly attractive.

She followed her twisting train of thought to the kitchen, hoping coffee would bring some clarity. Ben and Lily were already there, and mercifully, Ben had turned on the coffee maker.

"Good morning," Lily said when Kate entered the kitchen. "Thank you for doing this. It's a big help." Lily was dressed in a long skirt, denim jacket, scarf, and cute boots. She and Ben had to be at the church early to rehearse and sound check with the worship team. Ben stood by the coffee maker in jeans and an ivory sweater. His hair was longer than Chris' now, and Kate noticed the way Lily played with it whenever she walked past him. "How much longer is this going to grow?" Lily asked as she curled her fingers in his hair.

Ben shrugged. "Until the director says stop." He captured her hand and kissed her palm before scratching his head. "Which will hopefully be soon. It's driving me nuts."

"Too bad Chris isn't working on this movie with you." Lily accepted the cup of coffee Ben held out to her. He'd already added the cream and sugar she liked. Envy tugged at Kate's heart as she watched them. Ben noticed all those little details. He knew how Lily took her coffee; he knew which blanket was her favorite; and just the day before, he had stopped by a roadside flower stand on his way home from the studio and bought her a bouquet of sunflowers, which she loved. He even noticed the things Kate, her best friend for years, missed. Kate had never noticed that Lily didn't like blueberries, and yet, Ben picked all the blueberries out of her fruit salad without being asked. It was like they were in perfect sync, moving in a choreographed dance that wove between them, anticipating, meeting, and enfolding each other in every way. They shared something Kate had never experienced. She was starting to doubt she would ever meet someone who could know her that well and still love her.

Kate poured coffee into a large travel mug, suddenly sad that she didn't have someone in her life who knew how she liked her coffee. That was by choice, she reminded herself. She was alone because she chose to be. Involuntarily, her mind drifted to the sunrise shoot she and Chris had done. He had shown up with an extra-large peppermint mocha for her. He'd even added an extra shot of espresso. Her hands shook as she looked at the coffee in her hand. Chris knew her coffee order.

"I miss working with Chris," Ben said. "But I'm hearing great things about the documentary. Right, Kate?"

She nodded as she secured a lid on the travel mug. "It's going really well. The interviews he's done are incredible. I honestly don't know much about how the post-production side of the film works, but it looks like things are on schedule." Chris had been explaining the editing and scoring process to her, but he'd been so excited, she could only follow half of the conversation. She did know they were still on track for the film festival premiere, and as far as she was concerned, meeting that deadline was the finish line. "He also got an offer from a studio for the distribution rights."

Ben nodded. "I heard Ed Caine tracked him down. That could be a big deal. His studio has a lot of marketing muscle behind it."

Lily picked up her purse in a not-very-subtle reminder that they needed to go. "I thought he didn't want studio involvement."

Ben held the door to the garage open for them. "Not during production, but if the studio can get the film in theaters, it might be worth considering a deal with them. It will depend on the profit split and how much backing the studio is willing to give, but that's why he has you, Kate. To make sure he gets a fair deal, right?"

"That's what I'm trying to do." Kate followed Lily into the spacious garage and reached for a set of keys from the board by the door. Ben grinned as he snagged the keys to the black sports car first.

"Well," Lily said as pushed the button to open the garage door. "I hope he prays about it before making a decision."

So much for avoiding a discussion about Chris, Kate thought as she headed for the luxury sedan, while Ben and Lily got in the sports car. "Of course, he'll pray about it. It's Chris. He prays about everything."

Lily poked her head over the roof of the car. "That's not a bad thing, you know." Then she stuck her tongue out at her before disappearing into the car beside her husband. Ben revved the engine and raced out of the garage.

Kate followed at a more leisurely pace, sipping her coffee as she drove down the twisting road through the Hollywood Hills. No, it wasn't a bad thing to pray, but waiting for a sign from Heaven wasn't nearly as sensible as weighing the pros and cons and making an informed decision. That's what she did. She wrote lists and then made the most logical decision. Keeping her emotions in check was the only way to stay in control.

Chris hadn't said much about the distribution deal since he told her to be on the lookout for the paperwork. It had come in on Friday, and she'd only had time to give the document a quick glance. As far as she could tell, it was a straight-forward deal, but she wanted to do more research on it before giving Chris her opinion. She was hoping to visit some local entertainment lawyers and get their perspective on the numbers the studio was offering. She reminded herself to ask Ben for a few recommendations of attorneys he trusted. After all the work Chris had poured into the film, she didn't want to be the one responsible for it failing because she had been too proud to ask for help.

She pulled into the church parking lot and stopped. Chris' car was on the far side of the lot. She hadn't realized that he would be there this early, too. She parked next to his car, and a flutter swept through her stomach. She really needed to get that under control. She fluffed her hair, checked her lipstick, and went inside the church prepared to work. She was not, however, prepared for the smile on Chris' face when he saw her. The flutters were back, and they brought fluttery friends.

"I didn't know you were coming today," he said and pulled her into a hug.

The collar of his polo shirt tickled her nose, and as she peered over his shoulder, she caught a glimpse of Lily smirking at her from the platform.

She stepped away and then took another step back just to be safe. "Hannah asked if I could come by and help with set up." Lily whispered something to Ben as he plugged in his guitar, and Kate started to suspect Lily had involved Hannah in her matchmaking conspiracy. She sent Lily a dirty look, but Lily just laughed.

Did Chris notice? Did he know what Lily was doing? An embarrassed flush threatened to crawl up her cheeks. Kate quickly smiled to hide her anxious thoughts. "So, what am I supposed to do?"

Chris offered her his arm. "Follow me."

They spent the next hour setting up the coffee table on the old delivery dock outside, arranging an information table inside the foyer for visitors, and checking in with the other church members who'd come to serve that morning. Kate introduced herself, but Chris already knew everyone. It was busy, and Kate marveled that Hannah did all of this work every Sunday morning.

When the parking lot started to fill, Chris excused himself to the tech booth at the back of the sanctuary to start running the lights and music. Kate watched him settle in behind the mixing board, and in a split second, she decided to stay. She decided not to think about it too long. It was one service, and maybe when it was over, she and Chris could grab lunch. Not a date, of course, but food and conversation, maybe a Charlie Chaplain movie. She was walking up the aisle when the door to the sanctuary opened, and she froze. Trapped between the platform behind her and blocked by chairs on either side, she watched as her mother walked into the church.

Her mom was wearing black pants and a red sweater set and carrying a Bible. She looked like she belonged in the church, right down to the gold cross necklace. No one could tell just by looking at her that she had caused so much pain. The incongruity of it struck Kate like a wave of cold water. Her mother, pretending to be a sweet, Christian woman, standing in the sanctuary of a church like she hadn't abandoned her family.

Her mother took a step toward her, and Kate burst into action. She marched up the aisle, determined to walk past her without saying a word, but her mom touched her arm. "Kate, please."

"Please what?" she snapped, then looked around, worried that someone had heard her outburst. "Please stay? Please don't go? How ironic you would even think about saying that to me."

Her mom pulled back as if her words had burned her. "I just want to talk to you. To explain—"

"It's too late for that." She glanced at the Bible clutched in her mother's hands. "I wonder what that book says about mothers who abandon their children." She wanted to yell, to scream, to break down and cry, but she couldn't. Not yet.

Her mother didn't flinch. "It says that even if a mother abandons her children, God will not abandon them." Tears gathered in her eyes, but she stood firm. "Trust me, I know that verse well."

Anger built within her like flood waters against a dam. She wouldn't do this. Not here. She stepped around her mother and kept walking. She didn't see the people coming into the church, the pretty artwork on the walls, or the sunlight streaming in through the windows. She had to get to the door; she needed air; she needed to get away.

She rushed out the front door of the church, past the people streaming in. She didn't care what they thought about her. Digging in her purse, she tried to find her keys as she walked hurriedly through the parking lot, the chilly winter air stinging her face. Tears burned her eyes, and she blamed the wind. Breathe. She had to breathe. Keep it together until she was in the car. Keep it together until she was alone. Then she would fall apart. Where were the stupid keys?

She found them just as she reached Ben's car and yanked them out of her purse. One of the keys caught on the zipper, and they clattered to the ground. A curse flew from her lips, and she was tempted to throw her purse at the car. She bent down to get the keys, but before she could grab them, they were swept up in a male hand.

She reached for them, but Chris folded the keys in his hand. "You can't keep running, Kate."

Heat flared in her cheeks, and her hands balled into fists. She didn't want this. She didn't want any of it. She couldn't handle it. Not his kindness, not his concern, not the way her heart melted when he looked at her. It was all too much. Panic threatened to consume her. Was she mad? Was she hurt? She didn't even know anymore, and she was afraid to find out. "Leave me alone, Chris. This is none of your business."

"Wrong." He lifted his hand to her cheek and slipped his fingers into her hair. "You're my business."

He stepped close, so close she could smell his aftershave and the lingering scent of coconut sunscreen that followed him. He stood only a breath away, and she longed to touch his chest, to let her hands rest over his heart, to feel his blood pumping beneath her fingers. She wanted to be reminded that she was still alive, that she could still feel, that she wasn't an empty shell. She wanted to feel something, anything other than pain and anger. There had to be something more.

She looked away. In the distance, cars sped past; trees swayed in the breeze; and life went on. But not for her. She was trapped, stuck in an endless loop, and she didn't know how to break free. "I don't know what to do," she whispered.

"Yes, you do."

Kate shook her head. It was such a mess. Everything was happening at once. She couldn't think. Megan, her dad, her mom, Chris. It was too much to deal with. "I don't think I can do this."

"What about *we*?" Chris asked. "What if *we* do it? Together."

A shudder swept through her like a dam breaking or walls falling. She couldn't see what was waiting on the other side, but for the first time in six years, she didn't feel alone. "I'd like that," she whispered.

Chris pulled her into his arms. Her hands clung to his back, holding on to the warmth that spread through his shirt. She closed her eyes, desperate to disappear, hoping she would never come back, free from everything that was waiting for her outside of his embrace.

His head rested on hers, a weight and a connection she didn't want to analyze. She would think about it later. She would rationalize it, justify it, and figure out what it meant later. In Chris' arms in the parking lot, all she wanted was a few more moments of hope.

Chapter Twenty

CHRIS SAT ON A SURFBOARD, letting the water lap over the edge. The ocean was calm and flat. He normally wouldn't have come out on this kind of morning. The water was cold, and the chill seeped through his wetsuit and into his skin. It was a terrible irony that the water off the beautiful, sunny coast of Los Angeles was so cold. He glanced at his reason for crawling out of bed and braving the frigid water. Ben was lying on the board he had borrowed. That morning, Ben had spent more time in the water than on the surfboard, but Chris had to give him credit—he was learning quickly. He had been cast in his next film as a surfer who gets caught up in a murder investigation; so in addition to growing his hair, he was determined to learn how to surf, and Chris had volunteered to teach him. That was before he found out the teaching would take place in the freezing Pacific in March.

The thick marine layer hung low and heavy, blocking the sun. Gunmetal waves and steel clouds surrounded them in shades of gray. His feet were numb, and he looked longingly at the outline of his townhouse—his warm and dry townhouse. He loved being on the water, even if he was going to need three cups of scalding coffee to warm up. It was peaceful and quiet, two things he rarely got in the frantic pace of Hollywood. He hadn't realized how much he needed the time away until he'd paddled out from the shore. His mind was a jumble, and he wanted to find some clarity. He was doing his morning

Bible reading and spending time in prayer, but it seemed harder to hear from God recently, as if all the other voices and demands of the world were drowning out His voice. Or maybe Chris wasn't listening.

The movie was part of it. Ed had sent over the distribution contract, and it had been weighing on him. Kate hadn't found anything troubling in the contract, and she had spent a week consulting with other lawyers to make sure the profits and obligations were above the industry standard. She even suggested a few revisions that would give him more input in the marketing and allow him to retain a higher portion of the revenue. Before agreeing to anything, though, Ed wanted an early look at the film.

He'd only done a rough edit so far, and he was hesitant to let the executive see it, but he knew how the game was played. The studio wasn't going to put their name and their money behind a film without seeing it. Chris had been praying about it, waiting for direction, but he didn't have an answer. Maybe Ed showing up and offering the deal was the answer he had been waiting for, but he was too stubborn to see it. He'd talked to Kate about it, but she had been focused on the bottom line. She looked at the numbers, ran calculations, and made a practical decision. She was focused, determined, efficient. He loved that about her.

He loved her smile and her confidence. He loved the way she sat very still when she was nervous and the way she stood up straight when she was mad. He loved the tapping of her foot and her exaggerated sighs when he annoyed her. He loved the way she picked out the cookie dough chunks in her ice cream and saved them until the end. He loved her loyalty to her friends and the kind heart she tried to hide under stiff suits and big words. He loved it all.

He loved her.

The words weren't a shock to him. He'd known it from the first moment he saw her. She was sunlight and wildfire, strength and beauty. She was smart and funny, and she filled a part of him that he hadn't known was empty. When he'd held her in the church parking lot, he'd been so close to kissing her, to sweeping her in his arms and telling her how he felt, but he held back. She wasn't ready. She'd made that clear more times than he could count. She was hurt and angry, and she didn't want a relationship. She wasn't interested in love.

Or maybe she just wasn't interested in him.

The thought pierced his heart, and he smacked the water.

Ben looked at him from his prone position on his board. "Are you all right?"

Chris sighed and looked at the hazy sky in the distance. It wasn't that long ago, Ben had been in his place, in love with a woman who didn't want him. He'd stood by him, offered encouragement, pointed out the possibilities. He'd even volunteered to help Ben build a stage for the church just so he had an excuse to be around Lily. When things had been at their worst, he'd stayed with Ben in the hospital. Now that the tables were turned, he decided it was a whole lot easier to be the guy giving the advice than to be the guy hopelessly in love. But he didn't just need advice; he needed a miracle where Kate was concerned. "I think I'm in trouble."

Ben sat up on the board and pulled his feet out of the water. "Do not say shark."

Chris laughed. "No, not a shark. It's Kate."

"Same thing." Apparently satisfied that nothing with teeth was going to bite him, Ben let his legs slide back into the water. "The right woman will come up out of nowhere when you least expect it, latch on to your heart, and just like that . . . " He snapped his fingers, the crack loud and sharp in the quiet of the calm waves. "You're a goner."

Chris laughed. Ben didn't know how right he was. The surfboard rocked beneath him, rising and falling in a gentle motion with the undulating water. On the shore, early morning walkers paced the beach. It was too early for the tourists who would come out to spend the entire day on the sand. The overcast sky and cool breeze kept most people away, but it was his favorite time to be there. In a few hours, the beach would be full of beach towels and colorful folding chairs. The birds would be circling, waiting to dive down for a carelessly dropped snack. It would be as busy and chaotic as his mind.

"What's going on with you and Kate?" Ben asked. "And just so you know, Lily is rooting for you."

He watched the shore as he thought about Ben's question. What was going on with Kate? In the weeks since her mom had shown up at the Hollywood Mission, they had been having not-a-date nights at his place almost every night. Kate had decided they had to alternate between black-and-white and color movies. They bounced around the decades, a random smattering of Hollywood history. When he found out she had never seen *Rocky*, he insisted on an immediate watching. When Kate mentioned how many times she watched *Twelve Angry Men* in law school, he bought it. She spent the entire movie telling him every detail the movie got wrong about a courtroom. He'd been so happy to see the spark her eyes that he suggested three more courtroom dramas just to hear her point out the mistakes in them. He also made a note that if he ever made a legal thriller, the first thing he would do was hire Kate as his consultant.

But then she went home and left him with an empty house and a confused heart. Technically, nothing was going on, and that was the problem. He wanted something to go on. He wanted to hold her hand and pull her close. He wanted to laugh with her and take her in his arms. He wanted to share his work with her and listen to her opinions. He even wanted her loud sighs when he took too long to make a decision and her blurry-eyed grimaces when she woke up too early. He had twenty-four hours in each day, and he wanted to spend every one of them with her.

It was a problem.

Ben was watching him, waiting for an answer, but he didn't have one. He could play it cool, laugh it off, paddle in to shore, and forget he'd said anything. He could go back to overthinking and over-analyzing everything, stuck in Kate's not-a-date limbo until she went back to Boston and forgot all about him, or he could spill his guts to his best friend. He wasn't a huge fan of either option.

His drummed his fingers on his board as he watched the sun try to peek through the clouds. "I might love her."

Ben laughed, the sound echoing against the lap of the waves. "There's no *might* about it, my friend. You are head over heels for that woman."

"Is it that obvious?" he asked, but the grin on Ben's face told him all he needed to know. It was obvious to everyone except Kate. "What am I supposed to do?"

"It looks like you've got two choices." Ben held up his hand, counting the options on his fingers. "One, you swim to shore and move on. Play it safe and forget about Kate. Or two, you tackle the wave head on and risk the wipe-out. The question is, how much are you willing to risk?" He stretched out on his board and started paddling to shore, leaving Chris in his wake.

Chris followed, his hands cutting through the water with even strokes. If he took his shot with Kate, laid it all on the table and told her how he felt, it might be an epic wipe-out. He'd been tossed by heavy waves before, thrown around in the water until he couldn't tell which way was up. One early morning about three years ago, he'd nearly been crushed on jagged rocks. The waves had pinned him down, the sharp stones cutting through his wetsuit as he took hit after hit. The idea of telling Kate he loved her was far more terrifying.

*****

He walked into the office with a plan.

Well, not exactly a plan. He had a daring idea and a lot of prayer.

Kate was sitting at the desk. She had finally abandoned her slick business suits and was wearing a soft gray sweater and jeans. It set off the red of her hair, and she looked like a sunrise over snowcapped mountains. Her lips were turned down in a frown as she read the paper in her hand. He watched as she used a red pen to scratch out a few lines and scribble something in the margin. He would have been happy to spend all day watching her, and if he stalled long enough, maybe he could do just that and never have to open his mouth.

Calling himself every kind of fool, he crossed to the desk and stood in front of her. He hadn't put his heart on the line since Tessa. Ever since her betrayal and the ugly fallout, he'd been hesitant to get involved with anyone. There was so much at stake, so much at risk when you opened your heart to another person. If he kept his mouth shut, if he stayed in their not-a-date comfort zone, he would be safe on shore, but the shore would never satisfy him, not when he knew what was waiting for him on the waves.

She looked up and blinked. The green of her eyes sucked the air from his lungs. The words "epic wipe-out" echoed in his head.

"Dinner and a movie at my place tonight?" he asked, nervousness winging its way through his veins.

"It's a date," she mumbled and immediately went back to the papers scattered on the desk.

He put his hands on the desk and leaned forward. He wasn't going to sit on the shore anymore. He was going for it, the biggest wave he had ever faced. When she looked up at him, he held her gaze. "Yes, it is."

Her eyes widened. If he was going to wipe out, this was it. He'd left no room for doubt. This was a date. A first date. The seconds ticked by as she stared at him, confusion dancing in her expression, and he could imagine the thoughts rushing through her mind. He waited. The rocks were looming in front of him, and the wave was driving him straight toward them.

Her lips parted, and he held his breath. "Okay."

The word was a whisper, but it roared in his ears. He was riding the wave into shore. The only question now was what would be waiting for him on the other side.

Chapter Twenty-One

KATE STOOD ON THE WELCOME mat staring at the front door. She'd been there for at least five minutes, too paralyzed with indecision to knock, standing there like a door-to-door salesman who was hoping for a sale and expecting a rejection. She'd been here so many times before. Over the past few weeks, dinner and movie with Chris had become her favorite part of the day, but this was different. A date, he'd said, and for some bizarre reason she didn't fully understand, she had agreed. She was one knock away from dating Chris.

Chris.

Chris who had been a good friend to her. The man who had picked her up when she'd fallen apart and had never asked for an explanation. He'd given her a job when she needed one. He'd let her be a part of a film that she loved more every day. He was funny and kind, and she was about to ruin it all.

She didn't know how to have a good relationship. In the past, her relationships had been about distraction or diversion. She had only been looking for a good time, for a few nights of fun, and then she moved on. This was not that. There was no casual, no-strings-attached scenario with Chris. This was serious. If she knocked on the door and went inside, everything would change. She couldn't go back to "just friends" with him after this. It was all or nothing.

She stared at the number on the door, inhaling the sweet scent of honeysuckle blooming on either side of her. It wasn't too late for her to walk away. She could text him an excuse. She should be focused on working her way through the list in her purse, anyway. Her hand rested against the side of her purse. She would have to tell him. She'd have to be honest with him about the list. He had never looked at it or used it, but it had kept her up every night as she searched for information on the men. She couldn't keep it a secret. If tonight went well and they moved forward with a—she gulped—a relationship, she would have to find a way to explain it.

She shifted her weight on her feet like a runner looking for a good reason to change direction. What if it didn't work out? She would have to quit the film. There was no way she could keep working with him if they crashed and burned. It would be too awkward. She'd have to hide in her bedroom every time he came to Ben and Lily's house. This was a terrible idea. She did not have a good track record when it came to men. She didn't have the first clue how to make a relationship work. Growing up, she thought her parents had the perfect marriage, and look what happened there. Disaster.

She was a child of disaster. Why should she expect her relationships to be any different?

Her phone beeped. She dug it out of her purse and saw a text from Lily. *Don't be a chicken. It's worth the risk.*

Kate sighed. Lily had been ecstatic when she told her about the date-that-really-was-a-date. She'd helped her pick out an outfit, sat in the bathroom with her and gave her a lengthy list of all Chris's best qualities while Kate did her hair, and then made her promise to tell her everything as soon as she got home.

She stuffed her phone back in her purse without replying. She didn't know what to say. She didn't even know if she could knock on the door. Once it opened, it would be too late to change her mind. This was the last thing she wanted when she decided to stay in Los Angeles, and she had said those exact words to Lily when she made her change her outfit for the third time.

Lily's response drifted through her mind. *But what if it's the one thing you need?*

Her toes were getting cold as she stood in the cold night air. She'd gone back to her flashy high heels because they usually made her feel confident. Not tonight. Tonight, she felt insecure and confused, and no designer shoe could fix that.

It's worth the risk.

She lifted her hand, and before she could change her mind, she knocked quickly. She was already second guessing her choice, debating if she should jump into the bushes and hide, when Chris opened the door.

The sleeves of his blue dress shirt were rolled up, revealing his tanned forearms. He smiled, and she almost tripped over her own feet. Like a light flipping on, it suddenly all made sense. Chris made sense. It was definitely worth the risk.

She followed him through the house and into the smell of tomatoes and herbs. The lights were low, and candles burned brightly on the dining room table. Her stomach clenched, and her hands went a little numb. "No pizza tonight?" she asked, her throat oddly dry.

He shook his head, his sandy brown hair dancing at the back of his neck. "My mother insisted that I learn how to make at least one real meal before I left home. This is it."

A giddy dizziness swept over her. She'd never felt anything like it before, as if she was flying and swimming and soaring and diving all at once. It was like she had walked into a dream, a movie that had been made just for her. She wasn't sure if she wanted to sit down or throw herself into his arms and stay there forever.

She laughed at what she had become, but she didn't care. The candlelight stole her common sense, and she didn't want it back. She was ready to take the leap.

"I'm so happy you're here." Chris extended his hand. She intertwined her fingers with his. They connected like puzzle pieces interlocking, two pieces that had been separated but had always belonged together.

"Me, too," she said, stepping closer to him.

Candlelight danced on his cheek, a flickering glow that cast his face in red and orange. He smiled, and her legs turned to mush. It was only his presence, the strength of his body, and the warmth of his hand on hers that kept her standing.

Why had she fought it for so long? Chris was everything she could ever want.

And he wanted her, too.

The realization that he wanted her, that he cared about her, struck her with the force of a crashing wave. She didn't have to be alone anymore. Chris has seen her at her worst, and he was still here, still giving her his hand, drawing her close when others would have pushed her away. He was strong and trustworthy. She could give him her heart, and he would treat it like a prize, not a burden.

Could she give him her heart?

Her breath stuck in her chest as the truth of it screamed in her brain.

She had already done it. Chris already had her heart. She had just refused to see it until now.

Chris pulled her gently toward him, and she went willingly. His eyes smoldered with a passion she recognized, an intensity that sent wild dreams and desires flinging through her body. Heat leapt across her fingers, seeking the same flame that burned in his. If she leaned close enough, she could brush her lips against his. Her heart pounded in her chest as she turned her head to his. With her free hand, she shrugged her purse off her shoulder and dropped it on the counter that separated the kitchen from the dining room. She missed the counter, and it clattered to the floor, the contents spilling all over the floor with a loud rattle.

Kate cringed. That was one way to kill the mood.

Embarrassment flooded her cheeks as she knelt to clean up the chaos she had created. She grabbed lipstick, a pack of tissues, and her phone and stuffed them back in her bag.

Chris laughed and bent down beside her, scooping up her business card holder and an assortment of receipts and papers.

Kate gasped and reached for the paper in his hands. The list of names her father had given her.

Chris pulled back. He sat on his heels and stared at it. The notes she had made during her research crisscrossed the page. "This is the list your dad gave me." He studied it, scanning the careful notes she'd made beside the names. "What are you doing with this?" he asked.

"I . . . " Hurt flashed in his eyes, and regret filled her heart. "I'm tracking down the men from the club."

Chris stood, his eyes still focused on the sheet of paper in his hand. "Why? We decided not to use it for the film. We never used the list. It's been in a file somewhere since you gave it to me. Right?"

How could she explain? How could she make him understand what she had done? "I made a copy of it when my dad gave it to me. It's my own research, for something else."

"I don't understand. What are you using this for?" He walked into the living room, away from the mess on the floor, away from her.

Cold settled in her veins. She wanted to go back—to the day her dad gave her that envelope, to the day Chris hired her, all the way to the brunch when he first talked about the film. If she could just go back and tell him everything, explain it all. The clarity of her mistakes burst in her brain like a supernova. Everything she should have done, but it was too late. She was left with the chaos she had created, and there was no way to escape it.

"My sister was killed in a car accident six years ago. The man who was driving the other car disappeared. I've been looking for him ever since that night." The words tumbled out, as if she could stop the thoughts forming in Chris' mind. "That night in Norma Jean's, I saw him, the man who caused the accident." She followed him into the living room, the candlelight no longer reaching him as he stood in the shadows and continued to look at the evidence of her deception in his hand.

"My dad didn't believe me. But I know . . . " She stepped closer, willing him to believe her. "I know he's there. He's on that list somewhere. That's why I stayed in LA. I have to find him."

"Is this why you agreed to work on the film? To get this?" Chris looked at her, and the raw pain on his face broke her heart. "This whole time, you never cared about the film. You never cared about . . . " The word was unsaid, but Kate heard it. *Me.* You never cared about *me.* "It was about this list. This is the only thing you wanted." He paused, and she reached for him, but he stepped back. "And you used me to get it."

He turned and walked to the sliding glass doors at the far side of the room. Staring into the night, the reflection of his troubled face shone in the glass. She had done that to him. She had taken everything he had given her, every kindness he had ever shown her, and stomped on it, like a bug crushed under her foot. Regret wasn't a strong enough word for the emotion that consumed her.

"I'm sorry." The words fell flat, empty and useless, but she said them anyway. "I should have told you." She stood behind him, longing to touch him, but forcing her hand to stay by her side. Beyond his reflection, the ocean churned under a dark sky. Sea foam roiled on the waves, hitting the shore and receding again, pulled back in the blackness of the inky horizon.

"I can't escape that night, Chris. The sound of the crash, the fear, the smell of gas and blood. Megan was my little sister, and she died next to me. She was bleeding and scared, and that man walked away. He looked in the car. I saw his face, and I begged him for help, but he walked away. He left us there, and Megan died." Tears blurred her vision as the memories choked her. "I can't let him get away with it. As long as he's free, I won't be. I'm trapped in that moment, listening to Megan's last breath, stuck there forever." She put her hand on his shoulder, felt the tension and anger that tightened his muscles. "I know I was wrong. I messed up, and I'm sorry, but can you understand why I did it?"

He turned, and she wiped the tears away. He reached for her but stopped. He pulled his hand away, and she felt the loss, the connection between them crumbling, withering to dust and ash because of her.

"I understand," he said, and relief swept through her, until she looked in his eyes. Pain and disappointment raged in the blue depths. "But this," he looked at the paper that hung limply from his hand. "I don't know what to do with this. With us."

Her heart cracked under the weight of what might have been. Every dream she didn't know she carried was suddenly clear, brilliant, and beautiful just long enough for her to watch it die.

He held the list of names out to her. Revulsion filled her as she looked at the paper that hung between them, but she took it. Chris walked past her. He flipped on the lights and blew out the candles. The sudden brightness was a shock, a splash of cold water that shook her back to reality.

"She was my sister. I owe it to her." There was nothing else she could say. She'd made her choice. It was about Megan. It was always about Megan.

Chris put his hands on the back on one of the dining room chairs. The table was neat and pristine, set for a romantic dinner they would never have. She noticed the napkins and the flowers. He had gone to so much trouble, and now it was ruined. All of it was ruined.

He bent over the chair, his head hanging between his arms. If he was praying, Kate knew God wasn't going to help her. She didn't deserve it.

"I'll help you," he said, his voice ragged and rough. He stood and looked at her. His face was hard, his jaw clenched. "I'll help you find him."

Cautious happiness sprang to life in her chest. Maybe it wasn't a lost cause. Maybe there was hope for whatever they had been starting. "You will?"

He nodded. "I . . . " He stopped suddenly, as if he was about to say too much. "I care about you, Kate. It might be the biggest mistake of my life, but I do."

She recoiled, the sharp edge of his words driving straight into her heart. She wanted to say that she cared about him, too, that she was sorry, that she'd give anything to take it back. But she couldn't. There was no going back. All she had left was her pride. She stood straight and took his words, absorbing them, folding them into the regrets she carried. She earned his anger, and she wouldn't fight it.

Chris exhaled, as if all the energy had left his body. He sounded tired and sad, and it was her fault. "I'll help you find this man, help you get the closure you need," he said. "But after that, we're done. You can go back to Boston, stay in LA—it doesn't matter. Just stay away from me."

Chapter Twenty-Two

CHRIS SAT IN THE DARK screening room and watched his documentary flicker across the screen. It should have excited him, seeing his work on such a large scale, seeing the footage he shot and edited rolling by on the same screen that had shown future blockbusters and Academy Award winners. The screening room wasn't as big as a theater, but it was much larger than his laptop. For the first time, his work, the movie he had been working so hard to make, was playing on a big screen. The room was dark as he and Ben sat beside a collection of studio executives in the oversized recliners watching his documentary unfold before them.

He tried to concentrate on the images, the footage he had spent hours shooting and editing. He should have been looking for places to improve, area that could be tightened, edits that could be cleaner. He still had to finish the sound and music, the title cards, and the opening and closing credits. There were a thousand details still to be done, but the finish line was in sight. He was so close to being done, to seeing this through to the end, but he'd lost all of his momentum.

Kate plagued him. He couldn't think. He couldn't focus. Over and over, he replayed what she had done, how she had lied to him and used him. Once again, he was a fool. A blind, distracted fool. She had used him for his position, insinuated herself into his company, become a part of his film—all because she wanted that list.

Kate had never disguised her ambition or her independence. She didn't wait for permission. She took off running and left everyone else to catch up. He shouldn't be surprised that she had put her own agenda first. And yet, he was. He'd thought they had something different, that he meant something to her.

He was wrong.

He should be grateful no one knew about it. Tessa had destroyed his reputation and nearly ended his career. Kate had just broken his heart. She had used him and his film for her own purpose. She wanted revenge, and she had used him to get one step closer to it. He balled his hand into a fist and punched the padded armrest. If she had told him, he would have helped her. If she had been honest with him, he would have listened. Instead, she'd walked in shadows and half-truths, pretending to be on his side, pretending that she cared about the film, when all she really cared about was the list of names in her purse.

Ben nudged his elbow. He was seated next to him, concern etched on his face as he looked at him in the dim light of the film. Chris loosened his clenched fist and tried to relax. He needed to look like he was in control. He couldn't look like a director about to lose it over a woman who broke his heart—even if that's exactly what he was—not when the very people he needed on his side were sitting in the row in front of him.

Ed had brought in a few of the studio's marketing heads to watch the documentary. It was the last step before signing a deal. Once everyone was on board, they'd settle the final terms and sign on the dotted line. His film would be seen in theaters across the country, and depending on the initial response, possibly in theaters around the world. With the studio backing him, he had a good chance at not only making back the initial investment he and Ben had made but also turning a hefty profit as well. The studio had reach that he didn't, partnerships with theater corporations that would get the film in front of people. It was exactly the breakthrough he had been praying for. It was everything he couldn't do on his own.

He kept his eyes on the screen, watching Graciella's heartbreaking interview, but his mind kept drifting back to the red-haired lawyer who had stomped on his heart. She didn't know the depth of his feelings for her, and he was relieved he hadn't said anything. It was bad enough to be in love with someone who betrayed you; it would have been even worse if she knew he loved her. Rubbing his hands over his eyes, he tried to focus on the film. Loving Kate was something he would fix later. It would carve a hole out his heart to get over her, but he would do it. He had to.

At least he had the film. It wasn't finished, but he could envision the final cut. He was proud of the work he'd done. The work they'd done. Regret twisted in his heart like a sharp blade. He could see Kate's hand in every scene. He remembered where she was standing when they'd filmed a particular scene. He remembered how she complained when they'd gotten up early for the sunrise. He watched a street scene, remembering how Kate had dashed across the street to stop a car from driving past and ruining his shot. She'd been invaluable, and like it or not, she was a part of the film. In his mind, she would be in the shadows of every frame, a ghost of a presence that echoed in every scene. He would never be free of her. He was as certain of that fact as he was of his own name. Kate was imprinted on his heart, a brand he would carry for the rest of his life.

A smattering of applause broke through his thoughts, and he looked up to see that the film had ended. The temporary end credits rolled past, and Kate's name caught his attention. Kate Sullivan, the woman who broke his heart.

Ed was sitting in the row right in front of him. The producer stood and faced him, leaning against the back of the seat behind him. "Great work, Chris, really great. It's timely, powerful, and moving. It hit me right here." He tapped his chest, above his heart. "First class filmmaking."

The three marketing executives agreed, adding words like "amazing, moving, brilliant," as they stood in a line and applauded.

Ben slapped him on the back. "I knew you could do it." His grin was almost enough to banish the weight from his soul, but even Ben's approval couldn't break past the pain that set up camp around his heart. "It's an amazing film that will do a lot of good."

Chris tried to find joy in that. He was accomplishing what he set out to do, but it was hollow. He looked at the empty seat beside him. Kate should have been there. When he'd left the office that morning, he hadn't told her where he was going, and she hadn't asked. They were standing on opposite sides of a chasm, and the bridge that spanned the distance was gone, burned and broken.

Chris mumbled his thanks. He should be excited, but he wasn't. He wanted it to be done, so he could move out of the church and leave Kate behind. The sooner the film wrapped and he helped her find the man she was looking for, the sooner he could forget about her and everything she had made him feel.

Ed rubbed his hands together. "Let's talk details. The studio is ready to get behind this and give it a full push. It won't get the same build-up as a feature, but we'll make sure it gets plenty of press. Festivals, write-ups, a few op-ed pieces and it should have a good head start. With this type of story, we need to play up the human element, get people behind the cause, and that will get them into the theaters. Plus, with Ben willing to lend his support in the public relations campaign, we'll capture a big segment of the entertainment news during the release. With the right support, we might even be able to get it in to consideration for an Academy Award."

That got Chris' attention. An Academy Award. It was beyond his wildest dreams. He had been too scared to pray about something that big. It felt selfish, like he was asking too much. He wanted people to see the film; he wanted to bring it into the conversation, to get people talking about the horrors of human trafficking. But international distribution, awards—this was huge, and it was within his grasp. As everything with Kate fell apart, he was grateful he was doing one thing right. Seeing his film succeed would be a good consolation prize for having his love life reduced to rubble.

One of the marketing guys handed Ed a file folder. Ed removed a pair of reading glasses from an interior pocket in his sport coat and slipped them on. He peered at the papers hidden in the file. "We've got a few tweaks we'd like you to make to the final film, but once that's done, we'll be all set to hit the ground running."

Chris nodded. It wasn't unusual for the studio to want changes made in a film. He'd been in similar conversations before. There was a give-and-take between what the studio wanted and his vision as the director. There was always a compromise, a final agreement that would make everybody happy. He anticipated a request to add the studio name to the opening credits. It would go right after his own production company, 318 Films. Proverbs 31:8 had started him on this path. It was a perfect fit for what he was doing and what he hoped to achieve.

He pulled a notepad and a pen from the backpack by his feet. He had come prepared. Let the negotiations commence.

Ed noticed the pen and notepad, so he dove right in. "We'll want a title card, of course." Chris nodded. Of course. He rattled off a few minor changes, and Chris took notes. None of it was major. Ed looked at the folder in his hand and sent a sideways glance to the marketing executives. "There's one big thing we need you to adjust." He took off his reading glasses and crossed his arms. "You spend a lot of time in the film talking about God and hope and redemption."

A tight ball of dread settled in Chris's stomach.

"And that's all wonderful," Ed continued. "I know you're a man of faith, and I think that's great. Really great, right, guys?" He looked at the marketing executives, who nodded vigorously, parroting Ed's words. "But . . ." Ed paused and pursed his lips. "The studio isn't looking for a Christian market film. They want a broad appeal, something that will be accessible for everyone."

Beside him, Ben sat up straighter. "This film *is* accessible to everyone," he said. "Jesus is accessible to everyone."

Ed nodded. "Sure, sure. But in terms of the business side, the marketing, how we sell the film to theaters, we'll get more traction if the focus is on the human element and not so much on God. We need to appeal to a larger market."

Chris tapped his pen against the notepad. Something like numbness filled him. They wanted to cut his film up. That was the price of the studio's support. Distribution, awards, publicity, and all he had to do was take a scalpel to the only thing he had left.

One of the marketing executives stepped forward. "We came up with some suggestions after the first screening. Cut out the Manna Center and Jonathan Lopez, add some additional footage of the street scenes, what it looks like out there at night for the girls, bring in some of the danger and the more . . . " He hesitated and looked at one of the other men.

"We're thinking it needs more explicit details. To make it more powerful. Really bring it home." The trio of marketers nodded. Explicit. Gritty. God wasn't acceptable, but graphic details of abuse were.

A headache started to form behind his eyes as the young executive droned on about the changes they wanted made. They wanted him to cut out any reference to God, Jesus, redemption, or salvation. Focus on the human cost and highlight the good work being done by secular organizations. He was going to have to cut God out from the very project He had given him.

He raised his hand and stopped the list. "I can't cut out every reference to God. God is the reason for hope. He is the source of rescue. It's why I made this film."

Ed waved the marketing guys away. They stepped back without a word. "Chris, I thought you wanted to take a stand against human trafficking. I thought this film was about showing people the truth and inspiring them to get involved. God is great, but don't you want human intervention? Don't you want to see people stepping up to do the hard work, opening new homes for survivors, getting law enforcement to cooperate across state lines, assembling resources for the young girls and boys who escape? Isn't that what you're hoping this film will do? Isn't that more important?"

Chris stared past Ed's shoulder at the blank screen. He did want all of that. There were people suffering right that moment, and of course, he wanted to help—but at what cost? "God is the heart of this film," he said, but he heard the waver, the indecision in his own voice.

Ed sat beside him and leaned on the arm rest. "And there's nothing wrong with that. I applaud it, really. But if you want this film to go wide, if you want it to have a global impact, you need to make it palatable for everyone. If you keep this as a Christian film, you'll lose half your audience . . . at least. How is that going to help the victims? If you appeal to a broader audience, think of the good you could do. Wouldn't God want that more than having His name in the film?"

"Chris, don't." Ben whispered on his other side. "It's not worth it. You know what this film is supposed to be. We'll figure something else out."

Ed sat back and lifted his hands helplessly. "I believe in this film, Chris. I believe in what you're doing, and I know we can help. The studio can spread this message so much farther than you can on your own. We're ready to put all of our experience and assets behind it. What resources do you have? How many theaters can you call? How many reporters, editors, and influencers do you have on speed dial? Doesn't your film deserve the widest audience possible?"

Faith and reason warred in his head. *God*, he prayed, *what do I do?*

No answer came. He had been so sure he was making the film the way God directed, but what if he was wrong? What if it was supposed to be exactly as Ed said? What if the point was to get the message out? The studio could do that so much better than he could. Was that more important than keeping in a message about God? A message he wasn't even sure God wanted in the first place?

Unbidden, an image of Kate filled his mind. Kate walking into the waiting room at the hospital, the moment his whole world shifted.

Kate in his office, tapping her foot and sighing. Kate at the wedding, beaming with the first real, unguarded smile he'd ever seen from her. Kate at the beach, on his sofa laughing at an old movie. Kate's face when he confronted her about the list, when his world shifted again.

He'd been wrong about her, wrong from the very start. He'd fallen for her, and look what it had gotten him. Maybe he was wrong about the film, too. Maybe God had sent Ed and the studio's demands to get him back on track. If the point was to help people, shouldn't he go with the option that had the biggest potential? God was still God, even if He wasn't in the documentary. He sat in silence, the options waging a confusing war in his head.

Ben put his hand on his shoulder, grounding him, bringing him into the present, stepping into the conversation when he had lost his way. "Give us a few days to consider it," Ben said, and gratitude washed though him.

Time and space. That was exactly what he needed. Time and space and a blinking neon sign from God telling him what to do.

"Of course, of course." Ed stood again and patted Chris on the back. "Take some time and think about it." He scanned the pages in the file folder again. "We've got a pretty full schedule laid out for the release, and there are some extensive preparations, so don't take too long." He closed the file and handed it to Chris. "This is an important film. We can do great things together if you give it a chance."

He and Ben shook hands with each of the executives before leaving the screening room. They didn't discuss the offer until they were seated in Chris' car.

"You can't do it." Ben didn't bother with preamble, and he certainly didn't sugar coat his words.

Chris started the car. The engine hummed to life, but he didn't put it in gear. He gripped the steering wheel and stared at the road in front of him. "You heard Ed. The studio has more resources, more connections. With their backing, this film could make a difference. It could change lives, maybe even save lives. Isn't that what's important?"

"Is it?" Ben asked.

Chris slammed the car into drive and left the parking lot. He passed extras dressed in costumes, executives in golf carts, and tourists getting a backstage tour. It was the world he knew, the world he was familiar with. He should have stayed here and focused on the things he knew. He wasn't ready to step out on his own. If he did what the studio asked, if he changed the film, he could release it on a much bigger scale than he could do on his own. He could hand it off to the studio, let Ed and his team handle it. His part would be done, and he could move on, away from his little office at the church, away from Kate.

He drove slowly through the lot, conscious of Ben's silence beside him. Ben had made his feelings clear, but his career wasn't on the line. It wasn't Ben's name all over the documentary or his name that would be tied to it forever. It was his. It was a Chris Johnston project. If it flopped, he would never be able to escape that legacy. But if it became a studio project, if the studio backed it, he had a cushion, a safety net.

An ache to talk to Kate followed him as he maneuvered through the crowded lot. He'd talked about every aspect of this film with her. She knew the scenes he'd cut, the unexpected touches he had decided to add. They had argued about certain scenes, each of them making a case for why it should or shouldn't be in the film. They had rearranged the storyboard together. When she had trouble explaining how she thought a scene should go, he had taught her how to use the editing software so she could show him what she meant. Kate was the only other person who knew the film as well as he did.

But how could he trust her opinion? How could he trust anything she would say?

He drove past the security post and left the studio. As they drove back to the mission, he'd never felt so alone.

Chapter Twenty-Three

KATE SAT IN THE PASSENGER seat of Chris' car and stared into the Los Angeles night. They were parked in a residential neighborhood, waiting for one of the men from her list to come home, hoping to catch a glimpse of him as he walked to his front door. She'd used social media and public records to find photos of most of the men who had been in the club that night, but the ones she couldn't identify, she needed to see in person. Though she didn't deserve it, Chris had kept his word to help her. They worked their way through the names, waiting for Kate to make a positive identification, waiting for her to see the man she had spent six years looking for.

It had been the wrong man every time. Frustration clawed at her. A nagging worry that she would never find him grew with every disappointment, every photo that didn't match her memory. Doubt, the whisper she had kept at bay for so long, rose to a roar. Maybe she was wrong. Maybe she had thrown her life away, sacrificed her career, her family, and Chris for nothing, for a split-second glance that didn't mean anything. The possibility that she had lost everything she cared about and would have nothing to show for it made her sick to her stomach.

She snuck a glance at Chris. His jaw was clenched, and his arms were crossed tightly against his chest. He hadn't spoken more than a few words to her since they'd left the mission for their amateur stakeout. She tried to imagine how different the evenings could have been if she'd told Chris the truth from the start, if she had trusted him. It might have been fun. Coffee and snacks in the dim light of the Los Angeles streets. If she had let him in from the start, if he had been her partner instead of her prop, things could have been different. But it was too late for what might have been. The nights they spent searching for this man, this figment from her nightmares, were tense and quiet and full of regret.

She sipped lukewarm water from her reusable bottle. Chris wasn't slipping away from her; he was already gone. Only his word kept him by her side, his promise to help her find the man who killed Megan. Her time with him was ticking away. The sooner she found the man, the sooner she would lose Chris forever. Not that she had anything to lose. She didn't have a claim on him. They'd only had half a date, and that had ended in disaster. Whatever might have been, the fantasies she had concocted between his front door and the moment her purse fell to the floor didn't count. She had driven him away, and that was the end of it.

She popped the top back on the water bottle, and the click echoed in the awkward silence. Chris had never promised her anything. He'd never been more than a friend. She couldn't lose something she had never had, and yet she felt the loss, the emptiness of his absence, the space in her life where he should have been. Unbidden, a memory of the last night she had been in his house flitted through her mind. The candles, the dinner. It had felt like the start of something new, something that could have changed everything, but she had spoiled it. Looking back, she saw a thousand things she could have done differently, but none of it mattered now.

The quiet in the car was oppressive. Even his terse replies would have been better than the stone wall he'd put up between them. She cleared her throat, searching for something to say that would get him talking. "How did the meeting with Ed go?" she asked.

Chris kept staring out the windshield. His silence cut more deeply than anything he could say. Chris hadn't told her about the screening. She'd heard about it from Ben over dinner. He didn't say much, only that Chris had some big decisions to make.

These past few days, Chris had been businesslike and professional, and that polite distance hurt more than she thought it would. She missed his smile, his laugh. She missed the sand on his flip flops when he came to the office straight from the beach. He didn't tease her anymore or suggest tacos or movies. If he needed her to look at a contract or review a media release, he left the paperwork on the desk without a word and walked away. They worked side by side but worlds apart. Even now, only inches separated them, but it was a distance she couldn't cross.

She sighed and turned to the window at her side. Her breath fogged the glass, and she blinked back the sheen of tears. She didn't have the right to cry. It was her mess, and she would deal with it.

"It was difficult." Chris' rough and cracked voice startled her, and she whipped her head back to him. It was one sentence, but she would take it. "Ed wants a significant change to the film before the studio will sign on to distribute it. I'm not sure I can do it." His hands gripped the steering wheel, even though the car was parked.

Kate held her breath, afraid to say too much or push too hard. She wanted to blurt out another apology, to pour out every regret and mistake in her heart, to plead her case, but she resisted. More than anything, she wanted Chris back. The man who had believed in her and trusted her, who had pizza reheating down to a science. The man who had held her when she cried. She spoke softly, testing the water and hoping she wouldn't drown. "What change does he want?"

Lines of exhaustion creased the skin around his eyes. He looked defeated, worn down, and it was her fault. She reached for his hand, but he slid it out of her reach. "He wants me to cut out Jonathan and the Manna Center. He thinks the religious references make it too difficult to market to a secular crowd."

He went back to staring into the night, and she felt him retreating again. No wonder he hadn't signed the contract. She was surprised he still had it sitting on his desk. A month ago, she never would have imagined that Chris would consider cutting Jonathan from the film. He would have torn the contract up without a second thought. But now . . .

So much had changed, and she blamed herself. Guilt twisted in her stomach.

"Chris, I . . . " She stopped. How did you apologize for something this big? She hadn't just lied to him. She'd used him, and even when she had begun to fall for him, she had stubbornly clung to her own her agenda. Words couldn't make up for what she'd done. She needed to do something to earn his forgiveness, but she didn't know where to start. "I'm so sorry. For all of this. Please, can you ever forgive me?"

Chris lowered his head, and his hair fell across his face. She ached to brush the hair back, to see his face, to touch his cheek and tell him she would never lie to him again.

He swept his hair back, as he turned to face her. "I forgive you," he said, but the words were sad, like a mournful dirge playing at a funeral. "But I can't trust you."

"If you let me explain, give me a chance—" she started, but he cut her off with a shake of his head.

"I did give you a chance." The car was suddenly too small. There was nowhere to hide, no argument she could use to deflect the hurt in his eyes. He was right. "You were so focused on what you wanted, you didn't care who got hurt in the process."

"I do care," she said, a desperate hope filling her words. If she could just make him understand, make him see why she had done it. "I care about you."

"Not enough to let me in. Not enough to tell me the truth. The only thing you care about is finding the man who caused the accident."

A chasm opened in the car. It wasn't space keeping them apart. It was the weight of her deception. It was one more thing she had messed up, one more thing she could lay at the feet of the man she was searching for. If her sister was still alive, if her mother had never left, if she had never gone to Boston, how many things would be different?

"I don't know how to fix this," she said. The confession cost her. She was the fixer, the one who had all the answers; but this time, when it mattered the most, she had none.

"There's nothing to fix," he said, and the finality of his words stole the air from her lungs "I can't give you what you need. Only God can do that. You need to make your peace with Him, not me."

Kate expected resentment to flood her soul, but there was only emptiness. God. She had tried God. She begged and pleaded with Him, but He never answered. At least, He never answered the way she wanted Him to. She couldn't deny that doing things her own way hadn't been working out very well. What if she had been wrong?

Chris' phone beeped, and he looked at the text message.

"It's Jonathan," he said and started the car. "We need to go."

Involuntarily, her eyes darted to the door of the house they were watching. It was one more night of failure. One more night of not finding what she was looking for. It was also one night closer to the end of her time with Chris.

"Kate." It was the first time he'd said her name in days. That one word resonated in her soul and watered a dryness that had been starving her heart. "We'll come back. We'll find him."

She nodded. Chris turned the car around and sped into the night.

*****

Jonathan's text to Chris had been simple. *Come to the center. Bring your camera. You don't want to miss this.*

After a quick stop at the mission to gather the equipment, they raced to meet Jonathan. They were once again set up in the cafeteria at the Manna Center. It was almost nine o'clock, and Kate was already exhausted. The coffee in her hand was warm, and she gulped it down, hoping for a caffeine jolt. Jonathan, Chris, and Graciella were huddled together under the bright lights he had set up, and the camera was waiting nearby on a tripod.

Kate shifted on her feet trying to keep herself from collapsing. Jonathan hadn't told them anything more. He was doing a terrible job of hiding a smile as he checked his phone every few minutes. Even Graciella was confused as she sat on the same stool she'd used for her initial interview. If they were doing a follow-up, Kate couldn't figure out why they couldn't have scheduled it for a decent hour; anytime when the sun was up would have worked for her.

Jonathan glanced at his phone again and jumped up with an excited exclamation. "It's time," he said, his grin spreading across his face. "You better get rolling."

Chris grabbed the camera and hefted it on his shoulder. Kate moved to stand behind him, careful to stay out of the shot. It was a familiar dance they had done too many times for her to count during filming, and it brought a fresh wave of loss to her heart. Chris glanced over his shoulder at her, and for a moment, a shared sorrow linked them. Then Chris turned away, and it vanished.

As Jonathan walked to the door, Chris followed him from a distance. Graciella stayed on the stool, watching it all with a confused and sleepy expression.

Jonathan disappeared through the door. A minute passed as they waited. Excitement spread in the air, though none of them knew why. The door opened, and Jonathan walked in with a woman by his side. She squinted into the room, and Jonathan whispered to her in Spanish.

"Mami?" Kate turned. Graciella was standing, tears streaming down her face. "Mami!" She ran across the cafeteria, her flat shoes slapping against the tiles as she ran to her mother's arms, clutching her tightly as she cried.

Graciella and her mother clung to each other. Kate didn't need to understand the words to know what was being said. Graciella's mother touched her face and wiped her daughter's tears. Thousands of miles and nightmares had separated them, but now they were together. Jonathan stood to one side, his head bowed and his hands raised in prayer.

Chris shifted, his camera catching every angle. He stepped again until he was standing at her side. He lowered the camera and switched it off, letting the scene play out without film. Kate knew she wouldn't need a photograph or a movie to remember it. Seeing Graciella in her mother's arms was something she would never forget, even as she knew it was something she would never experience again. She would never know her mother's touch, her hug, to feel her hands on her face. She had dared to think that Chris could fill that void, give her the love that had been stolen from her, but she had been wrong. It was gone. Megan, her mom, Chris—all of it was gone.

Chris turned to her, and for a moment, he held her gaze. For a moment, they were together again, sharing an unspoken whisper only they could hear. But it was only a moment. He stiffened as if he had just remembered the reality they were facing, as if the memories had come flooding back, and he stepped away, leaving her in the shadows again, caught in a land between the world she had made and the world she wished for.

Chris and Jonathan were talking in hushed tones as Graciella and her mother sat together under the shining lights. Kate was alone, separated by the isolation she had caused, alone in the independence she had wrapped herself in. She couldn't bear to watch the scene unfolding before her. She was happy for Graciella, but that happiness was a mirror that showed her nothing but emptiness and solitude. If that was all she had left, so be it. She would finish what she started. Justice, revenge—it didn't matter. She didn't have anything left to lose.

Wiping the tears from her face, she turned and walked away.

Chapter Twenty-Four

CHRIS LOOKED AT THE FOOTAGE from Graciella's reunion. He knew exactly where it would go in the film. He scribbled notes on a sheet of paper, working out where to put the scene. As Graciella and her mom spoke, catching up on the time that had been stolen from them, he had interviewed Jonathan, who explained how they were able to track down Graciella's family. It hadn't been easy. They didn't have a phone to call or an address to visit. Graciella's family lived in a small shanty town outside of Mexico City called a colonial. The colonial itself was little more than a collection of plywood and cardboard houses put up by families who had nowhere else to go. Chris had seen something similar near Tijuana. Houses that disintegrated in the heavy rains, with dirt floors and no running water. Using Graciella's directions, Jonathan had sent a team into Mexico to try to locate her family. It had taken them three trips and what could only be described as a miracle for them to find her parents. The colonial Graciella had lived in had been destroyed, and her family had moved on to another. Once the team found her parents, they had to go through a lengthy process to get her mother here to see her daughter.

It had been after midnight when he sat down with Graciella and her mother. They had both readily agreed to the on-camera interview. Using Jonathan as an interpreter, Chris filmed their story. They told him how their family had been deceived and broken apart, a story he had heard repeated in dozens of different ways but always at the hands of selfish and evil men. When Graciella told her mother about some of the things she had endured, her mom wept and held her close, enfolding her in a love that couldn't be described, the love of a mother who would have given the world to take her daughter's pain away, to go back and do things differently. One decision had changed everything. One choice, one step, one word and it would have all been different.

Chris understood it, that wish to go back and make a different choice. It was so desperate at times, the hurt, the longing to go back, to do it over and make a different choice. He glanced at Kate as she worked on the other side of the office, wondering if she felt the same. If she was aching for a chance to start again, if she would make a different decision.

He watched the footage on the screen, humbled and honored by what he had been able to participate in, witness, and soon share with the world. People would see in Graciella the young girls and boys who were being terribly abused. Graciella would give them a voice. She would be the face people remembered when they heard statistics and numbers too large to comprehend. If he could put a face to the terror, a face to the crime, maybe then people would stop turning a blind eye and would be willing to stand up and fight. It wasn't too late. God was still breaking chains and setting people free. It was time for His people to get involved.

Graciella was going back home with her mother the following day. She might never know how much of an impact her words would have. She might not ever see the film. He didn't know what was in the future for Graciella or what would happen when she went back to Mexico.

He paused the footage and looked at Graciella's face, a young girl who had survived horrors he couldn't imagine. She deserved a voice. She deserved to be heard, no matter the cost.

He would tell their story. That was his responsibility. He was the storyteller, but it was Jonathan who had brought them back together. Lawmakers and the media might shake their heads and offer a catchy soundbite, but Jonathan was doing something. He wasn't speaking in hypotheticals. The Manna Center was offering practical help, meeting real needs in the moment, giving people resources they needed. Chris had seen lives changed there. As long as he lived, he would never forget watching Graciella's mom embrace the daughter she thought she had lost. Their family was whole again because of what Jonathan was doing. If he hadn't been there to give Graciella a place to stay, to feed her, and to help locate her parents, what would have happened to her? It was that very thing the studio wanted him to cut. They wanted him to ignore the work Jonathan was doing simply because he was doing it the name of God.

What was a tiny film compared to the power of God?

Maybe that was the point of all this. Maybe the whole point had been to show him that God was still working. He wasn't silent, and He wasn't absent. He was at work every day in people like Jonathan, in the people who volunteered at the Manna Center, in the anonymous and quiet men and women who showed up and served. Maybe God was giving him a chance to see life outside of Hollywood. Chris thought his career, his life, and his future depended on his films, on his reputation in the industry. God was saying it all depended on Him.

He drummed his fingers on the desk. Kate looked at him from the other side of the small room. They were back to working in the church because he couldn't stand seeing her in his home, not after the catastrophic dinner that revealed how broken their relationship was. It was bad enough when he went home at night and could smell her perfume on his sofa. She had rearranged the chairs on his deck, and he hadn't moved them back. Two days ago, he found a tube of lip balm that had fallen out of her purse. He had slipped it in his pocket to return it to her, but he hadn't done it. It was still sitting in the front pocket of his jeans, a small piece of her he couldn't part with. Once the film was done and they found the man she was looking for, they would go their separate ways. This film was the last connection he had with her, the last thread holding them together.

Chris looked at the distribution contract from the studio. He wouldn't let them silence Graciella. He wouldn't let them rob him of the story he wanted to tell. If God could reunite Graciella and her mother, He could do anything. He grabbed the contract and tore it in two.

Kate glanced up from the corner where she had been working. "Is that the distribution contract?" she asked.

He nodded and tore it again and again. It disintegrated into a pile of shredded scraps.

"Took you long enough," she said. No surprise, no second guessing. She picked up a wire garbage bin and swept the pieces across the desk and into the trash. "Maybe now you can finish this thing."

He closed his eyes and prayed. He didn't care what Kate thought of it. If this past week had taught him anything, it was that he had no idea what he was doing. He needed God's guidance. He needed God to tell him what to do. When he relied on his own judgement and his own timing, he made a mess of things. Just look at what happened with Kate. He thought he was on the right track, and the whole time, she'd been playing him.

When he opened his eyes again, he felt the weight of Kate's stare. She was watching him, her brows pinched together in thought. "What?" he asked.

"Did you get any answers?" A small smile curved the corner of her lips, and it sent a jolt of electricity straight to his heart. This was why he needed God's intervention. Clearly, he could not be trusted around Kate. It didn't matter what she had done. She smiled, and he wanted to slide across the desk, irresistibly drawn to her like a magnet attracting a coin. He had to stop it.

He shook his head. "Not yet, but I'll keep asking."

Kate was thoughtful. He recognized the way her eyes shifted from side to side as she worked through a problem. She stood on the other side of the desk, keeping distance between them. Their relationship was shattered, and they spent their time together trying to avoid the jagged edges. "Sometimes, I wish I had your faith."

Her words were so quiet, he almost missed them. "You can," he said.

She shook her head. "I tried once. God didn't listen." Sadness coated her words, as cold as their conversations had been. "My sister was praying when she died. She believed in everything the Bible says, and when she needed God, when she prayed for Him to help us, He did nothing."

Chris searched for the right words, even though he knew he didn't have them. He wasn't a theologian, and he wasn't a pastor. She should have asked Evan or Jonathan these types of questions, or even Noah. They were all more qualified to give her the answers she needed to hear. He was just a movie director. "Kate, I don't know why Megan died. I don't know why that man got away with it. But I do know that God loves you. I wish you could see that."

She stood in front of him, her hair pulled over one shoulder, her eyes raw and vulnerable. "That's not the love I'm looking for," she said. There was a question in her words, a whisper of hope that hung in the air.

One moment stretched into two. His mouth went dry. His common sense screamed at him. He couldn't give in. He couldn't go back. He had given her his heart once, waited patiently for her to see him, to notice him, and when she did finally notice him, it was to use him.

She waited, but he couldn't say anything. Holding the trash can against her side, she dropped her gaze to the floor and walked out of the office. Chris stared into the empty space she left behind. They'd go out again that night. Once more looking for any trace of the man she blamed for her sister's death. He was starting to think it was like looking for a needle in a pile of needles. One man out of the millions that lived in Los Angeles. But he'd promised.

He didn't know at the time how hard it would be to keep that promise. Being near her was torture. In spite of what she'd done, in spite of the lies and the half-truths, he still loved her, and he didn't know how to stop.

Chapter Twenty-Five

KATE SHOOK HER HEAD. OF course, it would be the last name of the list. It made perfect sense. After all the years of searching, it would have to be the last one. It couldn't have been the first name she searched or the first house they went to. She should have started at the bottom and then all this would be over. It was like some grand cosmic joke that she spent weeks researching and had nothing to show for it except for broken relationships and useless apologies. She was down to the last name on her father's list. It had to be him. There were no more names, no more leads. This was it. It had to be.

She glanced at Chris sitting in the driver's seat. He had kept his promise to help her, but she knew their time together was short. When this was over, he would be gone. Once she found the man she was looking for and knew who he was and where he lived, Chris would leave her. That thought hurt her more than she thought it would. She had spent so many years keeping people away, keeping them at arm's length, building walls to shield herself, that isolation had become a friend to her. In spite of her best efforts, Chris had found a way through all of her defenses. He'd grinned and teased and flirted his way right through.

And now, she was going to lose him.

He sat behind the steering wheel, his arms crossed over his chest as he avoided looking at her. The dingy yellow hue from the streetlight tinted his hair a golden blond. He made her laugh like no one else could. His stupid jokes and spontaneous taco runs had been like a hurricane blowing through the carefully constructed life she'd built. She tried to imagine what her life was going to look like in a few days when she wouldn't see him every day, hear his voice, or watch him deliberate over the smallest edit in the film. She'd sacrificed everything for Megan's memory. Once that was laid to rest, what would she have left?

She couldn't stay with Ben and Lily forever, but she couldn't go back to Boston either. Her career there was over. She wouldn't go back to her dad's house, not as long as her mother was there. Her eyes slid to the window, to the reflection of Chris' face that hovered in the glass. There was only one place she wanted to go, but in her obsession with finding Megan's killer, she had thrown it away.

"Kate." Chris' urgent whisper echoed in the car. He touched her arm, and she was transfixed by the sight of his fingers against her skin. Reflexively, she covered his hand with hers, soaking up the warmth of his touch. The feeling swept through her arm and straight to her heart—a connection, a touch she had been desperately longing for. He looked at her and searched her face. The silence was full of words that neither of them spoke. Emotions simmered in the tense air like bubbles under the surface that hadn't quite broken through. Slowly, he drew his hand back, taking the hope that had sparked at his touch with it. "Look," he said and nodded toward the street.

A man was walking up the sidewalk. His face was hidden in shadows, and Kate leaned forward, searching the darkness. He strode confidently through the night, a lunchbox swinging from his hand. He was in coveralls, and she could see there was a nametag stitched to the chest.

"Flip on the lights," she whispered.

Chris started the car and turned on the headlights. They lit up the sidewalk in front of the house they'd been watching in a circle of white light. The man kept walking, each step closing the distance between them.

Her heart pounded in her chest. It was the last name on the list. It had to be him. There was no one else left. She would finally see him. She would finally force him to acknowledge what he'd done. She would find a way to make him pay. There was no statute of limitations on murder. She would dig up every scrap of evidence they had, every clue the prosecutor missed. She would find new charges to bring against him. He would go to jail, and she would be free.

In less than a minute, he would be in their lights, his face clear for her to see. She gripped the door handle. Memories of flashing lights and breaking glass filled her head. The last time she'd seen his face, she was trapped in a car, blood dripping down her face. He had walked away then. She wouldn't let him do it again.

Yanking on the handle, she opened the door and stepped into the night.

"Kate, stop!" Chris called, but she slammed the door behind her.

Energy zipped through her body as she strode down the sidewalk. Not this time. He wouldn't walk away this time. A car door opened and closed behind her. Chris ran to catch up with her. She wasn't going to let him stop her, not when she was so close.

It hurt to breathe. Every breath was like a piece of glass forcing its way past her throat. Her hands trembled, but her legs continued to carry her forward. She was only steps away from him. A few more feet and she would know. A few more feet and she would make him pay. A few more feet and she would keep her promise to Megan. She just needed to see his face. She stopped under the streetlight, surrounded by the tainted, yellow glow, and dug her cell phone out of her pocket, pretending like she was going to make a call.

Chris appeared beside her. "What are you doing?" he whispered, and she shushed him.

The man stepped into the circle of the streetlight. His eyes darted between the two of them. "Are you guys okay?" he asked.

Kate couldn't speak. She couldn't breathe. Her body was frozen, trapped in the moment, paralyzed. Charlie. The nametag read Charlie. She read it twice to be sure. She swayed on her feet, and Chris put his arm around her shoulder to steady her. She leaned against him, certain that if hadn't been there, she would have collapsed.

"We're fine," Chris said, tightening his arm around her, accepting her weight as she struggled to stand. "Just a little lost."

Wariness creased his brow, but the man nodded. Charlie. His name was Charlie. With one more confused look at them, he walked away. He climbed the steps that led to the front door of the house and went inside. The door closed firmly, and the front porch light switched off.

Kate shook her head, trying to clear the confusion and the doubt that had fallen like a curtain over her thoughts. It wasn't possible. It didn't make sense.

Charlie Bishop.

That was the name on the list.

The last name.

Charlie didn't have a public social media profile. His profile picture was a photo of a dog. She had gone to his house to see him. To see his face. To confirm that no name change, no passage of time could change what he had done. But . . .

"It's not him." The night closed in around them as she forced the words past her lips, dragging them into existence.

"What?" Chris kept her against his side, and she was grateful for the contact, for his arm keeping her upright. If she'd been alone, she would have crumbled to the ground. He touched her chin and guided her face to his. Concern filled his eyes. Concern and something more. Something she wanted to believe was still there, something that she hoped she hadn't completely destroyed. "How is that possible?"

Kate shook her head.

Chris turned them back to the car, and she went without resistance. There was no reason to stay. That wasn't the man. She had never seen Charlie before. He had never invaded her nightmares. Those eyes had never seen her suffer or plead for help. That was not the man who walked away and left Megan to die.

How? The word bounced around in her brain. *How?* He was the last name. The last man from the club. She had gone over her dad's list with every tool at her disposal, used every technique she knew of. She had tracked them down, but none of them had been driving the other car.

Her dad's list.

She knew what she saw that night in the club. She was positive. After she had spotted the man, she'd gone to her dad and told him what she'd seen. He'd tried to dismiss it, told her to let it go. When she had insisted, begged him to follow him, to find out who he was, he'd stopped her.

"Leave it alone, Katie. It's done." Then he'd walked away. He was wrong. It would never be done, not until someone had paid for what happened to Megan and to her family. She couldn't leave it alone, and he knew that.

She stumbled to a stop, clarity exploding like a lightning bolt cutting through a storm.

Her dad had known. He'd been telling her to let it go, to move on, because this whole time, he had known.

There was another name on that list.

Chapter Twenty-Six

KATE STORMED UP THE FRONT walk to her dad's house. Faint stars dotted the sky, and the smell of a backyard fire pit hung in the air. Chris followed close behind. He hadn't argued when she asked him to take her straight to her dad's house. They had driven out of LA in silence. Kate's head was spinning with questions, even though she already knew the answers. Her dad had left one name off the list he gave her. The only name she wanted. The only thing she cared about, and he had sabotaged it.

She banged on the door. It rattled under the force of her pounding, and she ignored the sting in her fist. *Why?* She was too angry to cry. She wanted to kick something. She wanted to kick everything. The thin control she kept on her temper was snapping. Years of anguish were breaching the walls and threatening to overflow. Why would he do it? Why would he keep it from her?

Her dad opened the door, surprise written on his face. "Katie? What are you doing here?"

"I need to talk to you." She stormed in. "About this." She waved the list he'd given her.

Her dad was in the khaki pants and dress shirt he had probably worn to work. His shoulder holster was gone, but his badge was still attached to his belt.

"What's going on?" Her mom stepped into the living room, and Kate wanted to scream. She couldn't handle both of them. Not now.

"This doesn't concern you," she snapped.

"Katherine Marie, you will not speak to your mother that way." Her dad's eyes blazed. He wasn't yelling, but it was pretty close. Kate stood toe to toe with him, refusing to back down. She got her temper from him; let him deal with it.

"Joe, it's all right." Her mom's voice was calm and quiet compared to her husband's and daughter's. It had always been that way. Kate and her dad led with their temper while her mom and Megan were much more level-headed. In that moment, it was as if nothing had changed, as if the family dynamic had never been destroyed. Her mom playing peacekeeper between her and her dad. Kate almost expected Megan to poke her head down the stairs to see what was going on. But she couldn't. Megan was gone. Her mom had been gone.

"No, it's not all right," Kate said and shoved the list at her dad's chest. "Where is he?" Her dad took the list and sat on the sofa. "I went through every name on that list. I looked at every one of them. The man who killed Megan isn't there. Why?"

The clock in the hallway ticked, an echoing sound that set her nerves on edge. Chris stood by the door, watching the chaos unfold. It didn't have to be like this. The thought sang in her mind. Her life had been perfect. It had been wonderful. Until that night when everything had been destroyed. Someone had to pay for that.

Her dad rubbed his forehead, his shoulders slumped and burdened. "Joe?" Her mom sat beside him and put her hand on his back. Kate rolled her eyes and bit her tongue.

Her dad looked up at her, and she saw it in his eyes. He didn't have to say a word. He knew.

"Katie, I didn't want you to go through this. I wanted you to be able to move on. To have a life."

Chris stood beside her. She didn't know when he had walked over to her. He was just there, a solid presence beside her, one thing she could count on when nothing else made sense.

"You left his name off the list, so I wouldn't find him." It wasn't a question. Kate leveled the words like an accusation against her father.

He nodded. "After his probation ended, he changed his name and left the area. It didn't take much for me to track him down. I found him and kept an eye on him." He looked at the crumbled paper in his hands. "I don't know why he was at Norma Jean's that night. I didn't even recognize him. It wasn't until the officer gave me the completed list of witnesses that I saw his name and realized who he was."

"Why didn't you tell me?" Betrayal nearly drove her to her knees. "You knew how much this meant to me, and you kept it from me."

He lifted his hands helplessly, holding them up like he could offer an explanation, but there was nothing he could say that would excuse it. "You were so angry. I thought if you just had enough time that you would be able to move on. But when you came back for the wedding and saw Lily hurt, I knew you were still carrying it around." He looked at the list in his hand, at the decision he had made. "I was afraid if you found him, you'd do something you would regret."

Kate paced to the other side of the room, unable to contain the hurt that pulsed through her bones. "Megan was your daughter. Don't you care that the man who killed her is just walking around like nothing happened?"

Her dad sat back, weariness lining his face, as her mom took his hand in hers. "It was an accident, Kate. A terrible, horrible accident, but it was just an accident."

Kate stalked toward him. "You weren't there. I was. I saw it. I saw Megan die." The words impacted her parents like stones thrown across a chasm, and tears flooded her mother's eyes. "Everything that happened since that night is his fault."

Silence descended like a shroud. The wreckage of her life lay in broken pieces all around her. Kate didn't know where to start. She needed to see that man, to look him in the eyes, to tell him what he'd done; and this whole time, her dad had known. Her mom had run away. Her dad had lied to her. It was such a mess, and she couldn't find her way out.

She turned to Chris. She didn't deserve him, and yet there he was, in the middle of the catastrophe of her family. He opened his arms, and she walked into them, the only safe harbor she had left—and even that was only temporary. "It's going to be okay," he whispered.

But it wasn't.

She breathed in the warmth of his presence. Even this was broken. He didn't want her, not after what she'd done. He had made that very clear. He was a witness to her family dysfunction, and he felt sorry for her—that's all this was. She didn't have a future with him. She didn't have a future with any of them.

She stepped away and climbed the stairs. She knew what she had to do.

*****

Kate walked down the hallway. She passed her old bedroom, the room she had grown up in. There had been slumber parties and make-overs in that room. She had cried into her pillow after her first broken heart and sat there in defiance when she was grounded. She paused outside the wooden door and touched the dozens of holes from push-pins she had driven into the door. Her dad had threatened for years to replace it, but he never did. The holes remained, remnants of the dreams she had chased and the wild fantasies she had written on construction paper and stuck to the door. She had never wanted to be a lawyer. She was going to be a princess or a stunt woman. When she was in high school, she was certain she was going to be a doctor—until her first biology class. In college, she was pursuing a psychology degree. And then Megan died. There was nothing left of her in that room—no memory, no piece of her past that hadn't been overshadowed by Megan's death.

Next to her bedroom was Megan's. She opened the door and stepped inside. Even after six years, it still smelled like Megan. Or maybe she imagined the rose perfume scent. Megan had worn it for years. Kate had teased her relentlessly about smelling like their grand-mother's flower garden, but Megan didn't care. She liked it, and no amount of teasing could change her mind. Kate breathed it in and embraced the memories. Her sister's laugh. The way she slammed the door when she was mad at her. The folded notes she slipped under her door when she apologized.

She sat on Megan's bed. It was neatly made, just the way she had made it every day. Kate never made her bed. Her fluffy pillows and stuffed animals were usually in a pile on the floor surrounded by discarded sweatpants and rumpled pajamas. When Megan had been organized and neat, Kate had been carefree and unconcerned by the mess. Her mom pleaded with her to clean up, and she tried, but she usually ended up distracted by something she found hidden under her bed or buried in her laundry and promptly forgot she was supposed to be cleaning.

Megan was different. Megan was mature, kindhearted, and thoughtful of others. She had been everything Kate wasn't. The walls of her room were still covered with photos and mementos. Kate had woken up one morning in high school and decided to paint every wall in her room a different color. Megan thought she was nuts, but she'd helped anyway. When Kate offered to paint her room, she politely declined. Megan's room was one shade of gray; the decorations were color-coordinated, and all hung at right angles. Kate's walls were a mashup of clashing colors and lopsided pictures. It was the way she had lived. Wild and fun and never worried about the consequences.

Until those consequences killed Megan.

That was the day the color had left her life.

She wiped the tears from her cheeks. She owed it to Megan to do better. She went to law school and worked hard, the way Megan would have done. She learned how to organize her office and keep her study area neat. She abandoned her eccentric style and became more subdued. She tried to bring a piece of Megan with her, but it was never enough. She was never enough.

Kate stepped into the hallway and closed the door. She touched the little wooden sign with Megan's name on it, a trinket her parents had bought on a family vacation. Kate had no idea where hers had gone. She crossed the hall and opened the door to her dad's home office. Growing up, they hadn't been allowed in the room. It was off-limits.

Kate had snuck in more times than she could count, but she was always careful to stay away from his gun cabinet on the far wall, locked and secure. The room was filled with her dad's work. Files, photos, case notes—even as a child, Kate had been fascinated by the things he saw. He had tried to shield his daughters from the horrors he dealt with, to protect them, but Kate hadn't wanted his protection. She had been hungry for information, and she knew where to find it. His desk was usually littered with files and occasionally gruesome photos from the cases he was working on or cases he hadn't been able to solve. Kate had often dared her sister to come with her, but Megan never wanted to see it.

Kate went to the desk and opened the filing cabinet drawer. She flipped through the hanging manila folders, scanning the labels as she worked her way through the years of files he'd kept. It was a history of her dad's work, a timeline of his service on the police force. Her dad had always been a notorious notetaker and never threw anything away. She skipped over folders until she found what she was looking for.

She pulled out the folder marked Hannah Smith and laid it open in the desk. She read through the details of Hannah's report, the attempts to find Lincoln, and finally, the rescue from Norma Jean's. Kate ran her fingers down the list of names the officers at the scene had compiled. There was one name that hadn't been on the list her dad had given her.

Frankie Madigan.

She looked at the name, and revulsion swam in her stomach. She flipped through the file folders again, searching for a file that matched the name. When she opened it, her breath caught in her throat. A black and white mug shot stared back at her. It was the face that had haunted her dreams. The face that followed her across the country. The face of the man who had ruined her life. She ran her fingers across the image.

Frankie Madigan.

He could change his name, move away, start over, but she wouldn't let him escape what he'd done. She wouldn't let him forget the life he'd ended.

She yanked a sticky note free from the pad on the desk and scribbled down the last known address listed in the file.

It was finally time.

No one could stop her now.

Chapter Twenty-Seven

KATE'S MOM BROUGHT HIM A cup of coffee. He thanked her and held the warm mug between his hands. It was a small gesture of normalcy in a situation that made no sense. He was unmoored, tossed on the waves of the shifting sea. Kate. Her sister. Her search for justice. It was all a fog of questions and doubt, and he didn't know which way the shore lay. So, he held the coffee mug and waited for the storm to pass.

The three of them sat in the living room, absorbing the silence of Kate's escape up the stairs. Her parents sat in matching blue chairs next to each other while Chris sat on the end of the sofa. He was keenly aware of the empty space beside him. For months, Kate had been a fixture in his life. In his townhouse, watching movies on the sofa next to him, sitting in the small office at the church with her head buried in contracts and legal documents, or standing beside him as he filmed. She'd become a part of his daily life, and now that spot was empty. He had pushed her away, and the lingering emptiness was his reward.

He sipped the hot coffee, but he didn't really taste it. It was there, something to do with his hands, something to fill the void. Kate's parents looked tired and uncertain. He searched for something to say, some encouraging word he could offer, but he didn't have anything. All the light had left his life, stormed up the stairs, and disappeared. He had no idea what was coming next.

Detective Sullivan cleared his throat. "Kate just needs some time to cool off. She'll come around." They all nodded as if that was something that could be brushed aside, an argument that would be quickly forgotten, even though they all knew it wasn't. He patted his wife's hand. "This is my fault."

Kate's mom smiled at him sadly. "No, this was my doing. I should have stayed. I should have been here to help her. You did the best you could, Joe." She chuckled a little. "Kate has always been a wee bit stubborn anyway."

Joe laughed. "A wee bit? That girl could win a staring contest with a statue." He turned to Chris. "Once when she was about ten, she insisted that there was a mouse in our garage. I searched for it, but I couldn't find anything, so I told her she was wrong." He whistled and shook his head. "Well, that girl proceeded to stake out the garage. She set up a camera; then she made a nest in the car and waited. For four nights, she slept in that minivan, waiting for the chance to prove me wrong. And wouldn't you know it? She got photographic evidence of a mouse in our garage. She walked into my office and slapped the photos down on the desk like she'd found Hoffa's body."

Her mom shifted in the chair so she could look at Chris. "There was also a time when Megan was being bullied at school. Katie was maybe eight or nine years old. When she found out about it, she told Megan's teacher, but the teacher didn't do anything. So, Katie went to the principal. She marched right into his office and laid out her case. It was probably her first legal argument. She wouldn't stand by and let someone hurt her sister."

Chris leaned forward and rested his elbows on his knees. "What happened that night? How did Megan die?"

The Sullivans looked at each other, and an unspoken communication flew between them. Detective Sullivan sighed and glanced at the empty staircase. "Katie and Megan were going to a party. It was one of the last nights of summer, right before Kate was going to go back to college. A bunch of kids planned a party at Zuma Beach, and the girls decided to go. They were headed down Malibu Canyon Road. That road is so twisting with steep mountains on both sides, and it's hard to see what's coming around the turns. We're still not sure how it happened, but another car coming up the hill crossed the center line. He clipped Kate's car and sent them into a spin." His voice cracked, and he stopped to take a deep breath. His wife reached for his hand and gripped it tightly. "Katie's car hit the side of the mountain on the passenger side. Kate ended up with a severe concussion, a ruptured spleen, and broken ribs. Megan . . . Megan didn't make it."

Sorrow gripped Chris. Kate and her defenses, her walls, her tough exterior. It was all hiding a trauma he couldn't imagine, a loss that had haunted her for years. She had never spoken of it. She kept it all bottled up inside and didn't ask for help. Until him. She had relied on him, opened up to him, and he had promised to help her only on the condition that she would go away, leave his life forever. He'd been so wrapped up in his hurt and betrayal, he'd given her an impossible choice. "And the other driver?"

Detective Sullivan shook his head. "They couldn't identify a cause, and by the time he walked into the police station, it was too late to check him for intoxication. He was charged with leaving the scene of an accident. He got a few years of probation, community service, and a suspended license. The investigators ruled it an accident, but Katie . . . " He glanced at the stairs again as if he expected her to appear at any moment. "Katie never believed that. She was convinced it had to be alcohol-related. She couldn't believe it was an accident. She had to find a reason for it. She was so angry. She's still angry. I don't know how to help her. I thought by keeping this from her, it would force her to move on. I had no idea she was still holding on to it all these years later. She's always been so . . . "

When he paused, searching for the right word, Chris supplied it. "Strong."

Detective Sullivan nodded. "Exactly. She always seems so strong, as if nothing can get to her, but really, she's been suffering for a long time. I should have seen it."

Kate's mom sniffed, and tears pooled in her eyes. "I should have told the girls no that night. I blamed myself for it. If I'd made them stay home, none of it would have happened." She wiped her nose with the cuff of her sweater. "I couldn't handle the guilt. I started drinking. At first, it was just to get through the night. I needed it to sleep, to stop imaging those last few minutes of Megan's life, to stop imaging how I could have done things differently. Then it was during the day. Then it was all day. It was the only thing that made the pain go away. Except it always came back worse. Joe . . . " She smiled at her husband. "Joe saw it. He gave me a choice—rehab or leave. I left. And I regret it every day." Detective Sullivan squeezed her hand. Years had gone by, years of anger and hurt, and yet they were together again. "It took me a long time to get better. A long time and a lot of God." She looked at Detective Sullivan. "I didn't deserve your forgiveness."

Detective Sullivan stood and walked to the side of her chair. He knelt and wrapped his arm around her shoulders. "I'm just happy to have my wife back."

Chris sat back and tried to imagine what Kate had been through. Losing her sister and her mother, trapped in years of anger. It was no wonder she had been obsessed with finding the other driver. Guilt twisted in his gut. He'd turned his back on her. He had been so focused on himself, he hadn't even considered what had driven her to lie to him. He rubbed his forehead; he had done so many things wrong recently, he wasn't even sure there was a way back.

Footsteps echoed on the wood stairs, and all of three of them turned to watch Kate descend. She stopped at the bottom landing and looked at them. Her eyes darted to her parents and then to him. Without a word, she opened the front door and stepped outside. Chris followed her.

They stood on the porch, wrapped in shadows and moonlight. Kate stared into the distance as he stood beside her. He wanted to reach for her, to touch her and hold her, but he didn't know how. It would be easier to let her go, but he didn't know how to do that either.

"Kate," he began, his hands hanging helplessly by his side. "I'm so sorry about Megan. About what you've been through. I wish . . . I wish I knew what to say, what to do to help you."

"No one can help me," she said slowly, and his heart broke for her. For the years she had lost, the pain she had carried, the façade she had put up for so long.

"I can try," he said. "If you let me."

"You've always been kind to me, and you didn't have to be. I treated you badly, and I'm sorry." She looked at him. Streaks of dried tears tracked down her face. "I know it's too late for us. I ruined whatever might have been, and I will regret that for as long as I live. You've done everything you promised—and I'm sorry to ask—but there is one thing I need."

The sadness in her words and the finality in her voice troubled him. Nerves and worry coursed through him. He didn't want to lose her. He didn't want this to end. Not like this. "Name it," he said.

"Can I borrow your car?"

Chris took her hand, trying to hold on when she was already saying goodbye. "I can drive. Where do you want to go?"

She pulled her hand away and shook her head. "I just need a few minutes, to clear my head. I . . . " She glanced at the house. "I can't stay here right now. Please." The whisper stabbed his heart. He was one of the reasons for those tears. He had turned his back on her when she reached out to him.

He nodded and pulled the keys from his pocket. As he handed them to her, he tried to smile. "Don't forget about me."

She met his gaze with an intensity he didn't expect. Her hand lingered in his as she closed her fingers around the keys. "I will never forget you."

She stepped off the front porch and walked into the night. He watched from the porch as the car pulled away and disappeared into the darkness, red lights fading into the darkness as she drove away from him, and he couldn't shake the feeling that he might never see her again.

He went back in the house, praying as he closed the door, but the words were a tangled mess in his mind. He didn't know what to pray for. He didn't know what to do. He needed God to make sense of the chaos in his heart. Maybe it was too late for him and Kate, maybe there had been too many lies, too many hurts. Maybe there wasn't a way back.

He walked to the living room. Detective Sullivan was still by his wife's side, their heads bent close together. They looked up when he came into the room. "Where's Katie?" her mom asked.

"She said she needed a few minutes to herself. She took my car. I think she went for a drive to think things through. She's got a lot to deal with right now." He sat on the sofa again. He would wait for her to come back. Kate wouldn't disappear. She would come back, and they would talk. He had however long she was gone to figure out what he wanted to say. There had been enough lies between them. When she came back, they would lay all their cards on the table and start again. There had to be a way forward. He couldn't ignore what he felt. When she had said goodbye and walked away, he had known then he wanted her to stay, but he didn't know how to say it.

Detective Sullivan's brow furrowed. "Did she say where she was going?"

Chris shook his head. "No."

Kate's dad stood, his jaw tense. He paced to the window and looked into the blackness, then glanced over his shoulder toward the stairs. With a gasp, he turned and raced to the staircase.

"Joe?" Kate's mom called. "What's wrong?"

Worry ripped through him as he leapt from the sofa and followed the detective up the stairs. A light shone from one of the rooms down the hallway, and Chris went to it. Detective Sullivan was in his office, his hands braced on an old, cherry wood desk, his back hunched as he stared at the open files spread before him.

Chris stood behind him, trying to make sense of the paperwork.

"She found his name in my files," Detective Sullivan said as he turned away and crossed to a tall safe on the far side of the room. The combination dial spun in the quiet as Chris looked at a photo of Frankie Madigan. The man she had been looking for. The man she blamed for her sister's death.

"No." Behind him, Detective Sullivan exhaled like the wind had been knocked out of him. He turned to Chris, his face pale. "She took my gun."

Chapter Twenty-Eight

KATE PARKED IN THE SHADOWS in front of the small house. An iron fence ran around the perimeter of the yard. The grass was dry and patchy in places, a casualty of drought and the dry air. Bright flowers bloomed in the window boxes that lined the bay window. A white metal screen covered the front door, and a red tricycle and a soccer ball waited on the porch. The carport beside the house was vacant, an empty space of concrete. Kate double checked the address.

Light shone from the bay window, and the curtains were pulled back. Sitting in the car, she watched the people inside walk past the window. She waited. A woman walked back and forth several times. She appeared once again, this time with a baby seated on her hip. She stopped to talk to somebody and then walked away. Kate watched as a man rose. Blue light flickered, and Kate guessed he had turned off a television set.

She held her breath as he walked to the window. He stood in the light, looking out into the yard before he pulled the curtains closed. Every second of the past six years rushed to her brain, millions of fleeting moments, memories, and nightmares coalescing in that one moment.

It was him.

He may have changed his name, moved, and forgotten that night six years ago, but Kate knew the truth. That was the man who killed her sister.

She sagged against the seat and closed her eyes. It wasn't anger that engulfed her or even fear. It was cold resolve. After all this time, she was finally here, only steps away from the man who had killed her sister—the man who had destroyed her family and ruined her life. It would all end here.

Her hand curled around the handle of her dad's gun as it lay on the passenger seat beside her. She hadn't planned on bringing it. She hadn't planned on unlocking the safe and taking it. It had been a wild thought, a feeling that came out of nowhere, a siren call that she hadn't even tried to fight. The justice system had failed Megan. She wouldn't.

She stepped into the night, the weight of the gun heavy and cold in her hand. Her dad had taught her and Megan the four safety rules of firearms when they were in elementary school. She knew how to fire this weapon. She knew what it would do. *Don't aim your weapon at anything you don't intend to shoot.* The words echoed in her mind. Intention. Premeditation. Six years ago, her life had been irrevocably altered. Tonight, it would happen again. But this time, she was prepared.

She leaned against the side of the car, the metal numbing her back as she stared at the gun. Doubt crept though her mind, but she pushed it away. Her career was over. Her family was broken. Chris was gone. The only thing she had left was her freedom, but what good was freedom if she was trapped in this life of despair and hopelessness? She would give it up if it meant the emptiness would end. If she finished this one thing, if she made this man pay, then she could be free, even if that meant spending the rest of her life in prison. It was the only way to move on.

Headlights flashed on the street, and she turned toward the oncoming car, hiding the gun behind her back. As the car pulled to a stop, its headlights blinding her, Kate raised her hand to shield her eyes. When the lights dimmed, Kate blinked away the spots of light that danced in her vision as the driver's door opened and closed. She stuffed the gun into the waistband of her jeans at her lower back and pulled her sweater low to cover the bulge as the shadowy figure walked toward her.

"Katie, what are you doing?"

Her mother's voice drifted across the distance, and a pang of longing filled her. Her mother had found her. Relief like a child lost in a store and suddenly finding her mom swept through her, but she refused to feel it. Her mother shouldn't be here. She didn't want her here. The longing she felt was for the woman who had abandoned her. It wasn't for the woman who stood before her now. This was a stranger. A stranger who was getting in the way of her plan.

"Go away," she snapped, turning away and focusing on the house in front of her. "You shouldn't be here."

"Katie, don't do this." Her mom stepped closer to her, her face barely illuminated by the nearby streetlight. "It won't help."

Kate whirled on her, sparks of anger flashing to life like wildfire on dry grass. "What would you know about it? You have no idea what I need. You left, remember?"

Her mom didn't flinch. She faced her with a calm she'd never seen before, as if the most hateful words she could throw at her wouldn't make a difference. Peace filled her face as she withstood Kate's vitriol. "Sweetie, I spent years trying to drink away the pain of losing your sister. It didn't work. This plan of yours . . . " She reached her hand to the small of Kate's back, brushing her fingers against the concealed weapon. "It won't work either."

Kate stepped away, out of her grasp. "He has to pay for what he did."

"Katie, it was an accident."

She turned to the car and slammed her hands on the roof. An accident. It couldn't be an accident. It couldn't be bad luck or bad timing. Megan's life meant more than that. It had to be something more than a random accident. There had to be a reason. "He walked away," she yelled. "Don't you get that? He walked away and left us to die."

Her mom grabbed her arm. "He called the police. He was the one who called 911. He was the one who told the ambulance where to find you."

Kate shook her head. No. That wasn't right. Disjointed images from that night swirled together in her mind. The broken glass, the throbbing in her head, Megan's voice whispering prayers. The face that peered into the window. She saw him. She had looked into his eyes, and then he was gone. Was it possible? Had he called the police before he fled?

She paced down the sidewalk. She remembered very little about being in the hospital. The noise and confusion, the bright lights and the tubes. The ceiling rolling past as they wheeled her into the operating room. Her parents sitting beside her bed as she asked for Megan over and over until they sedated her. The weeks after the accident were a blur of pain and mixed-up memories. She remembered her dad talking to the responding officers, the prosecutor calling, but she couldn't remember the details.

When it was over, and she was home, her parents had turned into shells, empty husks walking around in a daze of grief. Her mom drinking. She remembered that. Her dad staying at work later and later. She overheard snippets of conversations. The investigators unable to find fault and ruling it an accident. Whispers of probation and community service. She hadn't asked any questions. She hadn't wanted to think about it. She didn't want to know. It was easier to stay in her room until she went back to college and tried to pretend it was all a nightmare she would someday wake up from. It was only when she got away, when she was in Boston, alone in her quiet apartment that the nightmares started. That's when she knew she had to do something, but by that time, everyone else had moved on. There were no more answers to be found.

Her mom stepped in her path, stopping her frustrated pacing. "Only God can heal the pain you're feeling. His grace and His forgiveness—"

Kate snorted. "Forgiveness? You think God has forgiven you for abandoning your family? You're wrong. There's no forgiveness for that. There's no forgiveness for what that man did. If he hadn't hit my car, Megan would still be here." Tears ran down her face as she let her emotions take control. "If we had stayed home, Megan would still be here. If I hadn't pushed her, if I had just let her read her stupid book, she would be alive. There is no forgiveness for that. I killed her."

The words leapt from her mouth like a lion breaking free from captivity.

She killed Megan. Her choices, her decisions, her car.

Her fault.

She stepped back, as if she could run away from the words she'd said, as if she could flee from the guilt that she'd carried for so many years. Her mom reached for her, but she walked away, desperate to escape the wave of guilt that was threatening to drown her. It was her fault. It was all her fault.

Megan's face swam in her memory. Megan had wanted to stay home. Megan never wanted to go to the beach. Kate had convinced her to go. She had begged and pleaded and coerced until she had said yes. All because she didn't want to go alone. Megan never should have been in the car. She should have been safe at home, curled up with the book she never got a chance to finish. Her sister was dead because of her.

All of the nightmares, all of the anger, it was because of her foolish decision. She touched the gun at her back. The person who needed to pay for Megan's death—the person responsible for it—was her. It had always been her.

A sob burst from her, a cry of anguish, and she fell to the ground. She sat on the sidewalk and cried.

"Oh, Katie." Her mom sat beside her and gathered her in her arms. Kate cried against her chest, weeping like she hadn't done in years. "It wasn't your fault."

Prayers danced over her head as her mom prayed for her. She rocked her back and forth the way she had done when she was a child and woke up in the middle of the night from a bad dream. But this was no nightmare. She had driven Megan to her death. No one could forgive her for that.

She squeezed her eyes shut and tried to disappear, but Megan's face filled her head.

Megan sitting on her bed with a book while she stood in the doorway and begged her to come to the beach with her. Megan rolling her eyes as she wheedled and whined and used every big sister trick in the book. Megan as they drove down Malibu Canyon Road, the radio blaring, as Kate sped down the twisting road.

The sun had set, and the sky was purple-black. The road was dark, the high mountain cliffs rising on either side. Kate had been focused on the fact that Kyle Miller would be waiting for her at the beach. She imagined sitting with him by the fire, maybe walking by the water with him. She hoped he would hold her hand. It was silly to think about flirting with him, considering she would be going back to school at the end of the summer, but she couldn't help it. She liked the thrill of it, the nervous tingling in her stomach.

As they drove down the canyon road, Megan said something, and Kate turned to look at her. Megan's smile turned to terror as the headlights blinded them. Metal crashed against metal. The airbag exploded from the steering wheel and hit her in the face. For a moment, she was buried in plastic, and then she flew back against the seat. The car spun wildly, and the side of her head hit the window. A deafening sound smashed against her ears as the car slammed into the side of the cliff. Her ears were ringing, and spots danced in her eyes. She rolled her head to the side. The passenger side of the car had folded in, wrapping Megan in a twisted metal embrace.

She looked at Kate, fear and pain filling her eyes. Kate had never felt so helpless before. She reached for Megan's hand and gripped it tightly. "Megan?" she whispered.

Her sister's mouth moved, but she couldn't hear the words she was saying over the high-pitched ringing in her head. She tried to lean forward, to find her purse and get to her cell phone, but she couldn't move. She was pinned beneath the seat belt.

"It will be okay, Megan," she said, but she couldn't hear her own voice. She wasn't even sure the words were coming out.

She tried to lean forward again when a face appeared in the window. He peered through the cracked glass. Blood ran down the side of his face from a cut over his right eye.

"Help," she said and raised her hand to the window, shocked by the blood on her arm. When had she cut herself? Why couldn't she feel it? "Please, help us." Was she speaking the words out loud? Did he hear them?

Deep brown eyes stared at her, then vanished. "Wait," she cried. "Come back."

Fear settled over her, cold and full of knives. Her heart raced as a wave of panic engulfed her. She pulled at the seat belt, but the latch was twisted, and she couldn't get free. She wasn't sure she believed in God, but she cried out to Him, anyway. "God! Help, please!"

Spikes of pain broke through the confusion. Her chest, her arm, her legs all screamed in agony. Tears ran down her face.

Megan's voice drifted through her panicked thoughts. She turned to her sister. "It's all right," she said, but she knew she was lying.

Megan's whispered words were so soft, so quiet, she strained to hear them. Her breath rasped as she spoke, but Kate couldn't hear her.

Then she was quiet. Her breathing stopped, and she was still.

Megan was gone.

Kate sat on the sidewalk in her mother's arms as memories of the crash assailed her. It was her fault. It had all been her fault. Megan dying, her mother leaving—she was the one to blame. If she'd stayed home that night. If she'd watched a movie or gone to the mall instead. If she had left five minutes earlier or five minutes later. She could have done a million things differently, and Megan would still be alive.

She'd spent years blaming the man who lived in the house right in front of her when she should have been blaming herself. She was the one who needed to pay. She was the one who couldn't be forgiven.

Her mom prayed. Her words fell like a cloud all around her. In the dim street, she was asking God for healing, forgiveness, and love.

As Kate listened to her mother's prayers, Megan's final words rose like a flickering spark from a pile of ashes. Words she'd forgotten. Words she'd buried under layers of anger, bitterness, and guilt. She had chased those words like she chased the man who had driven the other car; but in every memory of that night, every nightmare, the words were gone, lost in the ringing in her ears. It was the last thing she had of Megan, the last part of her sister, and she couldn't remember them. Until now. They came winging across the chasm of grief, an echo from her sister, a whisper that had been silent for too long, drowned out by her pain.

"Father, protect Kate," Megan had prayed as her life slipped away. "Watch over her and keep her safe. Help her to know how much You love her."

Megan's last words had been a prayer for her.

She pulled back and looked at her mom. Tears streaked her cheeks. "Mom," she whispered. "What am I supposed to do?"

Her mom ran her hand down her hair. "Give it to God, Katie. You have carried it for too long. Let Him take it from you. You don't have to carry this on your own anymore. He is right here, and He loves you."

Megan's words pounded in her heart, a drum beat that wouldn't stop, a knocking that wouldn't be silenced. It couldn't be that easy. She didn't deserve forgiveness. She didn't deserve love.

Still, the call hammered in her soul until it was irresistible. Fear clung to her. What if she turned to God and He rejected her? What if she opened her heart to Him and He turned away? Maybe she was better off the way she was. She knew she was guilty and broken, and she didn't deserve anything more.

She looked down at the sidewalk, at the cracked and broken places filled with dirt. "What if He doesn't want me?"

Her mom put her thumb under Kate's chin and tilted her chin up. "Katie, you're all He's ever wanted. Trust Him. He won't fail you."

Kate took a deep breath. She lifted her eyes to the sky, to the dark expanse above her. Her heart cried out to God. She breathed His name, and in that Name, a dam burst forth. She poured out her confession. She laid her heart bare before God and asked Him to forgive her. She lifted her hands and believed. In the midst of her pain, she chose to believe. In her doubt and brokenness, she brought all of it to God and let Him heal her.

Chapter Twenty-Nine

CHRIS PACED THE KITCHEN. WHEN they discovered the files and the missing gun, he had wanted to go after Kate, but her mom beat him to it. There hadn't been time to debate it. She had grabbed her keys and raced out the door, and he and Detective Sullivan had been left behind without a car to wait and pray.

And pace.

Back and forth he went, cutting across the tile floor with anxious steps. Kate with a gun was a nightmare he hadn't known existed. He worried that letting her mom go after her hadn't been the right choice. He should have been the one to go. He should have followed her and brought her home. He wasn't sure she would have listened to him—he wasn't sure she would listen to anyone—but he could have dragged her away if necessary to spare her from using the gun and destroying her life. She might have hated him for it, but he would have accepted that if it meant protecting her.

Images of Kate doing something stupid plagued him, scenes that played through his mind like a horror movie he couldn't escape. Kate firing the gun. Kate murdering a man. Kate going to prison. If it was a movie he was directing, he could have changed the ending, but trapped in this kitchen, he was helpless to do anything but wait.

He touched the piece of paper in his pocket. He'd written down the address at the same time as Detective Sullivan. He could still go.

He could call Ben and ask him to bring a car. He glanced at Detective Sullivan sitting at the table staring into his coffee mug. They could go together. Kate's dad could stop her before she did something they'd all regret.

He stepped toward the table, prepared to present his case.

"No," Detective Sullivan said, without looking up.

Chris stopped, the unflinching firmness in Detective Sullivan's voice as solid as the ground he was standing on. "No what?"

"No, we're not going after them."

"But—"

"Sit down, Chris."

Chris sank into the chair opposite the detective. He didn't want to sit. He didn't want to wait. He didn't want to watch the minutes tick away while he drank coffee and imagined a thousand terrible situations. He wanted to go after her. He wanted to do something.

"Kate needs more than we can give her," Detective Sullivan said. "She's been carrying this around for too long. Give her mom a chance. God was able to reach her when it seemed impossible. He can reach Katie, too."

Chris tried to relax. He tried to be patient, but anxiety rippled through him. He stood abruptly and went to the front door. Detective Sullivan didn't try to stop him.

The cool night air washed across his face as he leaned against the railing on the front porch. He stared into the distance and prayed. He couldn't save Kate, but he wanted to apologize, to tell her the truth before it was too late. Standing at the precipice of losing her, he prayed for one more chance, one more opportunity to tell her how he felt, to set aside the hurt and the mistakes and try again. The fact that he might never get that chance ate away at his soul. Missed opportunities, pride, and regret picked it apart piece by piece.

He couldn't wait anymore. He didn't care what Detective Sullivan said. He was going after her. He shouldn't have waited this long. He turned to go back into the house—he would borrow or steal a car if he had to—when headlights broke through the night, and he pushed away from the railing. He held his breath as he waited. The car crept up the street. His heart pounded as the car turned into the driveway. The lights dimmed as Kate's mom stepped out of the car and stood in the driveway. Disappointment racked him. It was too late.

Detective Sullivan stepped onto the porch. His eyes met his wife's eyes, and as she smiled, a second car appeared on the road.

Relief swept through Chris as hope leapt to life. He was running across the lawn before the car pulled to a stop. As Kate stepped out of the driver's side, he was there to meet her. He swept her into his arms, holding her close, inhaling her sweetness, as he lifted her off the ground, spinning her in a circle. He whispered her name against her hair as midnight enveloped them, cloaking them in its caress. Kate was here. She was in his arms at last.

Behind them, the front door opened. He glanced over his shoulder to see Detective Sullivan and his wife standing in the open doorway. Kate's mom smiled at him and shooed her husband back inside the house.

He lowered Kate to the ground but kept her close, his arms looped around her lower back. He wasn't going to give her a chance to run again. "What happened?" he asked.

She smiled and shook her head, like she couldn't quite believe what she was about to say. "God. God happened."

Joy flooded through him. He pulled her against his chest, his heart full of thanksgiving to the God Who had never given up on her. His head on hers, they stood as one, sharing the same breath, their hearts beating together, the separate roads they had been on finally joined.

Kate stepped back but kept his hands in hers. "I was wrong about so many things. I'm so sorry for lying to you, for using you. Can you ever forgive me?"

He lifted his hand to her face, cupping her cheek. She was so soft, so delicate. "Of course."

Kate turned her head, resting it against his hand. "I'm still not sure what happened back there. I went to his house prepared to execute my own justice. I was tired of waiting for God and the legal system to do what I wanted. I was ready to go to prison if it would stop the guilt and the anger I felt." She pursed her lips as she sighed. "When my mom found me, I didn't want to hear what she had to say. I didn't want to hear about God or love or forgiveness. I wanted him to pay. But then, something happened." She smiled as tears glistened in her eyes. "I remembered Megan's last words. She had been praying for me." A tear escaped, and she wiped her cheek. "Her last words were a prayer for me, and it took me six years to realize that God answered her. Everything she asked for that night, God did."

She took both of his hands in hers. "I don't deserve His mercy. I don't deserve His forgiveness, but I'm ready to accept them. And . . ." She looked up at him, and his heart swelled. The change in her eyes was incredible. Light shone through her, a light that could only have come from God. "If you'll have me," she said, "I will spend every day of my life showing you how much I love you."

Chris threaded his hands through her hair and cradled her head. "Kate Sullivan, I love you. Wherever we go, whatever we do, you are my happy ending." He looked at her, marveling at the woman God had led him to. Stubborn, independent, willful, vibrant, exciting, and wondrous Kate. From that night on, his heart would only belong to her.

She stepped toward him, melting against his chest, and he lifted her chin. She looked up at him, and he sucked in a breath.

Forever burned in her eyes.

Chapter Thirty

KATE STOOD ON THE SIDEWALK, staring up at the house. The tricycle was still on the porch. The metal screen door, the flowers in the window boxes. It was all the same, and yet none of it was the same. Chris held her hand as he stood beside her. Not long ago, she'd been on this same spot with evil in her heart and a gun in her hand. The thirst for revenge had driven her to the brink. It would have been so easy for her to go through with it, to take a life, to end hers, to give in to the despair and the guilt that had dogged her every step for six years. Whispers of accusation and condemnation had followed her across the country and filled her nightmares. It was the love of God that pulled her back.

It hadn't been an easy few weeks. She was trying to get to know her mother again, and it was harder than she thought it would be. When she accepted Jesus as her Savior, she thought that meant everything would be perfect. She expected to feel nothing but love and happiness, but the road had been rocky. She and her mom were working through it, but she found herself learning to forgive every day. Unexpectedly, resentment and recrimination would surge and threaten to destroy their growing relationship. She was choosing to forgive and to see the best in her mother. It was a hard habit to learn, but Chris was helping.

The day after she met Jesus, Chris gave her a Bible. She read it every day, diving in the same way she'd tackled complex law classes. She wanted to learn it all, to know it all. Chris reminded her that she would never know everything on this side of Heaven, but even if she couldn't learn everything, she would learn as much as she could as quickly as she could. She had wasted enough time on the past; she wanted to know what the future held, what eternity would be like. For the first time in her life, she knew what was coming. It might be a long way off, but one day, she would see the man who saved her—not from a car accident or from her own self-destruction, but the Man Who saved her soul, the Man Who loved her when she didn't deserve it and Who never gave up on her. She would see Jesus face to face.

Over and over, she reminded herself of the character of God. When her mom made her mad or when she struggled with old feelings of anger, she would look for a reminder of Who God was. In the sunset over the sea, in the laughter at Ben and Lily's house, in the love her parents shared, in the gentle way Chris held her hand—she saw little reminders of God in all of them. He was her Savior, her Father, her Protector, her Comforter, and so much more. When she focused on that, the emotions that threatened her peace would dissipate. Nothing could stand against the love of God.

She and Chris were nearly done with the documentary. It was going to premiere at the New Mexico Film Festival in two months. He hadn't looked for any other distribution deals. Together, they prayed for the right partner to come along. They trusted in God and His plans. The God Who had created the world and sustained it by His power knew every hair on her head. He definitely could handle a distribution deal for a documentary. The part of her that still longed for control and organization—the part that wanted to know what was coming around every corner—was making peace with her new faith. Trust was something she had forgotten, and slowly, day by day, God was teaching her how to do it again.

In that moment, trust was all she had. She stood outside Frankie Madigan's house with no plan, no agenda, and no idea what was about to happen. When she told Chris what she wanted to do, he hadn't hesitated. He'd grabbed the keys and driven her over. Standing on the sidewalk in the fading light of a spring sun, she wasn't sure she had made the right decision. She didn't know what she wanted to say to him. After six years, she had to see this through, but this time, she would do it with God guiding her. It wasn't about justice or revenge. It was about closing a wound that had been bleeding for too long.

"Ready?" Chris asked and squeezed her hand. The early evening breeze teased his hair, and she brushed it over his ear. He loved her. This man who had stood by her, shared his work with her, taught her what it meant to love freely and with abandon loved her. She could face anything with God as her guide and Chris by her side. Even this. She could face Frankie Madigan because she wasn't alone.

She nodded, and they walked up the cracked, concrete steps that led to the door. With a trembling hand, she pressed the doorbell. As it chimed in the house, she swallowed hard. Nervousness made her legs shake. Chris leaned over, his lips brushing her head with a lightness that took her breath away.

The door opened, and her throat constricted. Frankie Madigan stood in front of her. His hair was dark and wavy and shorter than she remembered. He was wearing faded jeans and a blue t-shirt. He could have been any man she passed on the street, a normal person who made a huge mistake, just like Kate had done. His brown eyes were guarded as he blocked the doorway. "Can I help you?"

"Um . . . " She drew in a ragged breath. Chris tightened his grip on her hand. She thought of Megan and the prayer that she had whispered. It had brought her here. Face to face once again with this man. A plea for help ran through her head and winged its way to God. She closed her eyes and exhaled. Whatever happened, God would be there on the other side of it. She was not alone. "I'm Kate Sullivan," she said. "And I—"

"I know who you are." He glanced over his shoulder into the house. From somewhere inside, Kate heard a baby laughing. He stepped onto the porch and closed the door behind him. The metal rattled as the screen door bounced back into place. "What do you want?"

Kate opened her mouth, then closed it again. What *did* she want? It was a question that had eluded her for years. What did she want? For years, she'd wanted to go back in time and change things. She had wanted to make this man suffer to erase the pain of her own guilt. Flashes of the past six years ran through her head. The nights she'd cried herself to sleep, the times she screamed at the sky, demanding answers from a God she said she didn't believe in but Whom she cursed nonetheless, and sitting in a car only steps from this door with a gun in her hand.

She didn't want any of that now.

Frankie was watching her, suspicion and wariness in his eyes, as she stalled. What did she want? She wanted Chris. She wanted a life filled with love and work that made a difference. She wanted her big, patched-together family. Chris, her parents, the Shaws, and Hannah. She wanted to walk where God led and hear His voice. She wanted to stand before Him someday and hear Him say, "Well done." To get all of that, she would lay down the baggage she carried. She would give it God and trust Him for something better. The more she gave up, the more she gained. She wanted to let go, to finally be free. She took a deep breath and surrendered this last piece to God. She would lay down her plans and her agenda and let God lead the way.

She struggled with the words. She had imagined this moment in thousands of different ways over the past six years. She had planned what she wanted to say to him, the accusations she would lay at his feet, the blame, the demands for retribution. She wanted to lash out. It was her chance. She had earned this victory. She had earned the right to berate him, to make him feel small and guilty and horrible for what he'd done. It was her right. She wanted to cling to her anger and her idea of justice. A familiar refrain coursed through her mind: if she didn't hold on to the pain, no one would care.

She inhaled a shaky breath. God cared. He held every tear she had ever cried, and He wanted her to surrender it to Him. To let Him take charge of the wrongs that had been done to her. She wasn't perfect, and she never would be, but she could do this. She could take this one step.

"I wanted to say thank you," she said. Frankie narrowed his eyes, his glance darting between her and Chris. "I just found out that the night of the . . . " She paused. Chris moved his hand to her back, a gentle reminder that he was with her. "The night of the accident, you called 911. You were the reason the ambulance found us. Thank you for doing that."

She had been hoping for some massive weight to be lifted off her, some immediate blessing to fall on her, but instead, it was peace that filled her heart. No matter what Frankie said, she had done her part. She gave up her claims on him and left him to God.

Frankie shook his head and leaned against the screen door, as if her words had knocked him off his feet. "I didn't mean to leave." He licked his lips as he stared at his bare feet. "I had to drive back up the hill to get reception. After I called the ambulance, I should have driven back to you. I should have stayed with you. But I . . . " He stopped and pounded his hand against his leg. "I was so scared. I left. I went home."

He wiped his nose, dragging his hand across his face. "I still don't know how it happened. I was driving up the hill, and then all of the sudden, your car was there. I never saw you coming. When the cops found me and told me your sister died . . . something inside me broke. I took the plea bargain, changed my name, moved away. I couldn't face what I'd done. I thought if I ran far enough, I could just forget it, but . . . " He paused, tears spilling down his cheeks. "I still see you every night. I see your face every night."

Two lives tied together by one nightmare. Every night that he had haunted her, Kate had haunted him. She recognized the guilt, the anguish on his face. It was the look she had seen every morning in the mirror. Her heart had been full of holes, her soul fractured and fragmented. He was living that same torment.

"It was an accident," she said. The same words her father had said to her. The same words she had refused to hear for so many years.

Frankie bit his lip and shook his head as if her words didn't make any sense. He looked at her, raw pain and hurt flashing in his eyes. "How can you come here and say thank you after what I did? How can you do that?"

How could she do it? How many times had she asked that same question? How could Hannah be filled with joy after all she had been through? How could Jonathan still believe after all the evil he had seen? How did Lily hold on to her faith when she couldn't walk? How did they keep going when everything around them fell apart? After years of searching, years of doubts and questions, Kate finally had the answer. It had never been far away. It had been right with her the whole time, waiting for her to open her eyes and see. God.

Kate smiled as the chains of the past slipped away. "I hated you for a long time. I blamed you for so many things because it was easier than blaming myself, but God showed me something better. It wasn't easy, and it still hurts, but you don't owe me anything." Tears pricked her eyes. "I forgive you, for all of it, because God has forgiven me."

A nudge stirred in her soul, a whisper in her heart, and instinctively, she recoiled, retreating back into her shell of isolation and heartache. She closed her eyes and prayed for strength. A warm evening breeze drifted across the porch, and she stepped forward. She would go where God led, wherever that might be. She wouldn't put limits on the One Who loved her limitlessly. She took another step toward Frankie and opened her arms. As the sun set beyond them, she wrapped her arms around the man she had spent years hating. He cried on her shoulder, and she cried on his. Wounds that had been ripped open in a terrible accident that had changed both their lives were finally healing.

Epilogue

KATE SAT BESIDE CHRIS ON the sofa watching the Academy Awards. She sighed in contented bliss as he massaged her tired feet. They had been working all day. The old house they'd bought in San Francisco needed more than a little tender, loving care. It needed a big dose of tough love. They had spent the past three months knocking down walls, ripping up stained and stinking carpet, and repainting every surface that didn't move.

Chris had managed to drop a hammer on his foot twice, and he'd nearly skewered Ben with a nail gun, but he was turning into a decent handyman. Jonathan, Ben, and her dad were taking turns giving him a crash course in basic construction and home maintenance. The San Francisco Manna Center would be opening next week.

Jonathan had been thrilled when she and Chris approached him and asked about expanding the Manna Center's programs for survivors of human trafficking. During the making of the documentary and in the months since its release, Kate and Chris had learned so much about the way victims were moved up and down the state. The magnitude of the problem and the way it was ignored stirred their hearts. After a lot of prayer, they decided opening a center in San Francisco would do the most good. It would provide a place of refuge and resources in Northern California, while Jonathan continued his ministry in Los Angeles.

Chris had committed the majority of his profits from the documentary to funding the San Francisco Manna Center, and in the end, it had been more than enough to buy the house and pay for the renovations. The day the film premiered at the New Mexico Film Festival, they had been approached by numerous distributors with each offer that came in topping the previous ones. Chris hadn't needed to change one thing in his film. It was exactly the way he wanted it to be. It had been distributed across the nation, and a few months later, it went worldwide. Graciella's story was changing the conversation about human trafficking on a global stage.

As the presenters on the television listed off nominees, Kate listened to her mom in the kitchen. Her parents had come up to help them as they remodeled the Manna Center. Each evening, she came home from her work at the Manna Center to the smell of her mother cooking dinner. For the first few weeks, Kate nursed a worry that one day she would come home and her mom would be gone. Every day, she forced that thought away, focusing on the gratitude she felt at having her mom in her life again. Her parents were working on their relationship, rebuilding the trust that had been broken, and Kate had to admit the feeling of family that greeted her every night was more than she had dared to dream about.

Applause echoed from the television as a woman in a gorgeous red dress accepted a gold statue, and Kate turned her attention to Chris. He hadn't hesitated when they decided to leave Hollywood. Though he hadn't intended it, the documentary had been his farewell to Hollywood, the legacy he would leave for his film career.

"Do you miss it?" she asked, and his hands stilled on her feet.

He tilted his head as if he was considering it. "A little. I loved making movies, and I'm proud of the work I did. Well . . . " He laughed and squeezed her toes. "Most of the work I did. There are a few early films that I wouldn't mind forgetting about."

She smiled at him, amazed at the man God had brought into her life. He was kind and faithful, and he loved her. That realization still made her stomach flutter. "Maybe we can go back someday."

He shrugged. "Maybe. Let's wait and see what God has planned."

"Of course, you're coming back someday!" Noah exclaimed. He was sitting on the other sofa, his arm around Hannah. They had come up just a few days earlier to help with the final preparations. Noah helped keep Chris from nailing his foot to the floor, and Hannah shared her story of survival with city officials to help build support for the grand opening. "You still owe me a movie about exploding aliens."

"Noah." Hannah smacked his arm. "Be good."

"I'm always good." He pouted. "Those guys," he said and pointed at Chris and Kate, "are the ones who moved away. Be mad at them."

Hannah looked at Kate. "I'm not mad at all. They're doing important work that is going to change a lot of lives. I'm proud of them. And you should be, too."

Noah grumbled about being outnumbered, and Hannah kissed his cheek. Kate marveled at how far she and Hannah had come. Hannah had been incredible over the past few days. Not only had she shared her story, she had also shown them how to reach out to the girls they were trying to reach and given them guidance on what types of resources and support the girls coming out of a life of sexual exploitation would need. The way God had knit them all together was amazing.

The host appeared on the television and announced the next award category. Best Documentary.

"Mom, Dad, it's on," Kate called. She sat up and scooted next to Chris as her parents hurried into the room. Chris reached for her hand, and she held on tight.

Kate turned to Chris. "Are you sad that we didn't go?" she asked. With the opening of their new center only a few days away, Chris had decided it was more important for him to stay in San Francisco.

Chris put his arm around her shoulders and held her against his side. "This is the only place I want to be."

Two celebrities walked to the microphone and announced the nominees for best feature-length documentary. Kate held her breath as the films were listed. Her dad thumped Chris on the back as the actor at the microphone said the name of Chris' film. "Well done, Son."

Tense silence reigned as the actress on the screen opened the envelope. She was taking so long, Kate wanted to reach into the screen and yank the envelope from her hands. "And the award goes to . . . *Out of the Ashes*, directed by Chris Johnston, produced by 318 Films."

Joy erupted in the small family room. Kate screamed and threw her arms around Chris. Her mom shouted a hallelujah as her dad swept her into a hug. Noah whooped, and Hannah cheered. All of their cell phones started beeping and ringing.

Tears of pride and happiness filled her eyes as she looked at Chris. "I'm so proud of you," she said. He grinned, and his smile melted her heart.

"Your name should be on that statue, too. There's as much of you in that film as there is of me." He touched her cheek and rested his forehead on hers. Applause blared from the television, and Kate closed her eyes, knowing she would never forget that moment.

They looked at the screen as the camera panned to Ben in the audience. He stood and hugged Lily, then patted the baby bump beneath her flowing ivory dress. His hair was short again, and as he walked up the steps to the microphone, Kate wondered if Lily was happy or sad about that change. His tuxedo was perfectly tailored, and he smiled broadly as he accepted the gleaming gold statue.

"I am deeply honored to accept this award on behalf of my friend, Chris Johnston. I know Chris would want me to give you his deepest thanks. He poured his heart into this film, and it shows. His commitment to shining a light in the darkness is reflected, not just in this film, but in every area of his life. God has done something powerful in this film, and He will continue to do amazing work through men like Chris who are willing to go into the dark places and bring the light of hope and the message of love. Thank you and God bless you."

Ben shook hands with the presenters and waved to the crowd as they walked off the stage. The broadcast cut to a commercial, and Chris and Kate collapsed onto the sofa. Noah, Hannah, and Kate's parents bustled around the family room replying to text messages and retuning phone calls.

Chris laughed and lifted her hand to his lips. He kissed her knuckles, just above the wedding band that gleamed on her finger. "I'll tell you what, if I ever get nominated for an Academy Award again, we'll definitely go."

"It's a date, Mr. Johnston," she said and snuggled closer to him.

"Yes, it is, Mrs. Johnston."

Author's Note

THOUGH THIS IS A WORK of fiction, human trafficking is a tragic reality plaguing our world. Current estimates say between twenty and forty million men, women, and children are trapped in modern slavery. This includes forced labor and domestic servitude, sexual exploitation, and child soldiers. It is a 150 billion dollar a year criminal industry that spans the globe. From babies to the elderly, our brothers and sisters are being abused in the shadows. Many who are lost in the world of modern slavery may never be rescued. These men, women, and children are image-bearers of God, and they are suffering the worst kinds of evil perpetuated by humanity. Who will speak for them?

We live in a world where slavery exists, so we must be people who fight for freedom. William Wilberforce, the great British abolitionist, said, "You can choose to look the other way, but you can never again say you did not know." We must not be people who look the other way when those around us are suffering. I encourage you to find out more about human trafficking. Learn to recognize the signs of someone caught in modern slavery and commit to praying for an end to this hideous practice.

If you are a human trafficking survivor or need to report a tip, you can contact the National Human Trafficking Hotline at 1-888-373-7888.

"Speak up for those who cannot speak for themselves" (Prov. 31:8).

Acknowledgments

Being a writer may be a solitary pursuit, but being an author requires a team. None of my books would exist without the steadfast support and encouragement of so many people. First, my husband, Paul. Thank you for being my biggest cheerleader and my greatest champion. Your love, patience, and perpetual optimism keeps me going. I love you, Marine.

To my children, Emily and Brett, who, once again, found ways to keep themselves busy so I could write, revise, and edit. Brett, thank you for your hugs when you saw me staring at my computer. Emily, thank you for reminding me (every day) that I should be writing.

Huge thanks to the incredible Kellie VanHorn, an amazing author and the best critique partner in the world. Thank you for reading my manuscripts, sharing your talent with me, and telling me when my characters are being brats. You are a blessing!

Once again, my deepest thanks to Ambassador International and the entire team who worked so hard on *Farewell to Hollywood*. Your continued support and enthusiasm for these books means the world to me. Extra special thanks to Katie Cruice Smith for her editorial skills and for her patience with all those extra commas that needed to be deleted.

And to you, dear reader. Thank you for being a part of my *Mission Hollywood* family. You're the reason I write. These books are for you.

To every one of you who sent me an email, message, or tweet asking "When is the next book coming out?," keep those messages coming! I cannot tell you what an encouragement it is to read your kind words.

Finally, my deepest thanks to God. I praise You, my Lord and my God, and I acknowledge Your love, grace, forgiveness, and holiness before the world. Let me always be counted on Your side.

Soli Deo Gloria

About the Author

Michelle Keener is a wife, mom, and the author of four books. She lives in Southern California with her retired Marine husband, their two children, and one spoiled dog. When she isn't writing, she is busy homeschooling, teaching creative writing workshops, or baking something involving chocolate.

Mission Hollywood

a Red Carpet Romance
Book One

MICHELLE KEENER

A Hollywood bad boy. A pastor's daughter.
What could possibly go wrong?

Movie star Ben Prescott arrives back in Hollywood after causing a scandal with his ex-girlfriend in Rome. Chased through the airport by paparazzi, he jumps into a limo hoping for a quick getaway. Instead he finds Lily Shaw, a pastor's daughter and preschool teacher. When the paparazzi capture a photo of the two of them together, Ben's agent demands that he do whatever it takes to keep the story from hitting the gossip pages . . . even volunteer to work at Lily's church.

Sparks fly as the movie star and the pastor's daughter work side by side. When Lily accompanies Ben to the premiere of his latest movie, Hollywood takes notice. Under intense media scrutiny and pressure from the movie industry, Ben must risk his career to follow his heart, but Lily wants the one thing he doesn't have, faith.

Mission Hollywood is an inspirational story about love, faith, and second chances.

Made in Hollywood

a Red Carpet Romance
Book Two

MICHELLE KEENER

When a pastor's son saves her life, can a prodigal daughter dare to believe in second chances?

Noah Shaw is almost thirty and he still doesn't know what he wants to be when he grows up. Torn between running his business as a limo driver for Hollywood's elite, and feeling called to ministry, he prays for direction. But he never expects that direction to include finding a woman near-death on the front steps of his father's church.

Hannah left her family and her faith when she moved to Hollywood looking for adventure. Instead of finding fame in the movies, she was lured into the life of an exotic dancer. Hopeless and ashamed, suicide seems like her only escape. Until the night Noah saves her life.

The Shaw family welcomes her into their home and gives her a chance to start over. When the shadows of her former life threaten to expose her past, she must choose between running away or fighting for the new life she's built and the man she's grown to love.

For more information about
Michelle Keener
&
Farewell to Hollywood
please visit:

www.michellekeener.com
www.facebook.com/mkeenerwrites
@MKeenerWrites
www.instagram.com/mkeenerwrites

For more information about
AMBASSADOR INTERNATIONAL
please visit:

www.ambassador-international.com
@AmbassadorIntl
www.facebook.com/AmbassadorIntl

*If you enjoyed this book, please consider leaving us a review on
Amazon, Goodreads, or our website.*

www.ingramcontent.com/pod-product-compliance
Lightning Source LLC
Chambersburg PA
CBHW051532260626
47170CB00003B/895